Gone Beaver

Gil Schriber

PublishAmerica
Baltimore

© 2009 by Gil Schriber.
All rights reserved. No part of this book may be reproduced, stored in a retrieval system or transmitted in any form or by any means without the prior written permission of the publishers, except by a reviewer who may quote brief passages in a review to be printed in a newspaper, magazine or journal.

First printing

All characters in this book are fictitious, and any resemblance to real persons, living or dead, is coincidental.

PublishAmerica has allowed this work to remain exactly as the author intended, verbatim, without editorial input.

ISBN: 978-1-60749-469-0
PUBLISHED BY PUBLISHAMERICA, LLLP
www.publishamerica.com
Baltimore

Printed in the United States of America

*I want to dedicate this book to the memory of
Joe Wallace,
fellow buck skinner, deer hunter,
turkey hunter, and most importantly.... Friend*

CHAPTERS

CHAPTER I: Westward 9
CHAPTER II: Chick 15
CHAPTER III: Three Friends 21
CHAPTER IV: Taking a Knife to a Gunfight 30
CHAPTER V: Big Cat and Many Horses 36
CHAPTER VI: Rendezvous and Uncle Jack 40
CHAPTER VII: Beautiful Woman, Dead White Man, Faithful Friend 45
CHAPTER VIII: Decisions Made 52
CHAPTER IX: Rendezvous Over 59
CHAPTER X: Jake's Stories 61
CHAPTER XI: Second Rendezvous 64
CHAPTER XII: Thanks to Chick 89
CHAPTER XIII: The Wedding 96
CHAPTER XIV: New Home 104
CHAPTER XV: Trapping Again 112
CHAPTER XVI: New Family 119
CHAPTER XVII: A Trip East 128
CHAPTER XVIII: The Rescue 145
CHAPTER XIX: Wapiti Meadow 161
CHAPTER XX: Wendigo 170
CHAPTER XXI: Third Rendezvous 183
CHAPTER XXII 195
CHAPTER XXIII: Jake's Revenge 201
CHAPTER XXIV: WOLVERINE 210
CHAPTER XXV: Eventful Elk Hunt 215
CHAPTER XXVI: Jake's Woman 226
CHAPTER XXVII: Little Storm 232
CHAPTER XXVIII: Mountain Justice 237

Gone Beaver

CHAPTER I
Westward

John Tucker is eighteen years old, and on his own these past two days. He had run away from an orphanage. In this year of 1830, an orphanage was equivalent to a prison. He had lost his family to cholera three years ago, and has been bounced around in four of these *homes* in that short period. Now he was free! Free to follow his dream so to speak. John does have an uncle somewhere out west. John used to listen to his Uncle tell tales of the *Western Mountain Man!* Trappers they were! Beaver trappers. And his Uncle "Jack" (That was his name), bombarded young John with these tales! Be they true, or not, John had decided a long time ago that he wanted to be one of these *Mountain Men!*

It has been five years now, since John had heard from Uncle Jack. Some of the other trappers who came back east occasionally had said they had heard that 'Ole Jack Tucker' had *Gone Under,* and was *Gone beaver!* This was mountain man talk for dying, or getting killed. Now John knew his uncle, and he did not hold with that belief.

Anyway, just maybe he could find his uncle, in those beautiful, and lonesome mountains that were calling him to them.

All that John had in the way of worldly possessions were the clothes on his back, and a very old butcher knife. The knife, he was able to steal, just before escaping that awful *home!*

Illinois is where John is right now, but he was determined to get to the mountains. For sure a horse would be quicker, but he had none, and no means of getting one. Stealing was not even an option. In fact he had hated the fact that he had stolen the knife. John was a big strapping young man, who had the personality to get along with most folks, unless provoked. That being his downfall at these last four *homes*.

John had known all of last year, that if he did escape, probably nobody would even come looking for him. He was just too big, and hard to handle, and besides, he was now eighteen years old. His only regret was Becky! She was an orphan in one of the *girls* buildings. They would pass each other while Walking in line to the mess hall. Since contact was not allowed, all they could do was smile at one another as they passed. He surely was going to miss those smiles! Now it wasn't hard to figure out how to get to the mountains, but between here and there were a pile of miles, and some very wicked rivers. Of course not to mention the grizzly bears, Indians, mountain lions, snakes, and very cold winters.

Although he was an excellent swimmer, he was concerned about the Mississippi. The *home* that John escaped from is on the Illinois side of St. Louis, so he didn't have far to go to find the "Mighty Mississippi."

Where John was standing, the river looked to be at least a mile wide. After pondering which way to go for a shorter crossing, he decided to go downstream. He had walked for about two hours, when he rounded a bend and saw that the river was narrower here. He did not know how strong the current was, so he needed something to hang on to. He found a good sized log on the bank and rolled it down to the water. Now all he had to do was hang on and paddle his feet. He put his arm around the log and pushed off. Immediately it started to roll, so he just sat astraddle of the thing just like a horse.

He wasn't even half way across, and already the current had taken him a long way downstream. As he approached what he considered the halfway point…….IT HAPPENED!

Another log, partially submerged, rammed his log, spinning him around and throwing him into that muddy water! The current was much stronger than he anticipated and both logs went speeding downstream, just out of reach!

Swim or drown, he thought to himself! Swim he did! Once in a while floating to rest. It felt like hours that he swam, and his arms were getting so heavy. He found that by just relaxing and holding his breath, he could just float and let his arms and legs rest. The only problem with this was the current kept trying to take him back out toward the middle. Finally he had reached his limit and he just let his legs hang down.

That is when his foot touched the bottom! He paddled his weary arms a little more and could actually stand. Now he walked to the beach, and just threw himself down, just out of the water. As he lay there catching his breath the thought went through his mind...*this is just the first of many obstructions on his way to the mountains.*

After laying there a while, he got to his feet and started his westward trek again. It was early summer, so he would just dry off as he walked. He needed shelter and he was now in Missouri where there were many caves. That being said (rather thought), he was now on the lookout for a small cave. He found a small stream that ran towards the Mississippi, so he followed it, as it too was leading west. He needed fire, and Missouri has no shortage of flint, so he soon found a nice piece. When he found shelter, he would build a fire. Dusk was not far off, when he found a small depression in the rocks. It was not a cave, but it would do. He rounded up some twigs and some larger pieces of wood. There was an old mouse's nest in the depression, so he picked it up and shoved it under the twigs. He then took out the butcher knife. As he held it over the tinder (Mouse's nest) he struck the back edge of the knife with the flint. After many glancing blows, a spark finally caught on the tinder! Then he bent down and blew lightly. The spark became a small flame that quickly spread from the tinder to the twigs, and finally to the larger pieces of wood. Now he would be warm, but he still had nothing to eat. It was already starting to get dark, so he couldn't see to hunt for food. This night he would have to go to bed hungry, but as exhausted as he was, it wasn't long before he was sound asleep.

John awoke the next morning rested, but very hungry. As he was getting a drink at the stream, he noticed shadows swimming around on the bottom. Trout! He had heard that they were very good to eat, but Illinois just didn't have any. What a breakfast they would make! If only he had a fishing pole? After trying to jump on them, he realized this process to be hopeless. He found a small pool where the trout were just laying there on bottom. He laid on his belly with his hands in the water, and sure enough, one came right over his hands! *"Gotcha"!* He said aloud as he tossed it on the beach. After that, he caught two more! He promptly cleaned them and poked a stick through each one, and propped them up by the fire that he had blown back to life. After eating his fill, he leaned back, belched, and decided this wasn't going too badly after all. After making sure his fire was dead out, he got up and headed west again. While walking, he was always on the lookout for edible plants, since it was summer, they were in abundance.

Missouri was not the wild west, so he did encounter a homestead once in a while. John's shoes have had it! So he would stop at the next house that he came to. John walked for the rest of that day, before finding a homestead. As he walked up closer, he noticed how run down this place was. John made his way around in front of the house and there they were sitting on the porch. A nice old couple with kindly looking faces. John walked right up to them and asked if he could work for an old pair of shoes? After looking him up and down the old man said, "What can you do?"

After telling him some of his skills, they invited him inside. While him and the old man were at the table talking, The man's wife was warming up leftovers.

Good God what an aroma, thought John. While John was wolfing down the leftovers, they laid out a plan for him to do a few odd jobs. They did have a pair of shoes, and as luck
would have it they were just his size. Apparently their last son had gotten married and left just a few months ago.

John worked very hard repairing this and that and after just two days, he had done everything that the old folks wanted him to do. In fact they wanted him to stay on for a while, but John was determined, so he politely refused and thanked them for the shoes.

After a few hugs and some farewells, John headed west. He felt bad about leaving, but the mountains were calling him westward. John knew that the old couple were lonely, and if it weren't for the mountains calling him, he would have stayed on a while.

GONE BEAVER

Anyone knew that to get to the mountains on foot was a monumental task, and John was up to it. Although a horse sure would make it a whole lot easier. The trail west was not hard to follow, even for a *Tenderfoot* like John. This part of Missouri was still populated pretty well, and all he had to do was ask directions once in a while. His goal right now was Independence. This was now the *Jumping off* place, so to speak, for parts west. Time was still on his side, as far as the weather was concerned. After all when you are 18, and healthy, and strong, you could overcome anything…Right?

He had gotten a large tin cup from the old couple, and strung it around his waist, so his hands would be free. This cup, he would use to boil food in. He did miss his coffee. Even at his young age, he liked a hot cup of coffee. Maybe the next place he came to, he could work for supplies, or money to buy supplies. He estimated that he had walked about twenty miles this day, and started looking for a place to camp. Most all these trails west followed, or at least crossed streams, so water was not a problem. He had been following one such stream for several miles now, and finally found a suitable campsite. There were some big rocks, and the stream was right there below them.

Now all he needed was something to eat. He pulled from his pocket a length of string, and a fish hook that the old couple had given him. He then cut a willow pole (there was never a shortage of them). After catching a grasshopper, and putting it on the hook, he tied the other end on the pole, and cast it out in the stream. Bam! Something hit him behind the head! He almost passed out!

After shaking his head, and clearing out the cobwebs, he slowly turned around, and this small old man with a very large club, said, "Yore on private property young feller!"

John stood up slowly, and told the old man he was sorry, but he did not know. As he was pulling in his fishing line with a nice bluegill on it. The old man said, "I'll take that for payment of You passing through my land."

John gave him the fish, and moved on down the trail, thinking *I guess everyone won't be as nice as the old couple.* John did not know how far this old man's land went, so he walked a couple more miles. The stream was still parallel with the trail, and there was still some light left, so he found another place to camp, and built his fire first.

As he sat watching the fire, he decided, *by God I'll not be run off this time!*

After lifting up a rotten log, and getting a couple worms, then baiting his hook with them, he cast out again and almost immediately caught a nice Channel Cat! He then pulled up several wild onions. He cleaned the fish and cooked it while eating the onions the whole time. Now with his belly not full, but comfortable, he lay back and slept.

CHAPTER II
Chick

Becky was kissing him and licking him on the mouth, and he was about to have a *hissy fit! Good Lord!* He sat up straight! *A Dog! A big hound dog had been licking his mouth!* The dog looked at him as if to say thanks, and was wagging his tail.

A dream, thought John. *Damn, but he wished it was not a dream. Oh well! This old hound must have smelled the fish on my mouth.* Now! Wide awake, he built up the fire and went to the stream to drink. As he was drinking the dog was right beside him drinking also. He reached over and petted the old fellow, and scratched him behind the ears. John thought, *at least now he had some company, that is, if the dog was a stray?* Maybe he belonged to the old man back up the trail? At least he hoped he did. If the dog followed him, then that would be some compensation for the old man's selfishness.

John stayed a little longer at the stream that morning, so he caught enough fish for both him, and the dog. Breakfast over, and moving down the trail once more, westward as usual, John noticed the dog stop. He also stopped. The dog was sniffing the air. *What did he smell?* Thought John. He himself tried to sniff, with no luck. The dog began growling very low! At this point John started looking around for a club, or rock, or something he could use for a weapon. He found a large branch, which seemed solid, and picked it up, and waited, watching where the dog was looking.

A black bear of average size stepped out onto the trail in front of them.

John looked down at the dog! It was gone! He could just see his tail rounding the bend back up the trail! *Some dog he is*, thought John. Then John looked back at the bear! It was running away too! *Do I smell bad, or what?* Thought John.

After thinking about it he decided that the bear scared the dog, and he, himself scared the bear. John was thinking, *these were not the bears that he would encounter out west*. He had heard his uncle Jack talk about the *Silvertips*. That is what the mountain men called the grizzly bear. *Lord he hoped he would not run into one of them! This black bear had done scared the living daylights out of him*. As John turned back, there was the dog slinking back, with his tail tucked between his legs. All John could do was just scratch him behind the ears. After all it is not the dog's place to save John's life. At least he did warn him. They continued westward. At this point in time John did not know how strong the bond between a man, and a dog could be.

They made about another twenty miles, even with the setbacks. As luck would have it, they found a good camping spot right on the bank of the stream. Now he didn't know about the dog, but John was kind of getting tired of fish. John devised a snare using the fishing line. He found a well traveled game trail and put the snare on it and went back to camp and waited. After

an hour or so, he went down the game trail to check on the snare. There caught in his snare was a nice plump skunk! Now what? It was caught by it's hind leg, and very much alive! He did not smell it yet, so it hadn't sprayed.

John knew that skunks could not see too good, so he slipped up on the back side, and cut the line by his leg. The skunk hit the ground running! Well...waddling as skunks do. John only lost about 3 inches of line, so he could still fish. He went back to camp, and there lay the dog casually eating away at a rabbit that he had caught. *Who is the hunter here?*, thought John. The dog had eaten the front part, so John picked up the rest, without the dog minding one bit. After skewering it on a stick, he propped it up by the fire, turning it occasionally. The fish had been good, but this was delicious.

Now kicked back, and resting, he was thinking that he had ought to name the dog. He would be thinking about this while they were traveling.

Traveling is just what they did for the next two weeks. Living off the land. Sometimes John caught supper, and sometimes Chicken caught supper. Chicken is what he decided to name the dog. John thought that appropriate, since the *bear* Incident. Eventually he just shortened it to Chick.

They began to pass a few houses, so John reckoned they were coming up on Independence. As they came into town, John was in awe of all the people. All kinds of people. There were mountain men, Indians, some foreign speaking people, and any number of bums, and panhandlers. The Indians are what bothered John the most, because that is what most of the panhandlers were, and some were so drunk, all they did was just lay along side the road. John had no idea that these Indians were nothing like the ones he would be confronting in the weeks to come.

He guessed the next step, was to try to find a job, so he could earn a *grubstake* to go into the mountains. He was willing to work, and could do most anything when he put his mind to it.

The first place he went was the blacksmith shop. This was not an accident, because John's dad was a blacksmith. A Ferrier to be exact. Meaning if your horse needed shoes, then Tucker's house was the place to go. James Tucker was his name, and before Cholera took him away, he taught young John everything he knew about the trade.

As John stood out in front of the blacksmith's shop, the *Smitty*, as they were called, appeared at the door, and just stood there looking John up, and down. John began to get a little nervous, until the man said, "Lookin fer a job young feller?"

John let out a breath, and said, "Yes Sir."

"Name ain't sir. It's Jeb." said the smitty. "You look like a man what's swung a hammer before, and from the looks of yer outfit, I would say you need the money."

John then looked down at his tattered, and filthy clothes, and wandered why this man would hire someone who looked like he did.

The *smitty* took him and Chick into his home behind the shop. As they walked through the door, Jeb hollered at his wife in the kitchen, who was creating these delicious smells. "Fix another plate Ma, we got company."

While John was on his second plate, Jeb began to ask the questions, who was John's father, and where was he?, and what in God's name was John doing in this crazy *Boomtown*? John told him, and also told him about his trip, so far. Jeb had heard John call his dog Chick, and he asked him about it. By the time John was through telling about the Bear incident, Jeb and his wife were roaring with laughter. They both said that was an appropriate name for the dog. Then they piled all the scraps on a plate, and took them outside, with Chick right on their heels.

Jeb told John that there was too much work for one man, and he was the only *smitty* in town. He did have a man working for him once, but he had gone west like most do from this town. There was a little room in the back of the house, and it had it's own entrance. That would be John's room. Jeb also said, "In the morning we will go to the General store and get you some clothes, then I want you to go jump in the creek."

The next morning, Jeb was as good as his word, and he and Chick were now down at the creek taking a bath. As it turned out, Chick loved the water, (at least he wasn't afraid of that too.) After putting on the new clothes he felt like a new man (well almost a man).

They returned to the blacksmith shop, and found it to be crowded with people. Jeb pointed to a leather apron hanging on a nail. John picked it up, and his new career began. It felt great to be back at the forge working the metal just like his Pa taught him. John lost count of the horses that they shooed that day, but when they finally quit, he was exhausted. After supper Jeb told John that he had never seen anyone work the metal the way John did. That praise was the best thing Jeb could do for John, and John decided when he did finally go west, he would give Jeb plenty of notice.

As the days went by, John got to talk to many people, and just about all had heard of Jack Tucker. A lot of these people were Mountain men, just like John knew he would someday be. As John was Making some tent stakes for this man, who was obviously a Mountain man, he noticed the big knife that he was carrying. He asked if he may see it, and the guy whipped it out so fast that John didn't see his hands move.

John appreciated good iron, and asked this man what he did with it? The man said, "Hand it back, and I will show you." John handed it back to him. In one solid blur, the knife was sticking in the wall behind John!

"How did you do that?" asked John.

"Lots of practice said the man." The man then said, "I have been watching you work the iron, and I must say that I am impressed."

John blushed and asked the man what his name was.

"Jim," he said. "Jim Bowie."

At this date in history Mister James Bowie was not popular yet.

John was so impressed with the man's skill with the large knife, that he asked him if he could try to throw it. Jim told him sure, and explained how to throw it.

John reared back and *let her rip*. Damned if it didn't stick right in the wall! He was hooked. John asked Jim if he thought that he would be able to make one for himself. Jim said, "Sure, if you find the right kind of steel."

After thanking Jim Bowie for the lesson, and the use of that knife, they shook hands, and Jim left. John hoped he would see him again.

Time was slipping away, and the mountains may have to wait till next spring. He was a patient young man, and besides, he was making good money, and having the time of his life.

Everyone has to see a Blacksmith sooner or later, so he got to talk to everyone in town. John listened much more than he talked, therefore learning much more about his beloved mountains.

As for Mister Bowie, he opened up something in John that nobody expected to see. Knife throwing became an obsession with John. When he wasn't on the forge, he was out back throwing different knives that he had made. He became very adept at throwing them, but as yet could not find one to match Jim Bowie's knife.

Finally, he went to Jeb with his problem. He asked him if he knew what kind of steel he could use that would come close to matching Jim's knife.

After thinking about it, Jeb said, "I think I have just what we need!"

He went over to a table at the wall, and reached under it pulling out this piece of steel. After bringing it out in the light, he told John that his father had brought this steel all the way from Sheffield England. Jeb said that he had not had a use for it until now. Jeb also said, "There are two more pieces under the table, so if you mess this one up, you got another chance."

John was so excited he about had a *hissy fit!* He could not wait until he got started on the knife. At the time he was backed up with making horseshoes, so he would have to wait. Meticulously he worked, catching up on his regular work.

His day over, and everything caught up, he cranked up the forge, because this was hardened steel and he would need more heat. As he heated, and pounded, a shape began to form, and pretty soon a knife that he was proud of emerged from the coals. After quenching it in oil and letting it cool down on it's own, it was ready!

He went out back at his throwing block (A cross section of a cottonwood log) and stuck a playing card on the log. Then he paced off about four paces, or around 12 feet and turned and threw! He could not believe his eyes!

The knife stuck right in the middle of the card! Now for the handle. He wanted something that would take a beating, so he decided on leather. The holes in the handle area of the knife, he had made when he forged it, so all he had to do was put two pieces of belt leather on each side with copper rivets. He would sharpen it on the grindstone, because this was not just a throwing knife, but also a working knife.

CHAPTER III
Three Friends

    Now he had his first piece of equipment for the mountains, and he had made it himself. As the weeks, and then months went by, he made two more knives out of the Sheffield Steel. Old Jeb said that he could keep them for himself, or sell them. Either way was alright with him. John had decided that if he did sell any of them, it would be to someone who would appreciate them. That someone came along just after John made the last knife.

    Jacob, was his name, or some called him "Quiet Jake." John did not ask at this time why they called him Quiet Jake. Out here, you don't ask questions, you just except things as they are. Eventually you find out what you want to know.

    Jake wasn't overly quiet that John could tell, so he guessed the name came from something else. Jake came to the smiths shop asking for John personally, so John took him aside

to find out what he wanted. Jake told him that he wanted one of those knives that he had seen John throwing out in back.

    John asked to see the knife that Jake was wearing. Jake took it out and showed it to him. After examining it extensively he gave it back to Jake. Jake looked puzzled, so John told him that he did not want to sell one of his knives to someone who did not take care of them. He then said that he would sell one to Jake.

Jake knew that John's last name was Tucker, and he asked him if he had any relatives out west? This shocked John to the core, and he asked him why?

"Well," Jake said, "I knowed a Jack Tucker."

You could have knocked John over with a feather! After John could speak again, he asked Jake about it.

"Back in twenty seven it was," said Jake. "Ole Jack and me were a trappin beaver over on the Muscle shell. We nearly went under that winter. It was so cold the trees were a poppin somthin fierce!"

"There was this cave what we wanted to stay in, but a derned ole Silvertip done laid claim to it! Yore uncle Jack didn't want no truck with a Grizz, so I slipped right on past that ole critter and found another way in!"

"We just holed up in that cave, with a few rocks tween us and thet ole Grizz!"

John was beside himself! For sure his uncle Jack was alive; at least he was three years ago! Jake was talking now, and john let him go on.

Jake said, "Some folks started callin me Quiet Jake, after the Grizz thing. Hell, a blind tenderfoot could sneak up on a winter sleepin Grizz! Anyway I thought you should know yore uncle was alive and well last I seed him."

Jake then said, "I aim on winterin down in Taos, but come the thaw, I could look ya up, and maybeso we could head on out yonder to find ole Jack!"

John told him that he would be looking forward to it. *That was that,* thought John. He was set! Now come spring he was going to the mountains come "Hell or High Water!"

Jake paid John for the knife, bade him farewell, and left. The price they agreed on was ten dollars (A lot for a knife). After Jake had left John opened up his hand that held the money that Jake had paid him, and there was twenty-five dollars in it! *Guess Jake really liked the knife,* thought John.

It was going to be a long winter, but that gave John the time to work, and make the money for the outfit that he would need come spring. There was no shortage of work, and John dove in with a passion. Even Old Jeb told John that he was working excessively hard. When he worked, he worked, but when he was not working, he was out in back practicing with his knife, and also a tomahawk that he had made. He was very good with either one of them.

It was a long winter, but John was so busy with the Blacksmith shop, that he did not have time to notice. After talking to all the Mountain men that he could all winter long, he thought that he pretty well knew what he needed to take to the mountains. He bought a blanket here, a canteen there, and all the hardware that he would need. The perishables, he would buy just before leaving. His reputation was growing, and not just the blacksmithing! John was getting to be known everywhere as someone who could handle a knife, and hawk! Lately he had been hearing that some of the mountain passes were beginning to open up. A sure sign of spring! The hard part about this whole thing was going to be telling old Jeb that he was leaving.

The time finally came when *Ole Quiet Jake* appeared at the shop one morning. He looked all tan as if he had been in a lot of sun, and John asked him about that.

All he would say is that he went a little farther south than Taos.

Jeb had seen Jake ride up, and he knew what that meant. He also knew that he would surely miss John, but a feller had to follow his dream. All this was going through Jeb's mind as

John came up on the porch. When John came into the house, Jeb had a big smile on his face. "It's that time! Ain't it?"

"I reckon," was all John could squeak out.

Damn, if he wasn't already sounding like a mountain man, thought Jeb.

Jake said that he had spent the night on the edge of town in the woods, and he was ready to go, so they left immediately. So many questions went through John's head, but he was learning to keep his mouth shut, and just wait until Jake was ready to talk. And talk he did! Jake told him about every plant and every animal they came across, and how they could be used. Jake knew that John would not be able to remember everything, but maybe when the time of need came, he would recall some of it. Everyone knew that experience was the best teacher, but out west, sometimes you did not live to get the experience! Besides, John was picking things up mighty fast, by Jakes way of thinking.

John was in the height of his glory! He was living his dream, and learning everything Jake had to give. While they were stopped for the night, John asked Jake if he had a particular destination, or was he just getting to the mountains the quickest way possible? Jake told him that he always had a destination, even if it was just the next draw.

They took turns hunting, and cooking. One day Jake would hunt, and John would cook. The next day it was visa-versa. This worked out well for both of them.

This particular day, was John's day to hunt, and he had been out a little longer than Jake thought he should be. Jake was just getting ready to go look for him, when John came into camp. John had a big Jack Rabbit by the hind legs.

Jake asked, "I didn't hear a shot, you get him with you're knife?"

"As a matter of fact, I did," said John.

Jake was not buying into that, and he said, "Let me see you stick this!"

He hung a leaf on the side of a tree. John stepped up to around 12 feet or so, and in one smooth motion, his Sheffield knife was sticking into the leaf!

Jake could not believe what he just seen. "I guess it is true then!"

John said, "What in Hell are you talking about?"

Jake said that when he was in Taos last winter, people were coming into town talkin about this kid in Independence who could throw a knife like no other!

John then told him that he had practiced all winter, when he was not working. He said that every time he went out back, ole Chick was always with him. At first, John would have to tie Chick up, because he would try to fetch the knife, or hawk. Later on, he got used to it, and he could then untie him. Jake said that it was good to have a dog along, because they could warn you of things that a man cannot hear, or see. John then told Jake that was not all Chick was good for, how do you think I got the rabbit? "Chick trailed him, and then flushed him out for me." Jake took the rabbit, and cleaned him. John put him on a spit by the fire. What they could not eat, Chick would take care of.

Traveling was much better than before John got to Independence. Horses, good friends, and the lure of the mountains! What more could a man ask for? Each day was pretty much like the rest, as they traveled across Missouri, and then into Kansas. Now on the western side of Kansas, the landscape began a slow, but sure change. The hills were getting bigger, and you could see for miles, when it was clear.

The last two days were overcast, and you could not see quite as far. Their routine was to get up before dawn, and have breakfast over with by dawn...

This day, with breakfast over, and them heading west again, John told Jake that they were going to get rain before too long. Jake said, "How do you reckon that?"

"That cloud bank in the west," said John. As John looked at Jake, he noticed Jake grinning very big! "What's so funny?"

Jake said. "Them ain't clouds Tenderfoot!"

John looked again very carefully, and saw snow capped mountains! *My God! The mountains! They were beautiful,* thought John. The questions started pouring out of John, and Jake had all the patience in the world. After all, he himself was a tenderfoot once. Finally, John wound down enough to let Jake explain that it would still take days to get there. After a couple days, they were in the foothills, and the game was everywhere. John saw Elk, Deer, antelope, and even a small heard of buffalo.

This one morning, about an hour before dawn, John awoke, to silence, deathly silence! No breathing from Jake, and no Chick anywhere! He slowly looked all around the camp, and Jake and Chick were gone! He started to panic, and the training kicked in! *Go slow! Be quiet, and keep low.* He was on his knees contemplating what to do when something cold touched him on the neck! Slowly he turned, and there was Chick, (he had touched him with his nose) and Jake right behind him! *How in the Hell did he do that?* Thought John. He would ask Jake later.

Now Jake had his finger to his mouth in the classic be quiet Position! "Indians!" Whispered Jake!

"Are they friendly?" asked John.

"Don't know yet" said Jake. "Have to wait till mornin ta see."

As daylight was just breaking, the travelers could just make out forms among the rocks, and when the sun finally made its appearance, there they were! It seemed that they were surrounded by Indians. When John turned to Jake, for answers, all Jake said was "Snakes!"

John knew from listening to the mountain men tell their stories, that Snakes meant Shoshone, and as far as he heard, they were friendly to whites.

One among them came forward and began talking in his own tongue and gesturing with his hands. Jake knew a little Shoshone, but he knew all the universal sign language, so he began communicating with the man. As Jake was signing, he was whispering to John that this man said we had some fine horses.

Jake got very testy about the horses, and even John could tell that Jake had told the man that they were not giving them our horses! Jake was gesturing, and pointing to the big knife on John's waist! John said, "What in the Hell are you doin?"

"Telling them how good you're knife throws, and that you had one in the saddle bag you might give them for crossing their land." '

"Not my Sheffield," said John!

"No! I meant one of those you made afore the Sheffield."

They had not saddled yet, so john reached down into his saddlebag and pulled out one of his knives. He held it up as he walked forward. Then without warning, spun, and threw it into a tree right beside the Indian!

Then John pointed to the knife, and then to the Indian. The Indian pulled the knife out of the tree, and looked at John. He pointed to himself, and said something.

John looked over at Jake, and Jake said, "He told you his name!"

"What does it mean? Asked John."

"MAN WHO KILLS DEER" said Jake.

John said, "I don't think that I can pronounce it, so I will shorten it to Killdeer." At that time a friendship was struck between the two men, that would last forever, although neither had any knowledge of it.

They then stuck a leaf on the side of the tree, and both went to throwing the knife, and their tomahawks. Killdeer was a good learner, and was sticking John's knife almost immediately.

Jake had already had some coffee made when he detected the Indians, and he invited Killdeer, and his five warriors to join them. As it turned out, it was the coffee boiling that the Indians smelled, and consequently led them to this camp.

Killdeer already had the knife in his waistband, and through talk and gestures, told them that he would have his wife make him a sheath for the big knife.

After the coffee pot was empty, they said their goodbyes and left. John asked Jake how he knew that Killdeer would like the knife.

"Didn't know, jest had ta tell em sumpin!"

John doubled up his fist, and hit Jake on the arm, knocking him over!

"He might have killed me!" Said John!

"Didn't though" did he? '

Then they both started laughing so hard that their bellies hurt. That's when they noticed Chick coming back into camp.

"Damn dog is a livin up to his name" said Jake. They started laughing all over again.

They broke camp, and started heading west again. Jake had told John that they needed to find a "Buffler" herd, so they could make meat, and jerky, plus tan a robe apiece for the coming winter. They were not into the big mountains yet, so the herds were somewhere close by. They would not be hard to find, because they leave a path a mile wide in some places.

They didn't find any that day, but there was a storm that night, and the lightning was flashing something fierce. Now it was thundering!, and Jake yelled to John

"Git everything, and head fer that hill over yonder!"

Just as they reached the top of the hill, John SAW the thunder! In the form of buffalo! Thousands of them stampeding across the plains! *Good thing Jake knew what that thunder was*, thought John, or they would be so much ground up meat, by now!

They finished out the night on that little hill, just in case! The next morning, John woke up to a churned up mess. All around the hill that they were on, there was nothing but destruction. Well they found their buffalo, now what? Jake told John that the buffalo probably only ran about five miles, or so. As it turned out, Jake was right.

They had gone a few more miles, and before they topped this big hill,

Jake had them pull up. Then they eased up the hill, and there they were, just milling around, about 50 yards out. John was surprised that the buffalo were still there, because he laughed out loud while they were crawling up the hill! There right beside him, crawling too, was Chick!, He looked so funny crawling up that hill! He heard Jake snicker too, so he didn't feel too bad.

Jake told John that the wind was right, and that is why they didn't hear them.

At this point, Jake whispered to John, "Crawl back down, and get the two 50 cal. Hawkin rifles!"

John did just that, and after he handed Jake his, he looked down at his own rifle, and "Bang!" Jake shot! That scared the daylights out of him, and he told Jake so. Jake said pick out one of the big cows, and shoot! As John was taking aim, he was wandering why the buffalo didn't run off after the first shot, and after downing one himself, he asked Jake.

Jake said, "They are confused!" "They know somethin is happenin, but they cain't smell or see us!" Jake shot his second Bull, then said, "that's enough! We will use the two bulls for robes, and the cow you shot for meat."

They skinned the cow, and quartered it, so they could get it back to camp. Then they went back for the bulls. This skinning was much harder, because they had to be very careful not to cut into the skin. After the job was done, they quartered these also, to take back to camp. John asked Jake why they were taking the meat on these, and Jake told him that they were going to make jerky, and pemmican. Naturally, John had heard of both, but was real curious as to how they were made.

The drying process was painstakingly slow, but this western sun was very hot, and by the end of the day they had a whole bunch of jerky. What was left, was pounded into cakes, with some suet added, plus some berries Jake had.

As for the meat, well they would carry it with them, using it all the while, until it got rancid.

That night, after they turned in, they let the fire burn down some. The night was deathly still. John had to go relieve myself, and as he was standing there, he noticed shapes dodging around, just outside the glow of the campfire.

Well he finished up right quick like, and went back to camp, and built up the fire.

Wolves were all around their camp, and as he started to wake up Jake, "I seed em," Jake said.

He got up, and they grabbed their guns! John asked him why they were this close to camp?

"Blood" is what he said! They smell the blood from the "Buffler we kilt!"

They started shooting at the glowing eyeballs, and were rewarded with a few yelps, and then they were gone! Jake said he would take the first watch, then John was to come, and relieve him.

He woke John about two hours from dawn, and John would say that was the longest two hours that he had ever spent. He knew that they were still out there, but they didn't try to come any closer that night.

The next morning Jake told John to throw a couple big haunches out on the edge of camp. He said maybe that would hold them off for a day or two.

They traveled all day, only eating some of their very own jerky for midday break. They seen nothing of the wolves, so he guessed Jake's idea worked.

They threw another big piece of buffalo meat out that night, all that meat wasn't going to last anyway. They heard the wolves tearing into it a little later, so they hadn't left the area. John guessed they would have to kill a couple more to convince them.

Jake showed him how to skin the three that they got the night before. He said they would be good medicine, if they were to come up on some more Indians. Jake said that there was a small "Tradin Post" right on up this trail a few miles, and maybe they could by a couple mules. They were getting a lot of plunder accumulated, and needed some way to carry it better.

CHAPTER IV
Taking a Knife to a Gunfight

They got to the trading post in the late afternoon. It wasn't much, just a shack, with a small choral behind it. As luck would have it, there were four mules in the choral. John asked Jake how he knew there would be mules here? Jake told him that he didn't, but prospectors, and Mountain men down on their luck were always tradin off their mules here. Jake bought one, and John bought another. Now they could carry most anything they needed. They went ahead and camped there that night. Jake brought out a jug of what he called "Taos Lightnin." John really didn't like the taste of whiskey, so he didn't drink any. "Ole Quiet Jake" wasn't quiet that night! He talked way into the night, in fact he was still talking when John went to sleep. It was sometime in the wee hours of the night, when John heard Chick growl. He had his ears laid back, and John knew something was about to happen.

Someone was trying to steal their horses, and mules. John jumped up and went running over there, and Chick was right beside him for a change.

There were two of them, and he didn't know if they were armed or not, but John hollered "Stop right where you are!"

They did stop, and turned around to face him.

One said, "Hell he ain't even armed."

John guessed they didn't figure a knife would count as being armed. One pulled out a pistol, and was bringing it to bear, when John threw the knife! That big knife caught him right in the arm he was aiming with, and the gun went off shooting himself in the foot! John had another knife, but didn't have to use it, because chick had the other man down on the ground! Chick had his mouth around the man's throat! All John had to do was say the word, and he told this man that. Needless to say, the man didn't move!

About that time, Jake showed up. John said, "I was wandering if you was going to miss the fun?"

"Did you shoot him?" Jake said!

"Nope, he shot himself."

Then Jake seen the knife sticking out of that guy's arm, and he said, "God Amighty" yore the onlyest man I ever seed who would bring a knife to a gunfight…and win!"

Then John told Chick to get off the other guy.

"What in the Hell are we going to do with them, John asked Jake?"

"Let's take em in to the storekeeper, and see what he says."

So that is what they did. There was no law of any kind out here, and they did need punished, so they asked the storekeeper what he thought. As it turned out the storekeeper did not hold with robbers, and he said that he had just the thing for them. They didn't ask all the details, but it had something to do with moving the outhouse to a different hole (That still needed to be dug)! They went back to their camp, and was too worked up to go right back to sleep, so they just sat around the fire and talked. They both agreed that Chick sure was nice to have around. After finally winding down, they did go back to sleep.

They woke up to an overcast, and gloomy day. Soon it began to rain, but they had all their stuff put away before it started. Now it was really raining hard. they went over to the stable behind the Trading Post, and stood under the roof until it almost stopped raining, then they mounted up and headed west once again.

The foothills that they had been traveling through, were now the beginning of the mountains! Those beautiful snow capped mountains that were all around John, seemed to be calling him. He had finally made it! Now if uncle Jack could be found, then he would be satisfied.

Last night, after everything happened, Jake had asked him why didn't he take a gun to go confront that guy? He honestly did not know, because he was a passable shot with a long, or short gun. The knife just seemed like part of him, and he could get it out quicker than any gun. He told Jake that, and Jake just nodded. Jake finally opened up to him about where they were going, and he explained how to get there, in case they got separated. Jake said there should be a rendezvous, over on the Green River, at least that's what he heard. John had heard so many stories about these rendezvous, that he just couldn't wait!

There were still a lot of miles between here and the rendezvous, and John still had a lot to learn. Every time they stopped for any length of time, John would be throwing the knife, and hawk at trees. Jake would just shake his head, and John told him that he had to keep it up to improve his skills. When he wasn't throwing, Jake was teaching him how to find places using landmarks, and what tracks to look for. They would eat the jerky, when they stopped for mid-day break, and along toward evening they took turns hunting, as was mentioned before.

This one evening Jake was out hunting, and hadn't returned yet, and it was almost dark. John was starting to get a little worried, when Jake came stumbling into camp, with an antelope on his shoulders! He told John that he spent all evening just trying to coax this critter into shooting range! He had hid behind a hill, and tied a white rag around his gun barrel, and stuck it up above the hill!

He said, "Them critters is mighty curious" and they come closer to investigate. "That's when I plugged thisn," He said.

That was some right tasty eating, thought John.

The next morning, as They were riding along a mountain trail, they both noticed it! Quiet! It was too quiet! Jake whispered to get off the horses, and they did. Chick was growling real low, so something was up ahead. They tied their horses, and mules to some trees, and crawled up the next hill. Then they took off their hats, and slowly peeked over the top. There were about a dozen Indians down there stopped, and discussing something in their own tongue. Jake motioned for them to back down the hill. When they reached the bottom, he said, "Those were Bloods, ifn I ever did see any!"

Damn! Even John knew that he meant Blackfoot! Bloods was what the

mountain men called Blackfoot, and they did not get along with anybody!
"Now what?" said John.

"They's too many ta have a tussle with," Jake said.

John agreed with him on that.

"Whar's Chick?" Jake asked.

John turned around and looked down the hill, and there was Chick down there where they had left the horses, and mules. John guessed he didn't want any part of those Indians either.

They got back down to the animals, and led them off the trail, just in case them Bloods came over this way. They waited about an hour, and saw nothing, so they crawled back up on that hill, with Chick right beside them. They peeked over, and saw that they had left.

After going back to get the animals, then going down to where the Indians were, they found sign on the direction that they went. Now satisfied that they were going in opposite directions as the Bloods, they continued on west.

Now at the very base of the mountains, they were seeing different animal signs. Once they saw some "Painter" tracks, as Jake called them. They were Cougar, or Mountain Lion, or Catamount tracks. Some of the mountain men called them all of those names. John didn't care what they called them, he really didn't want to see one, after hearing it scream all night long.

One morning, while they were taking a break, Jake told John that his uncle Jack used to winter right over the next hill. He also said that he would be long gone by now. The next morning John had Jake take him over to where uncle Jack used to stay, since it was just about a half mile off the trail. There was a well worn path leading up to a cabin right on the side of this hill, with a stream right below it.

They approached the cabin, and said, "Hello the cabin!" No one came out, so they went up, and knocked on the door. There was no one inside, so they went in. It was well furnished, and stocked with food. They were just standing there, when they heard this commotion outside! Chick was raising a ruckus about something. John opened the door, and peered outside at a very big man sitting on a horse, and pointing a 50. Cal. Hawkin right at his chest! He said in a booming voice "Who are you, and what do you think you are doin?

"That you out thar Half Pint?"

Well "Skin me fer a coon" is that you Quiet Jake?"

Apparently these two knew each other, so John said, "Ya mind pointing that there cannon somewhere else?" He did, and they stepped back out the door, and the friends slapped each other on the back, saying to each other... Hell I thought you went under back in 28!

And I done thought you were gone beaver last year. Jake drug out his jug, and John knew it was all over. He did get out of Half Pint, that he was watching the place for good ole uncle Jack, and he said Jack was on his way to Rendezvous. They went back inside, after taking care of the animals.

Of course Chick went in with them. It turned out that Half Pint was French, and they could not even pronounce his name. John asked about how he got this name, and said, "I know it's not because of your size!"

Jake chimed in at that time, saying "Hell he kin drink a half pint of "Taos Lightnin" in one swaller."

Jake introduced John, and before he even said his last name, Half Pint said, "Aint you thet feller what throws the knife, and hawk real good?"

"How did you know that?" John asked.

"Met a feller comin from Independence, said he seed this young blacksmith out behind the shop throwin Knives and Hawks like they was part of him."

After the name Tucker sunk in, Half Pint said, "You any kin to Jack?"

"I am his nephew," John said.

Half Pint said, "Damn, ya only missed him by bout a week."

John knew without a doubt that they would be staying the night right here. And that was ok, because they were friends, and out here that was important.

John and Chick bedded down on the floor, and went to sleep immediately. As for the two Mountain Men, John couldn't say when they finally gave it up.

The next morning They were up at dawn, and both men were in good shape, considering the jug they consumed. As they were leaving, Jake turned in the saddle and said, "Keep yer powder dry pard!"

Half Pint said, "Watch out fer the Bloods!"

As they were traveling along, Jake said, "It's time ta head north now."

He found this trail, and they turned onto it, and had the sun on their right. John asked how far to rendezvous, and Jake told him another week. He then said that, "We could step it up ifn you wanted."

John said, "No this pace is fine."

The scenery was absolutely beautiful as they traveled north. There were the mountains on their left, and lush green valleys to travel through, and the plains on their right. They saw antelope by the thousands, and buffalo as well.

Once when they were stopped for a mid-day break, they were sitting on top of this little hill, just watching this buffalo herd. Jake said, "Watch this!" And John watched as these wolves (They always followed the herd) were trying to cut a little calf out of the herd. Maybe they get lucky sometime, but not this time. Every time a wolf would get close to the calf, the wolf suddenly had several bulls to deal with. They did not want to take on a bull buffalo one on one. They kept trying the whole time the herd was moving past.

CHAPTER V
Big Cat and Many Horses

Jake told him that wolves were survivors, and eventually they would get a buffalo calf, or a sick, or an old cow. They moved on up the trail and made good time that day. Now they were finally getting low on fresh meat, so it was John's turn to go hunting this evening. As he was waking down this game trail following some deer tracks, Chick began to growl (a sure sign of danger)! He stopped immediately, and only moved his eyes. He could not see anything in front, or on either side, so he looked down at Chick, and he was looking up! He looked up, and just about messed his pants!

There, on a big rock was a cougar, and he was set to spring! The knife stayed in his belt, and he swung up the Hawkin, just as it sprang! The 50. Cal. Ball caught it right in the chest, and it was dead as it fell, but John could not get out of the way fast enough, and it crashed into him full force! It was almost dark, when he awoke.

Jake was pouring water on his face. He got up (Too fast), because his head was throbbing. Then he remembered! he looked around and saw that he was back at camp.

"How did I get back here, he asked?"

Jake said, "well twas getting kinda late, and I was just fixin ta go look fer ya, when Ole Chick came into camp, and wanted me to foller him. He led me right to ya!" Jake said, "when I got there, you was laying there with a big Painter" right on top of ya. I thought ya was gone beaver!"

Apparently John's head hit a rock when the cat knocked him down, and he could sure feel the gash, and goose egg on his head!

Jake said, "I gotta sew thet gash in yore haid, and it's gonna hurt some!"

Jake got a needle and thread out of his saddle bag, and commenced to sewing!

He was right, it did hurt! John didn't holler, but the sweat was running down his face when he finally finished! He told John that "it would heal jest fine ifn it didn't fester."

They skinned the cat, and Jake asked him if he wanted some of the meat? John said no, he could eat it if he had a notion, but something just didn't set right with John eating other meat eaters.

Jake did eat some of it, and declared it to be delicious. They were accumulating a lot of skins, and furs, and Jake said that would be good at the rendezvous. We could sell or trade them.

John started asking questions about the coming rendezvous, and Jake answered all of them. He told him the main thing to remember, is to have fun. That was what it was all about. Some of those ole boys have been out in the mountains for a couple years, and they had to "Let er Loose," as Jake would say.

They were now within two days or so from the site picked for this year's rendezvous. John asked Jake how the rendezvous came about. He knew why, but who started them? Jake said that he thought it was John Astor who first started them. Astor was a wealthy man, and thought this a good way to expand his fortune. He was right! He made a killing off the mountain men. They had no other way to trade or sell their Plews, save going clear back to Independence, or down to Taos.

They bedded down that night on a high plain that was prettier than any yet, and John thought *It just don't get any better than this*. As John was laying there with his head on the saddle, and covered up with a wool blanket, the ground started to shake! "Earthquake!" he screamed!

Jake said, "Git yer gear, and mount up, and pick up Chick when ya do!"

John did just that, and it was none too soon, because wild horses were stampeding right through where their camp had been!

Jake screamed, "Foller Me!"

John tried, but the wild horses were too many between them, by then. John angled off through the herd, and was finally out of them. After they passed, and the dust cleared away, he could not find Jake! He saw a horse down and thought, *oh no!*, but when he got there, he found it to be one of their mules.

Jake came riding down off this small hill, and asked, Ya all right?"

"Yep!" John said. And you?

He said he was ok. John asked him how did he know that the little hill was right there.

"Ya have to know all the time where to go ifn ya need ta."

John made a mental note of that. Chick was squirming around, so he let him down. What stampeded them horses, he asked? Jake said it could have been anything, a Painter, a wolf, a silvertip, or nothing at all.

"Wild hosses is notional critters," said Jake.

After they turned in again, John heard the horses in the distance begin to slow down, and then silence. He guessed they just had to run it out of their system.

The next morning they had to load all John's stuff on Jake's mule, for it was Johns that had gotten ground up in the dust last night. Like the tenderfoot that he was, He didn't grab the mule's reigns, like Jake did. He figured that he would be able to get out of the way. That would be a mistake that John would not repeat.

Now they were into the trees, and mountains again, and the trails were beautiful, but the beauty of these mountains, cannot really be written down on paper.

John was contemplating all this when Chick stopped, and his horse's ears perked up! Someone, or thing was off to the left somewhere! Thwack! An arrow was sticking just under John's saddle horn, and grazed his horse!

He started bucking (Which probably saved his life, as more arrows were flying all around him)! He had learned a long time ago how to fall off a horse, so he was ok, and he looked over at Jake, and he was off his horse, and taking aim with his Hawkin, at someone in the trees. John's horse calmed down, and he grabbed his Hawkin from the scabbard, and swatted him on the rump to get out of harm's way! Jake was reloading, and as John was taking aim on an Indian, he noticed out of the corner of my eye, that Chick was hiding behind a rock!

He could not help, but grin as he pulled the trigger! John guessed he would feel bad later about killing someone, but for now, all he had on his mind was to stay alive! It was over as fast as it had began, and the Indians were riding off to the west. It was just about then, when Killdeer, and about 25 warriors rode up to them. John was never so glad to see someone in his life!

After hugs, and pats on the back, they sat down and started to communicate. Apparently Killdeer, and his bunch were heading for the rendezvous too, when they heard all the shooting, and came up to find them fighting Bloods! John guessed they just liked to fight. They walked over to see the ones they killed, and was surprised to find two more.

Killdeer and his men were on the mark also! Some of the Shoshone were taking souvenirs from the ones that they killed, but John told them that he would just as soon leave them be. They looked at him kind of funny, but he guessed they didn't know that this was his first time to kill another human being!

Since they were all going to the same place, they decided to travel together. Safety in numbers, was always a good thing. Jake asked John what happened to Chick when all the fighting took place, and when he told him that Chick was hiding behind a rock the whole time, they thought they were both going to split a gut laughing.

Jake explained what they were laughing about to the Indians, and they started laughing also. After being around Killdeer, and his people, John noticed that they were easy to laugh, and told Jake so. Jake said, "Injuns was notional like the wild critters, but they liked to laugh when something was funny!"

CHAPTER VI
Rendezvous and Uncle Jack

They started hearing popping sounds in the distance, and John looked at Jake. Jake smiled, and said, "Ronnyvu"!

They had to bed down one more night before they got there, and John was amazed at the distance that the sound carried from the guns, and all the ruckus they were apt to make at rendezvous.

The next morning, he noticed Jake getting all spruced up in clean buckskins, and combing his hair, and primping like a woman, and he had to say just that.

Jake said, "everyone gets dressed in their best when they ride in for the Ronnyvu."

John guessed he was right, because Killdeer, and his men were doing the same.

They apparently had been to one before. John knew from talking to all the mountain men, that several Indian tribes participated in the rendezvous. Some said that it was rumored that the Bloods were even thinking about coming. John truly hoped not, because he knew first hand what they were like!

The next day about mid-morning, they topped this hill, and a grand spectacle lay before John's eyes! Down in this lush valley, were Tipis, and marques tents, and every kind of shelter you could dream of! The campfire smoke, just hung in the valley like fog. The tipis were on one end, and the rest were on the other.

What really caught his eyes were the horses! My god, there must have been a thousand of them down on the end where the tipis were. Now he could see why these Plains Indians were nomadic! They had to move, just to have grass for all their horses. And he thought it was just because they followed the buffalo. Jake said to John "Fire thet thar smoke pole in the air, and ride like the Bloods were on yer tail!"

Away he went, and Killdeer, and all his men too! John raised up the Hawkin, and touched her off, and away he went screaming like a Banshee!

The feeling that he felt could not be put to paper, but let it be known, that John Tucker was a BY GOD MOUNTAIN MAN, and was at rendezvous at last!

When he got closer, he noticed that the tipis were kind of in little groups. Killdeer and his bunch stopped at the first group. There was a lot of hugging and backslapping, in both groups, white, and Indian alike!

John was awestruck, and just followed Jake. He seemed to know where he was going. The smells were one of the first things that he noticed as they rode through camp! Cooking meat, raw furs, beaver plews, burning sage, and don't forget the ever present smell of horse crap.

Jake pulled up at a post that was driven in the ground to tie the horses to. John did the same, and they dismounted. This was a trader that Jake knew, and he had to say his greetings. Jake walked up to the man and hit him right square in the jaw! The man got up and did the same thing to Jake!

John was about ready to break them up, when they hugged each other, and slapped each other on the back! After they got done cussing each other, Jake turned, and introduced John to his brother! After he really looked, John could see the resemblance. His name was Robert, but most folks called him "Trader Bob." After they shook hands, Bob said, "Do I know you?"

John told Bob, Maybe it was his last name that is familiar.

Bob said, "You kin to Jack Tucker."

"Nephew" John told him. "Have you seen him?" John asked.

"He would be over with the Shoshones, I reckon. Seein as how he is married to one."

John was shocked! This was news to him, and he could not help wandering what his pa would think…His brother married to a heathen! Well he sure was glad that he didn't feel that way! In fact he could not wait to meet her. On that note, he told Jake that he was going to wander over to the Snake village. Jake said that he would be along shortly, because he wanted to see ole Jack. John had to walk the whole length of the encampment to get there, and the sites that he saw would make most people cringe!

Some guys were fighting, and some had Indian women down on the ground doing what men do! Nobody seemed to mind here at the rendezvous, he guessed you could do what ever struck your fancy!

As he was walking along, he was looking at this guy throwing a knife up in the air, and trying to catch it on the way down! John was so engrossed in this that he ran right into this giant of a man! Well the man didn't cotton to that, and he picked John up by his shirt front, and threw him up in the air, like he was a baby!

John was up instantly and the man, was just raising his hand to throw a knife! John did not even have time to think, and with the blink of an eye, John's knife was a blur as it pinned this man's arm to a tree that he was standing by! Of course the knife only went through the man's shirt. The whole area around them became quiet, as John walked right up to him, and pulled out his knife!, then turned, and walked on! As he was passing a trader, the man motioned for him to come over, and John did. The trader told him that nobody has ever bested Bull Baker, and that he had better watch his back. John thanked him, and walked on. He was just glad that he didn't have kill another human! One was enough for this trip.

He got to the Shoshone encampment a few minutes later. He had no Idea as to where to look, and he just kept walking past the tipis.

It was a warm night, and most everyone was outside their lodges at a cooking fire. As he was walking, and looking, a stick was thrust between his feet, and he went down like a ton of bricks!

He was up in a flash, and his knife was in his hand (this was automatic, it seemed.)! He turned, and found himself facing Uncle Jack!

"Ya gonna Stick me John?"

John looked down at the knife in his hand, and put it away. By then his uncle was giving him a bear hug, and slapping him on the back.

"I been hearin stories bout this youngen what gets his knife out real fast, and hits what he aims at!" "That be you"?

"I reckon." Was all John said.

Uncle Jack led John over to the fire, and stopped in front of this very pretty Indian woman and said, "this here is my wife! Her name is Antelope. Antelope, this here is John, my nephew."

John stuck out his hand, and then just about peed his pants, when she grabbed him, and hugged him! Then in almost perfect English, she said, "Glad to meet you John."

He could see his Uncle Jack out of the corner of his eye, just about to bust a gut, laughing! John was surprised, when Jack said that he knew ole Quiet Jake was bringing him to the rendezvous, and said so. Uncle jack said, not much happens out here without someone hearing about it. He then looked down, and said who do we have here? And John told him, Chick. Of course he wanted to know how he came by that name, and John had to tell him the story. After they quit laughing, he told them that Chick did help when the need was there. Uncle Jack said, "Aint nothin more loyal than an old hound dog."

They talked way into the night, and Jake never did show up. John kind of expected he was into the Taos Lightnin again. After these tough old mountain men get a good trapping season under their belt, they deserve to "Let er Loose!"

Jack and Antelope wanted John to stay there, but he told them that he had to get back to his plunder, and of course Jake. John went back to Jake's brother's lodge, and their they were both passed out right in front of Bob's lodge, with a jug sitting between them. He went, and tended to the horses, and mule, and then bedded down himself. As he lay there under the stars, he could not help but feel deeply satisfied, and even with all the commotion going on all around him, was asleep immediately.

He awoke with Chick licking his face! *Damn dog!* Thought John. *Gonna have to make him quit that, it always made him think of Becky.*

Wonder what she would think, if he told her that an old hound dog reminded him of her.

He got up and went down to the creek, to wash up some, and when he returned, Jake, and Bob were up, and already had coffee done. He didn't see Chick around, and asked Jake if he had seen him. Jake said that he reckoned Chick was over with the Injuns.

When he was making coffee, he spied him heading in that direction. Well there were a lot of dogs in an Indian encampment, and he guessed Chick found a good smelling female. He would not bother him, he would come back when he was ready.

They dined on a meal that Trader Bob set out. Bacon, eggs, and some biscuits that Jake baked. *My God, it was heaven, just eating someone else's cooking*, thought John, and he could not remember the last time that he had bacon. When you live like the mountain men do, the simple things are appreciated.

He was going to go back to uncle Jack's place, after he walked all around checking things out. Jake told him that he would meet him there, because he had to go "Knock ole Jack on his ass," as he put it.

Now John was sitting around the fire with his uncle, and Antelope. Jack told him what Jake did every time he seen him. Apparently Jack wasn't the one who got knocked on his ass. Jack went on to tell John about this game that he and Jake played. After not seeing each other for long spells, Jake would come up on his camp and sneak up behind him. Twice, he was able to come up behind him and tap him on the shoulder. Well naturally Jack would spin around, and knock him on his ass. Jack went on to say, "I don't know how in the Hell he can sneak up on me that way, but he aint Quiet Jake for nothin, I reckon!"

John thought that he would like to see the outcome of Jake's visit, but that was their game, and he would hear about it later.

There was a commotion out at the edge of camp, and John wandered over to see what all the hull-a-baloo was about. There was a small band of Indians coming into camp, and some were hollering at them, especially the Indian camp.

He asked this man that was standing there watching. "What's all the ruckus about?"

CHAPTER VII
Beautiful Woman, Dead White Man, Faithful Friend

"Blackfoot," was what he said!

Well that got his attention! As John was standing there watching, he did not see any that looked familiar. This was a small band, and did they look grand, dressed in all their finery. At this moment, John was concentrating on this one family. Their was a man, and his wife, and their daughter. It was the daughter that John was looking at, and he had never seen anyone so beautiful! Her dress was almost white, and decorated with beads, and porcupine quills, and died in different colors. He finally tore his eyes away from her, and following her horse was a dog, and guess who was following the dog? None other than Chick!

John watched where they set up camp, and since nobody got along with the Blackfoot, they set up a little away from the rest of the Indians.

Leave it to Chick!, thought John. Consorting with the enemy. *These people should not be his enemy*, thought John, *Hell he didn't even know them.*

As he was watching, they began to set up their camp, and John never saw anyone work as hard as those women. In somewhere around an hour they had their camp set up. John didn't know weather or not to go get Chick, or let him come back on his own. Him going to get Chick won out, because after all, he would get to see that beautiful girl close up!

He took a few steps in that direction, when a rope dropped around his shoulders, pinning his arms! He was jerked off his feet, and landed at the feet of Bull Baker! John himself weighed in at around two hundred pounds and this man pulled him off the ground like a sack of potatoes! While he was struggling with the rope, Bull pulled it tight, and was coming down with a knife in his hand!

John was powerless to defend himself what with the rope around his arms! All he could do was watch as he was surely going to be killed. A strange thought came to John at this time.

John was not an overly religious man, but Bull had this big grin on his face as he was bringing the knife down! John thought, *surely this man will go to Hell, since he obviously loved killing another man.*

Just as the knife was about a foot from his chest, a brown blur appeared out of nowhere, and Chick had Bull's wrist in his teeth! The momentum from Chick's lunge, spun Bull around, giving John enough time to free himself! As Chick let go to get a tighter grip, Bull kicked him in the head, throwing him about ten feet! He then raised the knife, as if to throw it at John! John didn't bat an eye, when his own knife came out in a blur, and was sticking in this giant's chest! Bull looked down at the knife sticking out of his chest, and then at John. The look that he gave John was that of a surprised mad man. He started to raise his knife again, but was too weak, and just fell over backwards! He was dead!

John had killed again! He knew that he should feel some remorse, but after all, it was kill or be killed, and this man kicked Chick so hard that he may be dead as well! It was just something he had to do.

He looked over at the friend who had just saved his life, and Chick was just laying there, not moving! 'Oh my God!' he thought, and was just about to pick him up, when a pair of brown arms scooped him up first!

The Blackfoot girl was holding Chick, and motioning John to follow her. Follow her he did, right over to the Blackfoot encampment! Apparently all had seen the fight, and the way Chick had saved his friend. They all just smiled as the girl, and John walked through the camp.

They stopped in front of a painted tipi, and the girl laid Chick down. John bent down, and he and the girl were petting Chick, when this very fierce looking man came out of the lodge! He motioned for John, and the girl to stand back, and they did. The man dug a very small horn container out of a pouch that he had around his neck. He opened it and got something on his finger. Then he reached down, and put his finger in front of Chick's nose. Chick sneezed, and sat up!

"Thank God!" John said aloud!

The girl looked at john, and said, "thank him," pointing to the man.

Chick was on them now, just licking away at both of them!

John felt around on his head, and felt a goose egg of a bump, but he would be alright. John then looked at the girl, and asked here where she learned to speak English?

She told him that a Missionary lived among her people, and he had taught her. John thanked her for helping Chick. She asked him why his name was Chick? John told her the story, and both were laughing before he finished.

When John looked up to thank the healer, he was gone! He turned to the girl, and asked her, her name. She told him that he would not be able to say it in her tongue, but the Missionary gave her the Christian name of June. Then June asked what John's name was, and he told her.

John noticed the man and woman walking up to them, and obviously they were her parents, because they were the same ones that he had seen riding in with her. June introduced them to John, and told John that they could not speak English.

Her parents bent down, and petted Chick, and said something in their own tongue to him. He asked June what they said to Chick? She told him that they called Chick a Little warrior. John smiled, and said that was true.

It was time for John to go back. He had to go bury Bull Baker! He asked June if he could come back later, and she said something to her father. As John looked on while they were talking, he could tell that her father was not too sure about him calling on his daughter. He broke in, and told June to tell him the he understood, him being a stranger, and white to boot. June finally turned to John, and said, "You can come!"

John grabbed her father's hand, and started pumping it! Her father looked at him like he was nuts, so John quit shaking his hand, and said thank you! June translated for him, and John turned, and headed back for camp, with Chick right on his heels.

When John got back to the area where the fight took place, there were a bunch of people standing there. At this time he thought, *were they going to hang him, or what?* It turned out, that his uncle, and Jake had witnessed the whole thing! Even him going over to the Blackfoot camp.

As John approached, everyone was slapping him on the back, saying what a good fight that was. Everyone wanted to see the knife that killed Bull Baker! It seemed that Bull Baker was known far and wide as a bully, but had no equal with a knife, until now.

Everything happened so fast, that John didn't remember pulling the knife out of the man, and wiping it clean, but apparently he had done so. He finally got away from all the people, and found his uncle, and Jake over at Jake's brother's trading place. All three men congratulated John on the fight, but John got no satisfaction from killing the man, and told the three that. Jake's brother asked John if he had gotten to know the Blackfoot. John said that he only met June's parents.

"Why do you ask," said John!

Trade!!! John! for the trade! Hardly anyone has been able to trade with the Blackfoot!

When John got to thinking about it, it made sense. Why else would the Blackfoot come here, if not to trade? He told Bob that he would ask June when he went back there later. At least, now he did not have to bury Bull, because the group said they would take care of it.

John headed back to where they had put their plunder, so he could find the wolf skins. He needed something to trade for some buckskin clothing, and maybe the wolf skins would work. As he was walking around looking at all the traders, it dawned on him that maybe the best place to find buckskin clothing would be in the Shoshone camp.

It took a while to find Killdeer's lodge, but when he got within sight of it, Killdeer spotted him first. There were a group of young men all standing around a log, with a knife sticking out of it.

Killdeer came over to John, and grabbed his arm, pulling him toward the log. When they got there, Killdeer pointed to the knife, and then to John saying something in his own tongue. All the young men came over and started patting John on the back. John realized that Killdeer had told them about a white man teaching him how to throw like that. He guessed that most Indians never threw their knives, because they might lose it to the enemy. Killdeer got a small piece of leather, and stuck it on the butt of the log, and pointed to John, then to the log. John knew he had to show them what he could do, so he walked off about four paces, turned and threw! They were in awe, because it was hard to see him even move, let alone stick the big knife right dead center in that piece of leather!

He did it a couple more times, just to show them that it wasn't an accident. Now they were all slapping him on the back, and saying something. John had no idea that they were calling him BIG KNIFE THAT NEVER MISSES!

After all the hooraying was done, he finally got through to Killdeer, that he wanted to trade the wolf furs. Killdeer took him, and of course Chick over to his lodge. While John waited outside, Killdeer went in, and was almost immediately back outside with a very young, and pretty girl, that he introduced as his wife through signs, and hand gestures. Again through signs, and gestures he was able to explain to her what he wanted. She went in and came back out with a very soft piece of leather, and held it up to John in a few places, marking it as she went. Killdeer was able to explain to John that he could come back in two days, and then they would see.

Now it was time to go to the Blackfoot camp, and talk to June. He tried to explain this to Killdeer, and all Killdeer would do was just grin that knowing grin that he had.

He shook hands with Killdeer, and he and Chick headed in the direction of the Blackfoot camp. Chick seemed all too eager to go over there. John guessed that he had an interest in that camp as well.

They walked up to June's lodge, and her and her folks were outside. John spoke to June's father first, as was proper in their culture. He then spoke to her mother, and finally to June herself. Of course June was translating everything that he said. John detected movement on his left, and there was Chick going around the back of the lodge with a female. John asked June if they could walk around the encampment, and talk. She asked her father, and he looked at John, with a look that said, "I will be watching you."

This was all new to June and she did not know why she was attracted to this young white man. Yes, she spoke their language, but that was because of the missionary who used to live with them. John was the only white person she had met other than the missionary. Why did he make her heart pound so? She never had these feelings before, and many young men have tried to court her.

June said, "This way," and off they went.

John was so impressed with the glowing beauty that June put out, that he could hardly talk at all. He did tell her that he had traded some furs for some buckskin clothing, because his were in such bad shape. She asked where he was getting these clothes from, and he told her. Ha!, she said, "I could have made you a better set of clothing!"

He told her that it would not hurt to have another set. John finally got around to asking her about trading with the white people, and she said that they would be glad to trade with them. He told her that he would bring Trader Bob over in the morning, and she said she would tell her father.

Women! John could make no head nor tail of them! It sounded like she had her feelings hurt when he told her who made the clothing, but he had no idea that she would make them. After all they had just met. Now, while walking along with her, he felt so flustered at himself, for not thinking of the right thing to say!

She must have detected this, because she told him to relax and just be himself. How could he relax, with her smiling at him that way. He finally took a big breath, and said ok, but he hadn't been around many women, so she would have to bear with him. They had pretty much walked around the whole Blackfoot encampment, and she said that they had better get back to her lodge, or her father would scalp John! John jumped, and turned, and looked at her, and then she smiled again!

Whew! She was just kidding! Well they had better get back anyway. John had some thinking to do, so when they stopped at her lodge, he bade her goodbye, and asked her if she would come over to the trader's place with her father. She said that she had to because her father needed someone to translate for him.

See you tomorrow then?

Yes! She said, I will look forward to it.

Just as John turned to leave, Chick got into step with him, and they made their way back to uncle Jack's lodge. As June watched John and

Chick leaving, she was reminded about the time another suitor had went away after a confrontation with her. This one left because he could not stand it that a mere girl could shoot a bow as well as him. That one was the pride of the village and had taken many coupes from enemies. June's father was not happy when that one left, because he would have been a good catch. This did not matter to June, because she had no feelings for him anyway. At least not the way she did about John Tucker. At that time she made a mental note that she would have to be careful, so as not to lose him as well.

When John got back, Antelope had a pot of stew on the fire, and said, "Are you hungry John?"

She then threw a large deer bone with stew meat still on it to Chick. It was funny to watch Chick trying to eat that very hot bone. First he would bite, it and then throw it up in the air. Uncle Jack had just stepped in, and was laughing, as he said, "I swear that mutt is trying to cool it off!"

Apparently it worked, because he was now just chewing away at it.

John could not remember when he tasted food that was so good. As he was eating away, the thought went through his mind, *that when in love, you lost your appetite. Love! Where in the Hell did that come from? He didn't have time for such foolishness. There were mountains to see, beaver to trap, and many more things to do that did not pertain to love.*

Uncle Jack told him to throw his bedroll over on the side, and he could sack out whenever he pleased. As tired as he was, right after he got done eating, he went to bed. Tired… Yes! Sleepy…No! Try as he might, he could not shut down his brain, he lay there for hours, and wanted to think of these beautiful mountains, and this very rendezvous, but alas… June was what he last seen in his mind's eye, when he finally did sleep.

CHAPTER VIII
Decisions Made

The next morning, after breakfast, he got uncle Jack off to themselves, and asked if he could talk to him. "Of course" Jack said. John did not know how to begin, so he started from the beginning. He told Jack how he met June, and of course it was all over camp about the fight with Bull. Jack listened patiently as John told his story.

When it was all said and done, Jack said, "look over yonder there at Antelope. She loves these here mountains, and don't mind me trappin, and she damn sure loves these here rendezvous, cause she gets fine cookware, and beads, and other things that strikes her fancy."

Are you saying that I should marry June?

At that Jack looked right into John's eyes, and said, "I'm a sayin foller yer heart. I did, and I would not have it any other way."

John then asked him if he knew any of the Blackfoot ways. Jack told him that he didn't know their ways personally, but that most Indians were the same in a lot of ways. He then told him to talk to her father, whenever he was around her. The father usually had the last word on most things. John thanked him for the advise, and said that he had better look up Jake, and see what's going on. They still had some trading to do, and he needed to buy some traps, and other equipment that he needed for life in the mountains. John's mind was jumbled as he walked over to Bob's place. He knew that he was hopelessly caught up in this age old thing called love, but he did need to spend one season trapping in the mountains, before he made any moves in that direction. *What were June's feelings? He did not know!* Women were a mystery to him, and he could not read them.

He got to Bob's place, and both Jake, and Bob were there. John had some talking to do with Jake. As far as Jake knew, he had just brought John to meet his uncle Jack and did not know that John wanted to spend a season with Jake stomping around the mountains, and trapping beaver. Jake offered John the ever present jug, and John passed on it, saying "That's ok, I never did develop a taste for that stuff." They made small talk for a while, and John asked Jake if he would take a walk with him.

Jake handed the jug back to Bob, and said, "Gonna take a stroll round camp, ya kin watch that for me till I git back."

As they started off, Jake could tell that John was troubled, so he just waited until John wanted to talk. Finally John started by saying, "are you going trapping when the rendezvous is over?"

"Yep" was all he said.

"Would you mind having a partner?" John said.

Jake turned to John, and said, "Thought ya had yer blood up over thet thar Bakckfoot gal?"

"I do," said John. John then told him that he did not even know if she felt the same way, anyway he wanted to spend a season in the mountains, trapping, before he took on a woman.

"Smart thinkin" was what Jake said. "Have ya asked her about it yet?"

"Nope" said John. I wanted to ask you if I could partner up with you, before I talked to her.

"Hell yes" ya kin be my pard" he said. As they were walking along talking, John noticed people waving, and greeting them when they passed, and he asked Jake about it.

"Hell boy you is popular since the fight with Bull! They all jest want ta say they knew the one what kilt ole Bull Baker!"

John did not feel popular, in fact he still had thoughts on the fight with Bull. Could he have done it differently? He did not know, but he did know that he did not like killing another human being. They spent the rest of the day buying, and trading for the things that they would need for the coming season. Now that they didn't have all the furs to pack around, there was enough plunder for one mule. John asked Jake how they were going to pack all the furs out on just one mule, and Jake said, "I will show you when we get em."

Now John could put it off no longer, he had to go see June! He told Jake that he would see him later, and then he headed for the Blackfoot camp. As always, Chick was right on his heels. After all Chick was the one who brought him and June together. The dog that Chick was interested in saw them first, and came running out to meet them. Chick, and her disappeared around in back of the lodge.

June's Father was the first one to step out the door, and he was looking right at John! John swallowed a couple times, then held up his hand in the universal sign for friend. They just stood there looking at each other, and all that came to John's mind was, *he knows, and he does not approve!*

As it turned out he did know, but approval may, or may not come about, depending on what John did in the next instant! John reached back behind himself, and pulled out the other Sheffield Knife. He held it out handle first to her father. No words were spoken, but John could tell that he was impressed. Of course this wasn't a trade for his daughter, and John made him see that.

Just about then, June appeared just behind her father, and she had the most beautiful smile on her face! John asked her if she could go for a walk again. She spoke to her father, and he looked at John with that look again, that said, "I'll be watching you!" *That was ok', thought John because if he had a daughter like her, then he would be the same way.*

Away they went walking slowly so as to take longer to get all around the camp. It was hard enough to talk to her just normally, but now he had something important to say. She could tell that he was nervous, and grabbed his hand. He just about had one of them hissy fits!, but when he looked down at her, she was smiling that beautiful smile, and he found his voice.

"I need to find out something," he said. She was looking at him questioningly. "I feel something for you, and I think you feel something for me. Don't you?"

She looked him right in the eye, and said, "Do you think we would be walking together, if I did not?"

"But what about your father?"

She told him that, that is all that they have been talking about these past few days. She said that her father was very impressed with the way you handled that big man yesterday. He also said that you were young for a white warrior, but knew how to fight, and would be a good provider.

Now that they knew each other's feelings, John had to see what she thought about him being gone for a season. There was no other way, so he just told her what he and Jake were going to do. Surprisingly she agreed to it. Women! John thought! You just could not predict what they would think, or do! She then told John that she, and her father had decided that her and John needed more time to make sure they were doing the right thing, and to see if they still felt the same, come Spring. By then they had walked all around the camp, and John squeezed her hand just before they reached her lodge, and said he would see her tomorrow. John thought it better to stay with Jake this night, because they had a lot to discuss about their upcoming trip. Bob had a lodge, but it was only for one person, so Jake, and John would be sleeping out in the open again.

There was still a little daylight left, and as John approached Bob's place, he could see a bunch of people standing around. John could see that they were throwing hawks, and knives at a block of wood, so he just stood on the sideline. Apparently Jake was trying to show them the same type of throwing that John had shown him.

About then someone in the crowd said, "There's John"!

That's all it took! Everybody was grabbing John, and saying "Show us how John!" John was stuck now! All he could do was comply to their demands. He stepped up to the throwing area, and in one swift motion, drew, and stuck his knife in the playing card that they had stuck up there. Then in a heartbeat, done the same with his tomahawk. He left enough room between his knife, and hawk, to stick his other knife right between them! All three weapons were sticking in the same card! Total silence surrounded the group, until finally someone said, "Damn!"

They had him repeat it again, and he did, with almost the same accuracy as before. Everyone was slapping him on the back, and congratulating him, and when all the hull-a-balloo was done, John noticed his uncle Jack standing off to the side, just smiling that devilish smile that he was known for.

It was getting on towards dark, and John asked Jake where they were bedding down. Jake pointed it out to him, and told him that he would be along shortly. John sure hoped Jake didn't get into the sauce too much tonight, because he had a lot to tell him.

After tending to the stock (Seemed like it was always him doing that now-a-days) he decided to turn in. As it turned out, Jake wasn't drinking this night, and he came along right after John turned in. John got up, and he and Jake started talking. All John really wanted to know was if Jake was really ready to take a greenhorn on as a partner? Then he told Jake about his talk with June.

After John wound down, Jake told him that he could not think of a single man that he would rather partner up with, than him. Now John asked Jake where they would do their trapping.

"The way I figger it we might mosey up to the Wind River Range. I hear tell we is in fer a tree snappin cold ass winter!" "Thet means the fur on them critters will really shine," and we could take out some right good plews!"

They talked for another hour or so, then John's eye lids started to get heavy, and he told Jake that he was going to sleep. One would think what with all the noise associated with a rendezvous, that you couldn't sleep, but they did.

The morning turned out to be cloudy and dreary. John went down to the stream to bath, as was his practice(One that the other men teased him about) constantly.

After he dried off, and was putting on his clothes, he remembered that this was the day to go check on his new buckskins.

Chick was laying up on the sandbar, as was his morning ritual. He would go into the water with John, but immediately turn around and go back up on the sandbar, and just lay there watching.

Chick suddenly stood up, and was looking just down stream. John looked down stream to see what had Chick's attention. Once again Ole Chick came through for him, as John stood there in the shallow water watching June walking out of the water as naked as the day she was born!

John knew that he should not look, but he could not tear his eyes away. She was as beautiful without clothes as she was with them.

As he was dressing, he glanced upstream every once in a while. June was also dressing, and John waited until she was fully dressed, and then he headed in that direction. Of course Chick was right on his heels. Far be it for him to miss anything.

She looked up as he approached, and did not seem in the least bit startled.

Clumsily, John said, "I could not help but see."

June just smiled, and said, "I was there before you were, and you were not the only one who saw!"

After their exchange of words, June told him that her father was waiting at the edge of the camp, and that she had better go.

John reluctantly agreed, but his heart was pounding so hard, surely she must hear it.

She then bent down and scratched Chick behind the ears, and then was gone.

In a daze, John made his way back to camp. As he walked along, his senses returned to normal. When he reached the camp, Jake, and his brother were drinking some strong hot coffee, and John thought that maybe that was just what he needed right about now. They were also frying bacon in a skillet over the fire, and did it ever smell good. John had the passing thought about Love, and loss of appetite again.

After breakfast, John, and Chick headed over to the Shoshone Camp. As they approached Killdeer's lodge, both Killdeer, and his wife came out.

They were both smiling, as his wife brought her hands around in front, to reveal a very soft, and beautiful pair of buckskins! Both shirt, and pants.

Killdeer made the sign for John to go inside his lodge, and try them on. While John was putting on those pants, he could not help but notice how they stretched, and moved when he did. Both pants, and shirt fit perfectly, and when John stepped out of the lodge, even Chick was smelling him up and down. John went over to the plunder that he had brought with him, and pulled out the three wolf skins that he had, and gave them to Killdeer's wife. It did not seem like enough, and John explained this through signs to Killdeer. At that, Killdeer pulled out the knife that John had given him, and made John see that it was indeed enough.

They patted each other on the back, and John started to hug Killdeer's wife, and caught himself. He looked at Killdeer, and all Killdeer did was shrug, so John hugged her.

John, and Chick made their way back to Bob's trading table, and there stood June and her father looking at what Bob had to trade. John just went over to his bedroll and watched, as the trading began. June's father could not speak English, but in no way was he hampered in the trading part. June translated for him, and it looked like everybody was having a good time. While in Independence, John learned from the Mountain men, that any Indian loves to trade. Before they left, John asked June to ask her Father if he could come and visit later. She did, and told John that it would be good if he came to visit, and then she looked John up and down, raising her eyebrow. Then they left.

After they had gone John asked Bob what he thought about trading with the Blackfoot. Bob told John that it was good to have the Bloods to trade with, but they were nobody's fool at the trading game. Jake was sitting over on the other side of the, table when he asked John, "Ya bout ready ta pull out a these here digs Pard?"

CHAPTER IX
Rendezvous Over

John looked over at Jake, and said, "Hell yes, but I have to make two stops before I leave."

Jake just grinned, and said, "I reckon."

They gathered up all the plunder that they traded for, and bought, and then said their farewells to Bob.

Of course the first stop was uncle Jack's, and Antelope's lodge. They were just finishing up breakfast when the two pulled up. Jack looked at them, and said, "looks like yer a goin trappin."

John, and Jake got down off their horses, and went over to the fire. Jake pulled back his fist like he was going to hit Jack, but just grinned, and grabbed him in a bear hug.

John stuck out his hand at Jack, and Jack just laughed and said, "I reckon I kin still hug my nephew!" At that he grabbed John in a big bear hug, and told him that he would be seeing him from time to time.

Antelope was not to be outdone, and she grabbed John, and hugged him also. They got back up on their horses, and leading the mule with all their plunder, and of course Chick following along, headed for the Blackfoot camp.

As they pulled up to June's lodge, both her father, and mother were out in front by the fire. June looked up at John and said, "my father said that we could go for a walk before you leave."

They got down off their horses, and Jake began signing to June's father.

It looked like Jake and June's father were getting along just fine, so John told them that they would return shortly, and off they went. Now John was holding her hand as they walked along. Neither had said a word. Finally John said It is only going to be about four months until we meet again. They stopped, and June looked up into John's eyes, and said, "a very, very long four months."

They were just walking along talking small talk, and when they got to the other end of the camp, John stopped, and grabbed her, and turned her around to face him!

While looking into those ebony eyes of hers, he bent down, and kissed her a long deep kiss, which she returned in full. They could each feel the other's heart pounding and at that moment, John knew that it was indeed going to be a long four months.

They made their way back to June's camp, and John "threw caution to the wind," as he hugged both June's parents. Now he hugged June, and said his goodbyes, and then they were leaving.

They must have went five miles before either man spoke. Finally, John broke the silence, by asking Jake if he ever had a woman.

CHAPTER X
Jake's Stories

"Course I did!," said Jake! "I had me the sweetest lil Flathead gal ya ever did see! She purely did shine, she did."

"What happened to her, said John?" John could see the change come over Jake as he said

"She went under back in twenty four."

Now John just settled back, because he knew that Jake was going to tell his story.

Jake began by saying that they had built a cabin up on the Popo Aggie, and all was well, until some bad men came. Jake had been out running his traps, when he had heard the shot. It sounded like it was coming from the direction of the cabin!

He then said, "I dropped everthin, and rode Hell bent for home!"

"I was too late!" he said. "She were a layin out in the yard, jest a hangin on ta life! Her dress was ripped, and there was a big slit all across her belly!"

"She tolt me thet jest afore they had their way with her, she shot, and wounded one with the pistol that I left for her!"

John could see the sadness in his eyes, as he went on with his story.

"Well then she closed her eyes, and went under, with her head a layin right in my lap!""I aint ashamed ta say thet I cried like a baby fer a while." I dug a grave, and put her in it, then I sorta went nuts! I caint remember everthin, but I knows I burnt down the house!"

He then said that he re-loaded the pistol, and got what he could carry on his horse, and commenced to tracking. He also said that those fools that killed his wife were not worried about anyone following them.

"They left tracks thet a blind tendrfoot could foller." Jake said, as he went on with his story. "They was only bout a hour ahead of me, so all I had ta do was wait til dark. I coulda slipped up on em, and kilt em all, but I wanted em ta know why they were a goin under one at a time!"

Jake then asked John, "ifn he was sure Thet he wanted to hear it all?"

"Well Hell yes, John said! I want to hear all about it."

He went on to say that he slipped into their camp after they went to sleep, and slipped right up on the closest one, and put his hand over his mouth, and slit his throat just as slick as a whistle. Of course the man did not have a chance to make any noise, so Jake just drug him out of their camp. Jake said he threw the man down in a draw. He then said, "Hell the critters got to eat too." Jake said that the next day, he watched from a small hill, as they awoke to find a blood spot where their friend had been sleeping.

"Twas plain as day where I drug thet guy outta there, but those two were not about to go see what happened ta their friend."

John could tell by looking at Jake that, that was just exactly the effect that he hoped for. Jake said that he followed them all the next day, and they was a long time going to bed. But finally, one went to bed, and the other stood watch.

He then said that the one doing the watching, was a nodding to beat the band, and Jake knew it would not be long before he was asleep.

Jake said that he went for the watcher this time, and had no trouble sneaking right up on that one either. He did this one a little different than the first one.

"I snuck up on thisn jest like the first, and slit his throat jest like the first, but I left a little present for the sleeper."

He told John that he cut off the man's privates, and left them laying right where the man was sitting.

John was thinking that, 'He sure was glad that Jake was his friend, and not his enemy!'

John asked Jake about the last man, and he said that he was going to do the same thing to him, but as he sat watching him the next day, he could tell that his work was done.

"What do you mean, John asked?"

He then told John that the last man just went off the deep end, nuts, or crazy, or touched, as the Indians say. Since he would not know why Jake was doing these things, Jake just left. After hearing Jakes story, and knowing how he, himself felt about June, John didn't blame Jake one bit.

CHAPTER XI
Second Rendezvous

Now they were two days from the rendezvous, and Jake had said that they were on their way to a valley way up by the "Stinkin Water," as Jake put it. Much later this would be called Yellowstone Park

Jake had told John that he needed to see the Stinkin Water. and that he would not believe it until he did. As they approached the base of the mountains, John asked Jake about the twin peaks to their left, or west?

"Them is the Teats," said Jake.

"Teats?"

"Yep, woman's breast," said Jake.

John did not realize that he was looking at what would later be called, "The Grand Tetons."

To the east of them were beautiful meadows, that were teaming with elk. John had never seen that many elk in one spot before!

That evening they dined on fresh trout caught from a stream that they had been following for quite a while.

John asked Jake why they were camped so far from the stream, and was told that the silvertips come down to get the trout, also, and they did not want any truck with them.

About that time they smelled this awful smell! Jake was about to tell John to draw his pistol, when a ball of fur about the size of Chick, jumped right into john's lap!

Chick was on it immediately, and pulling it off of John! This thing had Chick on the ground, just about ready to gut him, when Jake shot the critter dead!

Chick!" John screamed. Then he went over to Chick and was checking him out. There were a few slashes on his side, but they would heal, if it did not get infected. John then looked at his chest, and discovered that he, also had some slashes, but just in his buckskins!

"What in God's name is that thing?" asked John.

"Glutton," said Jake.

Jake could see that John was puzzled by the look John was giving him.

"Wolverine," said Jake. Thet is whut he is! "Meanest critter for his size in the whole world! Thet critter kills for the pure fun of it! He must have smelled the fish in yer plate!" Jake said. "Glutton aint fraid a nuthin!"

"What about that awful smell?" asked John.

"Them critters eat anything, even rotten meat, and then they roll in it, and also ifn thet aint enough, they have scent glands what stinks to beat the Devil!" said Jake.

John's appetite was spoiled, so he went over, and began skinning that critter, and what a stinking job that was. Jake told him that the fur from the "Glutton" would fetch a good price, because you usually can't get close enough for a kill.

Chick was licking his wounds, and appeared to be ok. John was very thankful that his friend pulled that critter off his lap. While sitting around the fire that night, Jake said that they would set out some traps in the morning, so they could start building up their plews.

The next morning they put out their traps, and when they ran their trap line, caught six beaver, and a muskrat. They would skin them when they found them, and when they got back to camp would stack them all together. This became a daily routine as they would follow this stream, trapping along the way.

One day, as John was down at the stream skinning a beaver, he heard a snort! As he turned around, he found himself looking into the meanest bloodshot eyes that he had ever seen! John's rifle was leaning up against a tree(a cardinal sin out west), but this giant Silvertip was between the gun, and him! No way would his pistol kill this thing!

Now the Grizzly Bear was standing up on it's hind legs (never a good sign)! John had just skinned a beaver, and had the skin in one hand, and the carcass in the other. He threw the carcass at the silvertip, and then it went back down on all fours, and was sniffing the beaver! That's when John took his chance!

He ran around the bear, and grabbed his rifle as he ran! When he turned around, there was the bear! Five feet behind him! How did they run so fast? He did not have time to contemplate! John pulled up the rifle, and shot point blank into the beast's heart from about three feet! In all this time he did not stop running, and could not believe that this bear could still be on it's feet!

On it's feet he was, and just about to swat John up aside the head, when a shot fired, and the thing finally did teeter a little! Jake had fired from the left, and got the thing in the heart also! John did not slacken his pace until he knew that thing was not going to catch him!

Now when John turned, he saw the thing fall, and now It was over! As John was walking up to the now dead grizzly, Chick came out of the bushes, and tried to put the very huge neck of the grizzly in his jaws. All he and Jake could do was laugh, because it looked like Chick was trying to claim this kill as his.

After they quit laughing, John asked Jake how he got here so fast, because he knew that Jake went upstream quite a ways. Jake said that he was already coming back, when he heard John shoot.

Now they had a bear to skin, and they set to it right away, because there might be more of them around here, and they might not be as lucky the next time.

After Jake listened to John's story about throwing the beaver carcass at the bear, he told John that he was very lucky, and that these critters were very notional, and you could never tell what they might do.

The next day it snowed, did it ever snow! The temperature had dropped drastically, but they were prepared for it with the supplies that they had gotten back in Independence.

Jake told John to take the bear robe, because he had earned it.

With the exception of the temperature, it was beautiful out here in the western mountains, and John never lost sight of that.

Where else could you pit you're life against nature almost on a daily basis, and when you were lucky, you would come out on top.

John still had thoughts about June, but you could not let them dominate you, or you would be dead! You had to be sharp witted at all times, because the alternative was not good.

While John was laying snuggled up in his new bear robe, he thought that June would be able to make a nice coat out of it. For a week or so things went pretty much the same day by day, except on this one day while John was setting some traps, he noticed that the forest had become deathly quiet! This was not a good thing! Many things could cause this, and none of them good! He stepped out of the water, and laid down his traps. Some birds flew out of the trees just across the stream!

Very slowly, John backed away from the stream, and into some large rocks.

Chick was looking in the direction of where the birds flew out of the trees, but he was not growling yet, so he at least hadn't smelled anything, or heard anything yet.

John just hunkered down in the big rocks, and waited. He didn't have long to wait! twelve Indians came out on the sandbar right across from where he had been.

John did not recognize the men, but they had their faces painted, so they were after someone, and not just a hunting party! They came across the stream, and were looking down at John's bait can, and also the peg that was driven into the ground to hold the trapped beaver.

Damn! He didn't have time to get the bait can! They might have overlooked the peg in the ground, but the can stuck out like a sore thumb. Even though it was a very small can, those Indians don't miss anything.

John's horse was just behind them hidden in the trees, but he might whinny at the Indian's horses at any time! As John sat there in the rocks listening to them talk, he could not understand any words, so he had no idea as to what tribe this was.

This was a land where many tribes passed through, because the hunting was excellent, and each tribe did not have far to travel to get to an enemy tribe, and make war. Most of these Indians thought the making of war was the most honorable thing that you could do.

They were looking in his direction! John was in the process of bringing up his rifle, when Chick turned, and looked behind them! Twenty feet behind them, came a warrior leading John's horse!

The only thing to do was to lay down the rifle, and put up his hands! Then he put a hand over his heart, and held up the other one in the universal sign of peace.

Chick was about ready to tear into them, so John reached down and comforted him, and talked him into settling down. Now they were all around him! The one that was doing the talking before, was looking at John' big knife sticking out of his sheath.

They hadn't tried to kill him, so that was a good sign. John knew that virtually all Indians respected skill with weapons, since this worked with Killdeer, just maybe it would work here. John very slowly pulled out his knife, and pointed to a tree that was about twelve feet away. He then pointed to the knife, and to the leader, and then to his own eyes, and turned, and threw! They all looked at each other, and at John. The leader pointed to the knife, and to John, meaning for him to do it again.

John had no problem with that, and he did it again, only this time, he stuck a leaf on the side of the tree. The Indians all grunted when the knife stuck right in the middle of the leaf! The leader began saying something to John, and John shook his head meaning that he could not understand. Then John started using sign language, and all was well.

Apparently they had heard of the young man who throws the knife very good.

As John was talking to these men, he could not help but notice how good they were dressed, and from what he learned from them, they were The Sparrow Hawk People, or the Crow, as they were known everywhere.

John was thinking that it was a good thing that he did not have June make his clothes, because the Crow hated the Blackfoot, and they would have noticed how his buckskins were made.

After he thought about it, he remembered that the Blackfoot were hated by everybody. Now that he was talking to them, Chick relaxed, and was quiet. Not much happens out here that don't get noticed by someone, and this band was no exception, because they asked John why he was seen in the camp of their enemies, the Blackfoot!

John did not quite know how to answer that, so he began by describing a woman, and that was all it took! They all started smiling, and pointing at John. Now that they were in a good mood, John asked the leader about the war paint that they wore, and he said Blackfoot, what else? *Oh great!,* thought John. *Well at least it wasn't June's band. They were many miles from here.*

The leader asked John how he felt about them killing the Blackfoot?

John just shrugged his shoulders, and signed that it was not his business, that they had been fighting as long as anyone remembered. They then told each other their names.

His name was hard to pronounce, but it had something to do with big bears, so naturally John shortened it to Bear, for future references. It was funny to hear the way Bear pronounced John. It came out something like Jong. Every time Bear said John's name, then John would laugh. When he did, Bear laughed right along with him.

So far, every tribe that John had, had an encounter with had a good sense of humor, and a ready laugh, when appropriate.

The Indians were wanting to go about their business, and John bid them good by, and they parted with "Good Hearts," as the Indians would say. John was done running his traps, and his feet, and legs were near froze to the point of no feeling in them, so he headed on back to camp. Jake had a hot pot of coffee sitting on the fire, and when John walked up, Jake said, "see any sign?"

"Some," was all John said.

Jake finally asked him what was going on out on his trap line? John told him about his experience with the Crow!

Jake said that he knew the man that John was talking about, and had actually wintered in their village one year.

"You surely do get around, you old He Wolf," said John.

At that, Jake just smiled, and said, "Look around you greenhorn, this here's my home!"

John just grunted, and poured himself a cup of hot strong coffee, and just kicked back, and let the fire warm his feet, and legs.

"We'll move on tomorry," said Jake.

Jake then told John that he did not like to trap a stream to death, but leave some of the critters for another time.

When John thought about it, that made a lot of sense. It's too bad all trappers didn't think like Jake, because, sadly enough there were those who would just plumb clean out a stream, or pond. Jake said that they would get everything ready to go, and when they got back from running their traps tomorrow they could just throw the morning's catch on the stack of plews.

John readily agreed, and said he would be ready when Jake was. They were both up early, and ran their traps, and were back at camp a couple hours after dawn. They then loaded the new skins on to the stack of plews, and headed out.

Cold he was, but John was as happy as he had ever been! They traveled north for two days, and John finally asked Jake if he had a place in mind.

"Dang it youngun!," said Jake. "I done tolt ya thet I allus have a place in mind!"

John just smiled, and said, "Kind of testy this morning, aint ya?"

At that, Jake loosened up a bit, and said, "I jest been thinkin on the times ya met up with Indians, and critters, and I warn't there ta hep ya! "Gettin ta be like yore own pappy, I am!"

John reckoned he was still a greenhorn and told Jake when you use you're head for something besides a hat rack, most times you come out all right. He was going on 20 years old now, and out here you grow up fast, or you don't grow up at all.

"You is right youngun, and I have purty well taught ya all I knows."

They camped that evening in a valley way up in the mountains, and it was as cold as John had ever been, even laying on a buffalo skin, and covering up with a bear skin, and blankets! Both slept close to the fire, and had wood within arms reach, so they would not have to get out of their bedrolls to add it to the fire.

The next morning they went down to check out the stream, and found it frozen solid from bank to bank!

"What do we do now, asked John?"

"Caint do nuthin here, said Jake.""Have ta go down offn this here mountain,"

"Too high up!"

They did just that, and John could feel, the difference as soon as they went down to the base of the mountain. Jake told John that the same stream ran right down to the bottom of this mountain.

As they were traveling along the base of the mountain, John began to notice animal sign that he had not seen up high. He did not have to ask Jake about it, because even animals were smart enough to come down off the mountain when it got that cold.

They found a nice camping spot close to the stream with a cliff to their backs, and Jake said that this was a good thing. After they had a fire going John asked Jake if he ever seen the "Wendigo" when he was by himself? John had heard the other trappers talking about it. It was supposed to be some kind of spirit, or something.

Jake looked John right in the eye, and said, "Course!"

John just settled back, because he knew Jake well enough now to know that he was going to tell a story, and when Jake told a story, John was right there to listen.

He started his story by saying that he had just gotten to the mountains, and was more of a greenhorn than John had ever thought of being. He could not remember the date, but he did say that it was before the Lewis & Clark expedition.

He was about Johns' age when he came to the mountains. He then said that he would have to backtrack a bit, so John would understand what he was talking about.

His folks and him were from Louisiana, originally, but had to move, due to an attack by River Pirates. He said that his father had run a ferry on a narrow part of the Mississippi, and these Pirates came looking for money.

It was in the middle of the night when they came, and everyone was asleep. They burst through the door, and shot his father just as he was getting out of bed, and he didn't have a chance!

His sister and him had beds up in the loft, so they didn't see them right away. There was a rope tied to his sister's bed, and ready to throw out the window in case of a fire, and he opened the window, and threw out the rope!

Jake then said that one of the pirates was rummaging through their stuff looking for something of value, and two more of the men were in the process of ripping off his mother's night dress! Jake said that his father's rifle hadn't been noticed yet. It was

leaning against the wall next to their bed. Jake knew without a doubt that his father was dead, so it was up to him.

His sister was now hiding in the root cellar...he hoped. Jake positioned himself right over the one attacking his mother, and jumped right on top of his head! He went down, and Jake reached for the rifle, turned and fired point blank at the man closest to him! Jake then looked at John, and said, "I kilt my first man, and I was 17 years old!"

He then went on to say that right after he shot one man, the other one bashed him on the head with something, but he didn't know what. Jake said that he woke up later, and was seeing double, but he was alive! That was more than he could say for his poor mother! Jake went on to say that those men must have thought that they had killed him(and they very nearly had). After stumbling around in the house, he found his father's old pistol, and headed for the root cellar!

Even seeing double, Jake could tell that he was too late! The door was hanging on it's hinges, and Betty, his 15 year old sister was gone!

Jake then looked John right in the eyes, and said, "I aint afeared ta say thet I cried like a babe for a spell, and then I was done cryin! I come up the steps from the root cellar, and then jest passed out!" He said that he woke up much later, because it was the middle of the day. When he sat up his aching head started to spin, and he had to lay back down. He reckoned that his skull was split, but there was nothing he could do for it, so he just laid there until he could move without getting dizzy.

Jake said it was all kind of fuzzy after that, but he remembered burying his folks, and saying some words over their graves! Jake said the bad men did not even bother to take the old rifle that was his father's.

Now it was time to find Betty! Jake got what he needed from the house, and set it on fire! He didn't even stay to watch it burn!

Naturally the men took the team of horses that his father used to pull the ferry, so Jake was afoot. He said that didn't matter, because he was going to find Betty no matter what!

Jake said that he followed their tracks for a week, but him being on foot could not gain on them any! He then looked at John, and said that he did find a piece of Betty's night dress, and as John looked at him he could see the tears forming in his eyes!

He told John that they were headed west into Texas, and every time he came to a town, he would describe them to the townspeople, but they all said that they had seen the men, but not the girl. Jake just figured that they had her tied up outside of the towns, so people would not get suspicious of them.

Now Jake had been following them for weeks, and they were on the southwest side of Texas. After all this tracking, Jake got to be able to read sign real good, and came upon a scene that made his blood boil! He came up to a campsite with three dead men in it! His dead men! Jake looked at all that happened right there on the ground! From the tracks, he could tell that a large group of Indians came upon the bad men, and Betty also, because her tracks were everywhere.

Now after all the towns he had came through, and the people he had talked to, he realized that these Indians were Comanche, and they took women/girls as slaves, or to trade! Jake said that he was now tracking Indians, and this was much harder to do, because when an Indian didn't want you to follow him, then you had a very hard time trying to. He followed this band for months, and when he would find someone willing to talk, was able to learn that this band would more than likely trade her off to another tribe, to be used as a slave, or if she was lucky enough as a wife.

Now he got a tip from a Mexican, that this particular band had a hideout up in the mountains, and he was also able to learn from him just where the hideout was located!

Young he was, but he had matured in ways that no man should have to endure!

The tip he got from the Mexican panned out! He was close to their camp, and him being only one man was prepared to trade for his sister. He did not have much to offer, but was willing to go into bondage with them himself, if they would free her in the near future.

As he approached the camp, he seen an Indian on a hill, and he knew that the man wanted him to see him! At this point Jake laid down his gun, and waited.

He did not have long to wait! A few minutes later about ten of them came riding right up to him! As they got closer, he thought that they were just going to run over him, and be done with it, but at the last minute they stopped their horses, and even as scared as he was, Jake was surely impressed with their horsemanship!

One among them came forward, and surprised Jake as he said, "Why do you follow us white man?"

"I want my sister back," was what Jake said.

Like most Indians, they respected bravery, this man was no exception, as he said, "you are too late, white man! We know you follow us, but we trade her to my cousin." Your heart is good for you to have come so far, and for that you may live!"

Jake then asked where his cousin lived. The man just smiled, and looked Jake in the eye, and said, "I will tell you, but my cousin will not let her go!"

He then explained to Jake where to go, and smiled again, when he said, "I will even leave you're rifle, because you will need it where you are going!" Then they all raised their rifles and whooped real loud, and were gone as fast as they had appeared!

At that, Jake said, "got a powerful thirst on, jest hang on a minute there Youngun!"

He went over and got out his jug, and John knew there was much more to his story, and he couldn't wait to hear it!

He told John that he went and found the camp of the one that was the cousin to the one that he had talked to.

"I jest walked right up on it!" said Jake. "The next thing I knowed, I was surrounded by those buggers!"

He then said that their leader came riding up, and was just about ready to stick a spear into his gut, when Jake's sister came running up to them! Jake said that he didn't recognize her at first, because she looked just like all the other Indians! She pleaded to this man to let him live, and she was saying it in his language! After he got to thinking about it, it had been almost a year that he had been tracking his sister, so she would have had time to learn some of their tongue.

Jake said that he watched his sister, and this man exchange looks, and knew that his sister was lost to the ways of the white people, and these Comanche had taken her heart! She then told Jake that this was her husband, and Jake said that was impossible, because she was only 16 years old! She told Jake that she was happy, and that he could stop worrying over her!

At this time Jake looked at John, and said, "What could I do?"

"What did you do?" Asked John.

He told John that the Indians knew that he was Betty's brother, so they did not treat him badly, and that he and Betty talked way into the night, until Betty finally convinced him to just leave, and come back at another time to visit.

The next morning Jake did leave, and he would go down there through the years just to visit, and in fact that is where he wintered this last year, instead of Taos.

After telling the story about his sister, Jake looked at John, and said, "the reason I got this here jug, is cause now I will tell you about the Wendigo!"

John sat back again, and just listened.

Jake went on with his story, as he said, "well after I left the Comanche, I headed north into the mountains." He then said that he had learned how to live off the land while trailing his sister. He told John that his father's rifle was a small bore, but he was a good shot, and he shot an elk, and tanned the hide, because where he was, it was mighty cold! He then said that he went down to a town, and made some money to buy a Hawken 50. Cal.

Jake looked over at John, and said, "when you is alone in the mountains is when you hear the Wendigo!" He told John that there was a blizzard, and he was in this cave for shelter, and the wind was howling something fierce outside!

He then said that you expect to here the howling outside, but this awful howling started a way back in the cave that he was in, and it was definitely not a wolf! For three days, and nights the blizzard roared outside, and this thing howled inside! "Wagh! It liked to have done me in, I surely thought I was gone beaver!," said Jake. When the wind finally quit, Jake said that it was so deathly still, and that was almost as bad as the howling inside, and out!

Jake said that when he went to the entrance to the cave, and looked out, he could see human footprints twice the size of his own, and they came from the very cave that he was in!

He told John never to tell a soul about this, because after seeing the tracks, Jake lost it, and started running through the snow, and not knowing, or caring where he went!

He could not run too far, because the snow was so deep, and after running himself out, he realized where he was, and went back to the cave to get his possibles, and the elk robe. Jake looked at John, and said, "sooner or later any man what lives by his own self will see, or hear the Wendigo!"

Now all that John could do was just marvel at the experience that Jake had to offer, and he surly was glad that he had partnered up with this mountain man! John knew that his uncle would have taught him the way of the mountain man, but he was busy with his new wife, and that was ok.

Jake told John that he was all talked out, and was going to turn in, cause they would set out their traps in the morning. John said that he was going to have another cup or coffee, then he was also going to turn in.

Much later, Chick was starting that low growl of his, and it was the middle of the night. The only thing that John moved was his eyes, and he was scanning all around, but could find nothing out of the ordinary, so he scratched Chick on the neck, and relaxed.

It was a good thing that John did not get too relaxed, because "All Hell Broke Loose" in the next minute! There were men (shadows) all around them, and they were moving in, and taking things from their camp!

John, and Jake both exploded out of their bedrolls, with guns blazing! After the two pistols that John had were empty, he then used his knife! He did not throw it, he fought hand to hand! He would stab one and another would take his place. John was getting tired of all this killing and sneaked a peek over at Jake to make sure he was ok. Finally they left!

It was over as fast as it had begun, and there were dead, and dying Indians all around them! John looked over at Jake, and said, "Who are they?"

"Diggers!" is what Jake said. "They is about as poor a redskin, as there ever were!"

As John was looking at the five that they had taken out, he could see that this was true, by the way that they were dressed, and the weapons that they used! After they had reloaded, John asked Jake if he thought that they would be back, and Jake said probably not, after losing five men.

"Ya hurt bad?" asked Jake.

For the first time, john looked down, and noticed a gash in his left shoulder. He could not believe that a knife made from flint could cut so good. Jake had John take off his buckskin shirt (it would have to be sewn also), so he could get to the wound.

He told John that it was going to need some stitches, and John said go ahead! Sweat was pouring off John's forehead as Jake sewed up his shoulder with sinew that he always carries with him! Then Jake took something out of one of his bags, and started chewing on it. He chewed until this stuff was a paste form, and then smeared it all over the gash hat he had just sewed up.

The "Diggers" did not come back that night, but Jake thought it better not to put out any traps right in this area, and they would just move on down the trail.

The two men, and their animals traveled all the next day, and the scenery changed drastically once again. Now they were in foothills with good graze for the animals, and what promised to be a very productive beaver pond!

Jake said that this would be a good place to spend some time, and catch some beaver in the bargain!

Catch the beaver was what they did, and when Jake declared it time to move on, they had gotten as many from this one pond as they already had from all the trapping they had done! Jake said that they had enough plews for the spring rendezvous coming up in a couple weeks.

John could not believe that it was that close to rendezvous time, and he asked Jake about it. Jake told him that the rendezvous was at Pierre's Hole this year, and he calculated that from where they were now standing, it would take two weeks to get there, while pulling these here critters what are loaded with prime plews.

Two weeks! Where did the time go? Thought John! He was going to see his June! "Did she know where to go." He said out loud. Jake just looked at him, and got this wicked grin on his face!

"Didn't you tell her?" Asked Jake. Jake could see the panic written all over John's face. John looked at that grin on Jake's face, and knew without a doubt that he had been taken in by him! John hit him so hard that he summersalted backwards spilling coffee as he fell!

Now they were both laughing so hard that Chick must have thought they were crazy, because he cocked his head off to one side like dogs do when they are curious, and that made the men laugh even harder.

After they calmed down, John was able to get out of Jake that his brother had told June's father where to go to trade, and of course to meet up with John in the Spring.

The next morning they were up early putting away supplies, and securing the plews on the mule, and horse.

When they left the camp, John had mixed emotions about leaving, but he really wanted to get back to June, so he was ready.

The mixed emotions that John had in the first week of their two week journey to find the rendezvous, and June were slowly dissipating, now that they were getting close. He and Jake were sitting around the fire talking, and Jake asked John what he was going to give June's father so that he could marry her.

"What do you mean?" asked John.

"Well skin me fer a coon!" said Jake. "Ya mean ta say ya aint got nothing to give her father? Soons we gets ta the rendezvous ya gotta trade some of yer plews fer hosses!"

Now John was getting worried, and he asked Jake if he thought there was enough plews in his share to get some horses, and then he wanted to know how many horses it would take. Jake told him that four aught to be enough, and yes he did have enough beaver plrews for that many horses, and still have a right smart amount left over.

As the night progressed, John bombarded Jake with questions! Some about the wedding, and some about living on their own, and every thing a young man would be curious about.

Jake was very patient, and tried to answer most of the questions, because he knew how John felt, from his own memories of the "shinnin" times he never got to spend with his own new bride! Finally they turned in, and it was a beautiful night! It was still cold, but not like before, since Spring was right around the corner, and they were a lot lower down the mountains now.

John was awakened with Chick's low growl again, and was wide awake, and looking with his eyes, and moving nothing else. As he was looking out in the darkness, he thought he could make out a shape of a man, but it was just too dark to be sure.

He cocked the pistol that he always had when he went to bed, and it was as loud as a gunshot, or so it seemed.

"You goin at shoot me, nephew?" said uncle Jack.

"I waren't goin ta let em shoot ya, ya damn idjit!" said Jake from his covers.

Finally John said, "Come on in uncle Jack."

Jack materialized out of the darkness, and came over and gave everybody a big hug, and patted Chick on the head. Then he whistled, and Antelope materialized also!

How did they do that? Thought John.

Everyone got another hug from Antelope as well! They all sat around until first light talking, and getting re-aquainted again, John told his uncle about his plans when he got to the rendezvous, and both Jack, and Antelope were almost as excited as John was.

Antelope was a good source of information about getting married, but was not sure of the Blackfoot custom, so she told John just to ask his intended bride about it when he got there. Jack told John that if they left as soon as they broke camp, they could be at the rendezvou site the next afternoon.

As luck would have it, they ran into Killdeer's bunch the very next day. They were all glad to see each other, and it looked like John was going to be riding into his second rendezvous with the same Indians as he did the first time.

This time John prepared himself for the doins, by sprucing up just like the others, and when they got there, they all fired their Hawkens into the air, and yelled at the top of their lungs, as they sped into rendezvous.

The women that were traveling with them, just held back, and waited, and then picked out their campsite, and commenced to putting up the tipis, and unpacking everything.

After John got slowed down, he started looking around for the Blackfoot camp, and did not see it! He was starting to panic, and good ole Jake came to the rescue, when he rode up to John and said that the Blackfoot always like to be the last ones here.

He then told John that his brother, Trader Bob said he asked June's father, and was told that they would wait until everybody was there before they entered, because they knew they were feared, and no one would think that they were sneaking up on them.

This time Jake, and John pitched their camp right next to Antelope's tipi. It is Antelope's tipi, because most Indians believe that the woman owns the lodge, and she puts it up herself. After they got settled in John told Jake that he was going to pick out some horses.

John knew that Killdeer would be glad to trade some horses for some of the stuff that John had, and their herd was enormous!

Also their were some Nez Pierce here, and their spotted horses were coveted by everyone, Indians, and white alike.

Killdeer's lodge(rather, his wife's lodge) was not hard to find, and they were out in front cooking something on the fire when John walked up. Hugs were had by all, and Killdeer's wife was checking out John's buckskins to see how they were faring out.

Of course she saw the repaired slash, but did not say anything.

John told Killdeer what he was doing as to taking on a new bride, and Killdeer's face lit up, as did his wife's. Killdeer immediately offered John two horses, and when John asked what he wanted in the way of trade, all he did was shrug his shoulders, and indicated that they were a gift to a friend.

John started to protest, and then remembered how proud these people were, and changed his mind. Killdeer went on to explain that he could always catch more horses, but he could not make a knife like John had given him.

They then went to the Shoshone's horse herd to pick out two. John went back to his camp to show the horses to Jake, and to pack up a mule with Plews, and skins to trade for two more horses. Jake did a double take as John walked into camp leading two fine horses, and then he asked John how he did it, since he didn't take any furs or anything else to trade. John told him all about it, and then he started loading up some of his share of the plunder on the mule.

While he was packing the mule, he told Jake that he was going over to the Nez Pierce to trade for two of those spotted horses. All Jake could say was……."Good luck, them pierced noses think right highly of their ponies, and so does everyone else!"

John then told him that he had a plan that just might work, but if it didn't he would only be out one of his knives, of which he could make more when they went down to a town. Jake asked him what kind of plan did he have that those Indians would trade their coveted spotted horses for. All John said was, "come see for your own self."

By now John was very good with sign language, so he would not have any trouble communicating with the Nez Pierce.

Jake dropped what he was doing, and went with John over to the Nez Pierce camp. As they got there, they could not help notice why everyone wanted one of their horses, because they were magnificent by any standard. John was leading the mule, and the two horses that he had gotten from Killdeer. As they came up to the camp, a few Indians came over to them, and one asked what they wanted by signing. John pointed to their horse herd, and made sign for trade, then held up two fingers for two horses.

The group of Indians all started laughing, and pointing to John's trade goods. John then got down off his horse, and made sign that he would put up his two horses for one of theirs, if they would have a contest with him.

They all looked surprised, and asked what kind of contest. John explained that he would stand about 12 feet from this log that he would prop up, so the end showed about 3 feet off the ground. He then said that their best archer could stand with him, and he could use his bow, and John the knives, to see which one was the fastest. They all started to laugh, until John put up a playing card, and said that the arrows, or knives had to be both inside the card. At that, they all looked at one another, and were discissing it. One of them looked at John, and said in broken English that they knew who he was, but they would still do it.

John knew that the first arrow would get there before his knife, but while the Indian was knocking the second one, John's knives would both be sticking in the card.

The Nez Pierce had another discussion, and finally one of them came foreward. John had one of them hold a piece of cloth, and when he dropped it, the contest would begin! The man dropped it, and immediately there was an arrow sticking in the card. Luckily it was off to the side a bit, so John in a blur of motion had his two knives sticking into the card! The Nez Pierce did not even have the second arrow all the way to the bow yet!

They all had a look of wonderment on their faces, including Jake! All Indians love to gamble, and John knew this, and was not surprised when they asked him to do it again, for another horse. John made sign for one more time, and said two for one again?

Of course, the one said in English. Jake was just standing back there shaking his head, he was as flabbergasted as the Indians, because he had no idea that John was that good.

The same thing was repeated, but this time one of John's knives grazed the arrow, cutting off feathers but still going into the card. All the Indians were patting John on the back, and congratulating him on his prowess with the knife. Then they led him over to their horse herd.

John motioned for Jake to come over, and help him pick out the two horses, because Jake was better with horses than John. They picked out the two they wanted and the Nez Pierce were still patting John on the back, and smiling. John was sure glad that they were good losers, because he had seen some that were not. They were just people, like whites, and they had their sore losers, but not this bunch.

Now he had his horses! All he had to do was wait!

John had now been at the rendezvous for two days, and still no sign of the Blackfoot! He was getting very impatient, and everyone noticed it. When he would be talking to someone, all of a sudden he would just start staring off into space. This happened more, and more, until Jake finally took John aside, and asked him what was wrong.

She aint here yet, was all John could say.

Jake knew exactly how John felt, so he did not give him the ribbing that

GONE BEAVER

he normally would have. John looked so forlorn that Jake took him over by the fire, and had him sit down. Jake then placed a cup of steaming hot coffee in his hand. He wasn't done yet. Then he poured a little Taos Lightning into it. John did not even see him pour the whisky into his coffee, he just automatically took a sip. He spat it on the ground, and looked at Jake!

"Got yer attention," said Jake. "Go ahead and finish it."

John did finish it, and it did make him feel better, but he still could not see what some folks saw in the stuff.

"Watch yer dog," said Jake.

"What do you mean?" Said John.

"When the Blackfoot start to git close, Chick will notice, cause he's got a nose fer a certain female that's with em, and kin smell em long before you can see em."

At that, John perked up a bit, and went about finding Chick. He could not find him! John went to all Chick's favorite places, and he had many. Everyone in camp knew about Chick, and how he saved John's bacon a time or two, so he was well fed by all.

Exasperated, he went back to camp, and told Jake that he could not find Chick anywhere! After listening to John's very worried explanation about not finding his friend Chick, Jake just got that devilish grin on his face! This infuriated John to the boiling point, and Jake could tell, so he then said, "Chick has gone ta lead the Blackfoot in ta the rendezvous!"

Now John quit shaking, and looked at Jake like he was nuts. Wait a minute! Chick would not leave the area unless he had a good reason, and it was not hunger, since he was fed by everyone. At least it wasn't hunger for food!

Maybe Jake was right, and Chick did go out to get the Blackfoot! That would be great! John decided to make his wait easier by going to check out the sites here at the rendezvous. He had already been to Trader Bob's place, and Jake and his brother were well into their jug about now, so he would not bother them by hanging around waiting.

At almost every trading place John stopped at, the people were very friendly. Some were naturally friendly and some were just that way because John was the man who put Bull Baker under. *Man? Yes he was a man now!* He had killed, and he had trapped in the "By God Rocky Mountains," and now he was going to embark on another journey! A journey called marriage!

John went back to his camp, and got the mule with all his trade goods on it, and went back to Trader's row. This was his second rendezvous, so he knew how to trade his plunder with care, to get the things needed to make it through till next rendezvous.

The trouble was, he was now going to take on a wife, and did not know for sure just what they needed, so before he traded too much more, he decided to go talk to his uncle Jack. Jack had already done most of his trading, and was just sitting around the fire smoking his pipe, when John walked up leading his loaded mule.

Uncle Jack motioned for him to come and set a spell, and John did just that. He asked his uncle every question that he could think of concerning taking on a new bride. As before Antelope was very helpful in that department, and before long John was beginning to relax a bit. John wrote down the things that Antelope told him to get, so he would not forget something that would be needed at a later time. As John was getting up to leave, he heard a commotion at the south end of the rendezvous encampment.

When he strained his eyes, he could make out riders coming in, so he left his mule ground hitched, and went to check it out. They were Indians! Blackfoot Indians to be exact! His Blackfoot Indians!

John did not know weather to run to meet them, or just stand there and wait for them, so he just stood there, and watched as they went by looking for a place big enough for their horse herd.

She was there! Right in front of him now!

The horse that she was riding was right behind her father, and mother, and she looked absolutely beautiful! As she passed, she turned to look at John, and smiled, and held her hand up, meaning to wait.

Wait! How could he wait? John knew that he had to keep to their customs, but after a whole season without seeing her, this was going to be the longest hour or so that he had ever spent! He just stood there, until the whole small tribe passed, and then Chick came running up to greet him!

John kneeled down to scratch him on the neck, and the female that stole Chick's heart also came up for some attention. John had two hands, and he used them to pet both animals. Now John went back to his camp to wait, and Chick and his mate came with him. Jake was there, and as John and the dogs walked up. He bent down and petted both animals, and said, "so this is the critter what Chick has taken up with,huh?"

John sat around talking to Jake for an hour or so, and then started to get fidgety. He stood up to go to the Blackfoot people, and turned, and there they were! June, and her Father!

He about had one of his Hissy Fits, then said out loud, "how do people keep sneaking up on me like that?"

June laughed out loud, and even her father was grinning. John opened up his arms, and looked at her father questioningly! He nodded his approval, and June was in his arms! She smelled of smoke, sage, and some kind of wild flower, and John drank in all of that, and the feel of her in his arms! She told John that her father said that she could stay here until he was done talking to Trader Bob, then she had to return to their camp when he went back.

John had so many questions that he did not know where to begin, so he started with asking her if she was sure that she wanted to marry a Fur Trapper, a white one at that! She looked John in the eyes with those large Doe-like ebony eyes and said, "like I said before, would I be here if I did not?" The questions started pouring out of John, as he asked if they would leave the village, or have to stay afterward, and what did the ceremony consist of?

June just smiled that beautiful smile of her's, and said, "we can do what you wish. After we are married I will belong to you!" June pointed to the horses at the edge of John, and Jake's camp, and said. "I see you have more horses. Is ther a reason for that? Also you have two of the Nez pierce's spotted horses. What are you doing with those?"

John started to answer, but she was grinning, and said, "I am not supposed to know!"

At that, John thought it better to not say anymore about the horses, because he did not want to ruin the wedding. She was smiling, so four horses must be a good price.

June's father was back, and June beckoned John to follow them back to their camp. Just before they left, John noticed her father look at the extra horses, and especially the spotted ones! John could have sworn that her father showed some emotion by grinning ever so slightly. Both June, and John were watching Chick, and his new mate running, and playing. June told John that more than one couple would be joined together at this rendezvous.

After they reached the camp, June's mother came running out of her tipi, and gave John a big hug, then said something in her own language. John asked June what she said, and June said, "she said it is good to see the young white warrior with the big heart!"

John asked June why she said that, and June said, "because of your fight with that big white man, and then your softness for Chick right after."

June told John that she would have to ask him some questions as well. She then told him that she would have to translate for him, so there were some things she needed to know.

John said, "Ok go ahead."

"We will have to break our tradition, so we can arrange for our wedding to take place, so when do you want to get married?"

"Is now too soon?"

"Yes!" Bring the horses to my father's lodge tomorrow, and tie them out in front for everyone to see. "Then wait for my father to send for you."

"After you get here just follow along with what I tell you, and the ceremony will take place."

So many thoughts were going through John's head, and it was a long time before he could get some sleep that night, but finally he did, and he woke to June kissing him!

As he opened his eyes, Chick and his mate were standing over him. Chick did it again, only this time John dreamed it was June, instead of Becky. John got up, and went down to the stream to wash up, after all, this was to be his wedding day, and he wanted to be clean. He went back to camp, and located Jake, and told him that the next time he seen him, he would be married. Jake congratulated him, and patted him on the back. Now John had to tell his uncle Jack, and Antelope, so he went next door, and rattled some elk hooves that were hangong by the door.

"Come in," said Jack.

John entered the tipi, and moved to the right as was custom.

"We been hoping you would come see us," said Antelope. "These are for you," said Antelope, as she held up two beautifully beaded knife sheaths, for his now famous knives.

"I can't accept those, said John."

"It is a wedding present," said Jack.

Antelope insisted on making those for you, and I know you can use them. All John could do was give her a big hug, and he did just that.

"Now here is what I am giving you, and I don't want any argument."

Jack went over to the edge of the tipi, and uncovered a small forge, and all the hardware involved with it. John went over, and ran his hand over everything, and when he looked at his uncle, there were tears in his eyes. When finally John could talk, he asked Jack, "Just how in the Devil did you get a forge out here in the mountains?"

Jack told him that this guy got tired of toting the thing around, and it was too hard to get coal for it. He then said, "the guy damn near gave it to him just to get shut of it!"

Jack said that if John ever wanted to make things on it, that he could get the word out that he needed some coal, and many of the trappers would bring a little when they returned from a town.

"Blacksmiths are hard to come by out here, so they would not mind keeping you stocked up," said Jack.

Now John had everything that he needed to start a family. The only thing missing was his bride. The day was going to be a long one, because all he could do was wait. The custom was to put the horses in front of the father's lodge before daylight, so they would be there when the village woke up. He knew that he could sneak in there before daylight, the problem was to try to get some sleep, and with all that he had on his mind, just how was he going to do that!

John decided that he needed to try to get some sleep, so he turned in early, so he would be up before dawn. Sometime way before dawn he woke up, and went down to the creek, as was his ritual. After washing up, he then went and got the four horses that he was going to use for the ceremony. John walked the horses over to the Blackfoot camp, and just went over to June's father's lodge, and tied them to a peg that was in the ground just for that purpose.

After he got back to camp, he decided that this was just too easy. Little did he know that June, her father, and mother, and many others of the tribe were listning, and grinning to themselves as John tied the horses to the peg, then returned to his camp.

Now what? Wandered John. Just wait, he guessed. John built up the fire, and put some coffee on to boil. After the coffee was done he got a cup, and just kicked back and waited.

CHAPTER XII
Thanks to Chick

Daylight was now at hand, and John walked over to the fire, and was reaching for the coffee pot, when Chick came out of nowhere, and tripped him! John stumbled so as not to hurt Chick, and as he was falling, a shot rang out from the trees behind them!

Something thumped John in the chest like a sledge hammer, and he went down, with the coffee pot flying out of his now, numb fingers! John's uncle Jack, and Antelope were both out of their lodge at once! It was not unusual to hear a shot at a rendezvous, but this early in the morning could only mean that someone was hunting, and nobody would hunt this close to camp.

Jack got to him first, with Antelope right on his heels! As Jack rolled John over, he could see the hole just to the right of John's heart. John was breathing, but very raggedly! A whole crowd of people were gathered around, and June who had been walking over to get John, broke through all of them to discover John laying In his uncle's arms.

"Let us take him to our Medicine Man," said June. Jack and Antelope both agreed, and Jack scooped him up, and started off. Jake had been at his brother's lodge when the shot was fired, and he told his brother, "Thet thar were a Sharps ifn I ever did hear one!"

Now after watching Jack carry off his friend, Jake began asking questions. After talking to several people, Jake learned that there was a buffalo hunter in camp who had a Sharps.

After asking all around Jake learned that this buffalo hunter had broke camp last night, and was gone this morning. Jake finally learned the man's name, and this man's last name was Baker! Relative of Bull Baker? Jake did not know, but he was going to get him.

The shot had came from just south of the camp, and it was a long one, as buffalo hunters are apt to make. Jake told everyone to stay away, so as not to ruin any sign that was there, and off he went!

Tracking was what Jake was best at, and he had no trouble finding where the shooter had laid in waiting for the right shot. Jake could not help but wonder why the man missed. Buffalo hunters rarely missed with those Sharps rifles. Little did Jake know that Chick had made John stumble at the crutial moment, therefore saving his life!

Jake found which way the man went, so he went back and got his horse and gear that it would take for this task. He knew that vengence should only be the Lord's, but that was his friend laying back there, and he had done it for his wife, and he would do for John! In fact nobody better try to stop him!

Meanwhile, back at the Blackfoot camp, everything was chaos! What was supposed to be a verry happy day turned out to be a tragic one. June never left John's side, except to get him water when he needed it. After Jack looked at the wound, he said that the bullet passed clear through, as Sharps are want to do, and he thought it missed the lungs by a fraction! Infection was the worse thing to look for now.

The Medicine Man had mixed up a poultice of some kind, and after cleaning the wound had put this on and bound it up with very soft beaver skin. Now all they had to do was wait!

That night, as expected, a fever came upon John with a vengeance! June was at John's side constantly, and anytime he would be conscious for a short period, It was her face that he would see.

This waiting game was very hard on everyone who cared for John, and that was many, including Chick who also never left his side.

Only one person did not have the luxury of worry, and that was Jake. Jake was closing in on this cowardly man who kills from hiding, and when he caught him (which WAS going to happen), This man's life was going to be short lived!

Cowardly this man was, but he was very smart when he knew someone was following him, as he surely must. He had put gunny sacks, or something on his horse's hooves to eliminate the imprint. This made it a little harder for the tracker, but this man did not know "Quiet Jake!"

A good tracker could anticipate which way his man was heading, and by doing this go around him, and lay in waiting. This is just what Jake had done. Jake was on a boulder the size of a house, and the man had to pass right under him. This man was a buffalo hunter, so Jake had to be very careful!

As this man passed under him, Jake dropped a looped rope over his shoulders, and pulled the man right out of his saddle. Jake kept the rope tight as he climbed down from the boulder, so the man couldn't get the rope off.

This guy was kicking, and screaming obscenities at Jake, so Jake just did what was natural. He pulled out his tomahawk, and smacked him in the head with the side of it!

While the man was out, Jake tied him up real good so he could not escape. After all………..he had some answering to do!

Jake went through the man's things trying to find something to link him to Bull Baker, and was rewarded with a letter that was in his saddle bag.

Reading was not Jake's most favorite thing to do, but he could get by if he took his time, and he had plenty of that.

The letter was from a fellow buffalo hunter (Jake guessed even some of them could read, and write if they had to.) This friend of his was telling him about his brother getting killed. The letter explained about Bull getting killed at the rendezvous by a young blacksmith who was very good with a knife. No animosity was held by Jake, because all this person was doing was informing this man about his brother getting killed. He did not say anything bad about John, so Jake would not try to find him.

As the would be murderer was lying there, Jake was surprised at the difference between the brothers. Where Bull was a giant of a man, this guy was small.

Jake figured that a Sharps rifle made any man a giant, but to do it from hiding was too much to stomach.

The man was starting to come around now, and Jake dumped the man's canteen on his face, bringing him wide awake!

The man was staring at Jake with the meanest, coldest eyes that Jake had ever seen! Jake decided right then that this guy had killed before, and probably from hiding, just like he tried to do with John. Jake looked right into those small evil eyes, and said, "Ya didn't kill him, coward!"

The man reeked of old blood, and unwashed body odor, and Jake had to back away! Jake had been around many buffalo hunters, and they all smelled bad, because of all the skinning they did, and you expected that, but this man was awful smelling!

An idea began forming in Jake's mind.

Jake picked the guy up and laid him across his saddle, and tied him on. The man was still screaming, and Jake brought out his tomahawk, and showed it to him. He shut up right quick like! Jake went and got his horse, and led the other one with the man tied to it, down to the stream. As they reached the water, Jake untied the rope that held the man to the horse, and just pushed him off into the very cold water. All tied up like he was, the man could not swim, and Jake just sat on his horse watching, and just when the man thought he was drowning, Jake pulled on the rope bringing him to the surface.

Jake did this for about a half hour before he decided to call it quits. He then drug the man out of the water, and just let him lay there. The need for revenge was there, but now Jake was older, and did not have the heart for torture as he did with his wife's murderers. It was getting late, so Jake just let the man lay there while he went about building a fire, so he could cook up something.

Back in the Blackfoot camp the vigil was set! Someone was always with John. When someone had to go, then someone else would relieve them. This went on all night, and now it was dawn, and John had been quiet for a little while, and June felt his forehead, and smiled for the first time since he was shot. June went out of the tipi, and told uncle Jack, and Antelope, and her parents, and everyone she saw that the fever had broken, and she thought that he was resting now.

It was June's morning ritual to go down to the stream and bath, and now that John was resting, she did just that. When she returned to John's side she learned that he had been coming awake for the last few minutes. She bent over to kiss him, and her wet hair brushed his face, as he whispered, "Are you an angel?"

When she looked at him, he was smiling!

He tried to set up, and was immediately pushed back down by June.

"You need to rest," she said.

John did not argue with her, because he thought he would probably pass out if he did set up.

"What happened?" asked John.

"You were shot," said June.

"By who?" said John.

We are not sure, but some say that a buffalo hunter shot you from hiding. You're friend Jake has went after him, and we will know for sure when he gets back.

John looked at June, and said, "May God Have Mercy On His Soul, cause Jake sure will not!"

"I guess the wedding is on hold for now, huh?," said John.

Until you are ready was all June said.

John looked at her, and grinned.

"Why are you smiling,?" asked June.

Seeing you with you're wet hair reminded me of the time we were bathing at the same time. June smiled, and said, "we will have a lifetime to get to know each other, and the sooner the better!"

John just smiled, and said that he would be able to sleep now, and hoped she was the first thing he saw when he woke up!

Jake rode into the rendezvous two days after John's fever broke, and the first thing he did was go to see his friend. Naturally John wanted to know what Jake did with the man who shot him, so Jake threw back the tipi door, and said, "Thar he be!"

John looked out at the man draped across the horse, and asked if he was dead.

"Nope! Reckon I brung him back fer some good ole ronnyvoo justice," said Jake.

John just laid back then, because he knew that there was nothing he could do for the man, even if he had the notion. A small crowd began gathering around the man Jake had draped over the horse, and Jake just led him over to the middle of the rendezvous.

Jake stood up on a trader's table, and quieted down the growing number of people.

After they all quieted down, Jake said, "Y'all know how I get when someone I care fer is hurt, well I aint goin ta give in ta revenge, and let it take over my life like it has before! I ain't no talker of big words, so I will jest say thet y'all kin do with him what ya want." At that Jake stepped down off the table.

A man everyone knew as the preacher came out of the crowd, and patted Jake on the shoulders, and told him that he was proud of him. Jake just grunted, and kept on walking toward Jack Tucker's lodge, rather, Antelope's lodge. He needed to talk to somebody about why he let the man go, and Jack was his long time friend.

Jack had just returned from all the hullabaloo that Jake had created, when Jake walked up. The look of worry was all over Jake's face, and Jack asked him what was up.

Jake cut right to the chase, as he said, "Ya know how I feel about yer nephew, and ya know me, now why in Hell didn't I kill thet feller?"

Jack pondered this for a while, before he told Jake that he was probably just getting older, and had killed enough men in his life, and he had heard what Jake had said about revenge taking over his life. He then told Jake that there was nothing wrong with him, and that everybody changes with time.

Apparently that was all Jake needed to hear, because he then asked for a cup of coffee, and just kicked back, and the look on his face softened up a bit.

On the fourth day after he was shot, John was sitting up and eating like he had never had eaten before. John kept asking when he and June could get married, and if the horses that he had left tied at her lodge were enough! June was very patient with him, and would just smile, and tell him that the horses were enough, and they would be married when he was able.

The man that shot John was still alive, and that was a wonder in itself, since there was no law this side of the Mississippi! All the men at the rendezvous had a meeting, and most just wanted to skin him alive, but the preacher talked them into a more just punishment. Bull Baker's brother was to be hanged the next morning at sunrise! This was as good as the preacher could hope for considering who he was dealing with.

They were as good as their word, and the next morning the would be murderer was marched out under a giant cottonwood tree with a limb just right for the job. His hands were tied behind his back, and he was placed on a horse. He was then asked if he wanted a blindfold (Which he declined), and the preacher stepped up to say a few words. After the preacher was done, someone slapped the horse on the rump with his hat, and it was done! The man died fast enough so as not to be in pain very long.

John laid in the medicine lodge and could not help but hear some of the goings on, but he was not a vindictive person, and he would just as soon that he did not have to hear.

Justice was swift out here in the mountains, so John would not dwell on this. After all, he had a wedding to think about!

People were in and out of the Blackfoot camp checking on John, and this was a good thing, because the Blackfoot were not usually accepted by anyone. John's strength was returning daily, and after the first week, he was able to stand without help. Now he was walking (slowly) all around the camp.

CHAPTER XIII
The Wedding

They decided to have the wedding the next week. John insisted that he was strong enough for the ceremony, and June agreed. June had this ornery streak that would come out at times. This, in no way detracted from her inner beauty. In fact it added to it. When they were alone, June looked at John, and said, "I know you are strong enough for the ceremony, but what about after?"

June had this wicked grin on her face, and after saying that, John turned beet red, which made her laugh out loud.

They had the ceremony the next week, as planned, and that was the last week of the rendezvous. John was so nervous that he did not even feel the wound in his upper chest, although, if he moved too fast, or a certain way, then he would definitely feel it.

John was dressed as good as he could be, and was waiting for June to come out of the tipi, as was the whole camp. When she finally stepped out of the door, John, and all the village sighed, as she walked up to John! Beautiful could barely describe what she was! June's mother, and some other older woman was standing there with John, and when June joined them, a blanket was thrown over the young couple!

As they were under the blanket just kissing away, someone was saying words in the Blackfoot tongue, and before John knew it, it was all over! The Blanket was pulled away, and June said to John that they were now man, and wife. She pointed to a lodge over on the other side of the horse herd, and said that is our wedding lodge.

Off they went all through the camp, with people cheering, and pointing, and laughing.

While John was recuperating him and June had planned what they would do until John was ready to travel. They had planned to live with June's people for the first year, and then go off on their own.

Now they were staying in the wedding lodge, and would stay there even when the camp left to go back to their summer encampment. When John was able to travel, then they would go to where this band of Blackfoot were spending their summer.

John was young, and strong, and healed quickly, and the days passed with no complications, and they got to know one another both Intimately, and spiritually.

One morning John awoke, and told June that Jake, and Jack, and also Antelope were still camped at the rendezvous site, and he had to go talk to them. June agreed, and said that she would take down the lodge, and make ready to leave, while he was talking to his uncle, and friend.

It was a short walk, but John wanted to see if he could ride ok. John saddled his horse, and of course Chick, and his mate had to go with him. They got to Jake's camp a short while later, and John decided that it would be no picnic, but he would be alright to travel. As John was climbing down at the fire, Jake said, "Bout time ya came a callin!"

John punched him in the shoulder, and said, "I reckon I'm strong enough now!"

Jake was rubbing his shoulder, and said, "I reckon!"

Chick went over to Jake, and was licking him on the hand, and every once in a while would look at his mate. Jake got the meaning, and scratched Chick's mate on the neck. Now all was well, so Chick settled down beside John.

John told Jake that he was now married, and Jake said, "I knowed thet, I seed ya my ownself!"

"When?" said John.

"Me, Ole Jack, and Antelope were a standin at the edge of the trees watchin the wedding. What's yer plan now Tenderfoot?" said Jake.

I reckon we are going to live with her people for a season, then go on our own.

"I called ya a tenderfoot, but ya ain't. Ya got the mountains in ya jest like me, so er ya goin ta take her with ya?"

"Been thinking about that," said John. "I reckon I will set up this little forge that Uncle Jack gave me, and go to blacksmithing again," said John.

Then he told Jake what his uncle had said about people up here really needing a blacksmith.

"Got a place in mind?" said Jake.

"Thought maybe you could help me with that part," said John. "If I build a cabin, I want to be able to look out the front door, and see the mountains within a half day's ride," said John.

"I'll ponder on thet a spell," said Jake.

"Appreciate it ole pard! Now I need to go next door to see my uncle, and aunt, so stop by our lodge, before you leave, so you can tell us where to go."

John went over to his Uncle's and aunt's lodge, and scraped on the door. The flap was thrown aside, and his uncle said come on in. As John went inside, he could tell that they were packing to go, so he made it short, as he told them about his plans.

After John got through telling his uncle about his plan to be a Blacksmith, and try to make a home on the edge of the mountains, his uncle agreed with him whole heartily.

Jack told John that trapping had been a good life for him, but he did not have the skill for working the iron that John had. And besides the beaver trade was about washed up anyway. He told John that there may be a few more good years left, but not enough to make it your lively hood.

John then told his uncle that he would not trade the two years trapping in the mountains with Jake for anything in the world. They said their farewells then, and Jack, and Antelope hugged John, and said that they would find him when he got settled. After all nothing happened in these mountains without Jack Tucker knowing it!

John returned to Jake's camp, and it is Jake's camp now, because everything that John had owned had been taken to the Medicine Lodge when John was recuperating.

Jake told John that he had thought of the perfect place to build a cabin, and he would help him do it. Jake broke camp, and John went back to June to see how she was doing. John could not believe his eyes! June had everything ready to go, including the tipi. After thinking about it, he decided that Indian women had been doing that for as long as anyone remembered, so this was just another day for June. John told June about Jake finding them a place, and asked her if that was ok, seeing as how they would not be with her people.

June's only reply was, "You are my husband, I go where you go!"

Now Jake was coming into their camp, and he was ready to lead John to the place that he had in mind, so they all headed in the direction of the Grand Tetons.

Jake asked John if he remembered the place where they seen all the elk, and John said that he did, and that would be a perfect place to set up a small shop, and build a cabin. John explained to June where they were going, and she knew the place, and said that it would be a place that her people would visit when they could.

The place they were going was later known as Jackson Hole.

While they were traveling toward the Grand Tetons, John had asked Jake what his plans were for the coming season, and they had talked about it for a while, and Jake decided that he would stay in that area to trap. That way he could come down from the Tetons, and come to John, and June's place for good "vittles," once in a while.

They had been traveling for a week now, and the routine of taking turns hunting returned, and on this day it was John's turn to hunt. John was off his horse examining a track when an arrow just missed him and crashed into a rock! When he turned, there was an Indian knocking another arrow, so John shot him. He was immediately surrounded by many Blackfoot warriors! John tried to greet them in their tongue, but was hit from behind and knocked unconscious. When he awoke, he was tied face down to a horse and entering into the Blackfoot village. They had him tied to a pole and every time he tried to speak, someone would hit him with a club. His wound was beginning to hurt something fierce and he could see that it had opened up, because his shirt had not been repaired yet and there was blood coming out of it.

He was starting to get light headed, but he definitely woke up when this man pounded him in the chest right over his wound. He thought he heard a scream and realized it to be he himself doing the screaming. Now he gritted his teeth and looked this man right in the eye when the man hit him again. He could feel himself slipping away, but he was able to spit in the man's face before he passed out!

June was heating up the last of their venison, and Jake was sharpening up his knife, when they heard the shot. Chick was in camp with his mate, which was unusual, because he always went where John went.

Chick immediately took off in the direction of the shot, and Jake was hard pressed to keep up, but he did not lose sight of him. When Jake got to the scene, Chick was already sniffing around, so Jake just stood there, and let him go, because he did not want to ruin the scent with his own.

It was apparent what had happened. A large group of Indians had come upon John, and one of them paid with his life. By looking at the scene, Jake could tell that John had shot one before they took him, and from the looks of things, John put up a good fight, even in his somewhat weakened condition.

Chick took off in the direction that he thought that they had taken John, and Jake stayed back long enough to check out the scene. Jake could not tell what tribe took John, but every indication said Blackfoot!

Don't thet beat the devil!, thought Jake.

After looking around, Jake found a broken arrow that had obviously missed John, and struck a rock. This find confirmed what Jake had thought, they were Blackfoot. This band of Blackfoot would have no knowledge of John's marriage to one of their own, and therefore had taken him prisoner to go back to their village, and do very bad things to him. Instead of taking off after Chick, Jake went back to camp to get June. She would be needed when they got to the village. It was amazing to Jake that June would have anticipated the need to travel, but when he reached their camp, June was ready to go.

Jake explained to June what had happened while they were heading in the direction that Chick went, and June said that they did not have far to go, because there was a village about a half day's ride from where they now were. Jake was not sure about the way of the Blackfoot, but when most Indians took a prisoner, they would have some kind of ceremony before they tortured him too much. He expressed these thoughts to June, and she said that he was right. They would have a ceremony before they hurt him too much. June biggest fear was the condition of John's wound at the time they took him! If it was opened up again the Blackfoot would have fun shoving things into the hole! She had witnessed this before, and the man had died from this torture.

June did know the band that lived here, but not too well, and she may not be able to convince them that John was her husband, or they would not even care, since he was white! They heard the drums long before they got to the village, so they knew that John was at least, still alive. June told Jake to stay at her side no matter what, and they would just ride right into the village. As they approached the village, the drums stopped abruptly, and dogs started barking. One dog in particular came out to meet them, and of course it was Chick.

Chick wanted them to follow him, but they could not. At least not right this minute. Protocol demanded that they see the chief before they did anything else. June remembered this man, and also remembered that it was his village that she was in when they tortured that man. As they rode through the camp, Jake was hit with small sticks, and pelted with horse dung! It was obvious what these people thought of the white man.

A hush went through the camp as they rode up to the chief. The chief motioned for June to get off her horse, but Jake was to stay mounted. June did as he asked, and got down off her horse, and immediately started talking in their own tongue.

After many minutes went by with both talking back and fourth, June finally turned to Jake, and said that this man remembered her, and would hold off the torture until all the village was satisfied with the reason that June married a white man. June told Jake that it was very important what she said to the chief next, and asked if Jake could come up with something that would help explain why she married a white man!

The only thing Jake could think of to tell the Blackfoot, was that all the Black foot did not hate the white man as they do, and all the white men did not hate the Blackfoot!

He told June that after she said that, that she should say that her man thought that by him marrying her, their children would be the strongest, and bravest to be found anywhere! Jake knew that these people put strength, and bravery above everything else.

June agreed with Jake, and proceeded to tell the chief just that! After listening to June, the chief turned to his elder tribesmen, and told them what she had said, in case they did not hear her. All of them were nodding their heads in agreement, and they all decided that this was as good a reason to marry a white man as there ever was going to be.

Now all that was left was to free John, and that is what they asked the chief. He told her that since she was one of them, that she could go release him.

This chief also told her to hurry, because not many in this band trust the white man, and he could not be responsible for what a young man might do. They did not have to tell June, and Jake to hurry, because they wanted to get john, and get out of here as fast as possible. They were led to a gathering of people, and there was John tied to a pole right in amongst them! John was barely conscious, from the torture that he had already endured, so they had to do most everything themselves. People were shouting, and throwing things at them while they were cutting John away from the post, but at least the chief's word held off the worst of it!

Finally he was free, and he collapsed in Jake's arms! At this time Jake noticed the blood on John's chest, and determined that his wound had opened up. He sure hoped that these people did not shove anything in the wound hole, as June had said that they have done in the past. Jake set John on the horse, and jumped up behind him to keep him from falling off, and with June leading the way headed out of the village, and started for their camp. Chick had been with John the whole time, but obviously could not do anything.

Jake, and June had both seen him, but did not want to show a weakness by petting a dog! Now they were back at their camp, and Jake got down and took John off the horse and laid him on the ground by the fire, and covered him up with a blanket. Chick immediately came over and began licking him on the face. John opened his eyes, and smiled, because Chick was doing that sideways look that dogs do when they don't understand something. Both Jake and June seen this, and decided that everything was going to be ok, if his wound did not fester, and he did not get another fever. John slept the rest of the day and night. When he woke up the next morning he was very hungry, and thirsty. Needless to say, June was right there feeding him, and giving him water, not to mention hugging, and caressing him now and again.

Now John was sitting up, and he wanted to tell them what happened. He had a good audience, because both Jake and June wanted to know just what happened.

John told them that he was checking this stream for beaver sign, even though they were not trapping, he could not resist checking it out. He just bent down to look at a track a little closer, when an arrow whizzed past his ear, and hit a rock, shattering it. Then he said, "I spun around just in time to see this warrior aiming his bow for another shot!"

"I shot him before he could release another arrow, and then I was surrounded by Blackfoot. I tried to speak a greeting in their tongue, but was hit in the head from behind!" He then said, when he came too, he was laid over a horse, and just entering their village. Someone pulled him off the horse, and then they beat him, and tied him to a post.

He kept passing out, but he did remember that every time he woke up someone hit him in the wound in his chest making him pass out again. John looked at both Jake and June and said, "there was this one man who done the hitting, and I can see his ugly face every time I close my eyes." When I get better, I am going to find this man, and he will know some pain! This I will pledge to!" At that he looked at June and said that he was sorry that this man was a Blackfoot, but this was personal now. June told John that she was ashamed that this band were Blackfoot, and that she understood, and she herself wanted this man to feel pain.

CHAPTER XIV
New Home

John said that he was a patient man, and he would wait until they were settled, and he would be back strong again. John was getting stronger by the day, and on the fifth day after his capture, he told June, and Jake that he was ready to travel. They traveled for three days, with Jake doing all the hunting this time. Of course John pleaded with Jake to let him help, but Jake just told him that he needed to build up his strength some more.

The Grand Tetons were now just to the west of the travelers, and John still wondered at the sheer beauty of them. When the sun came up, it shined on all the snow caps, making them stand out even more. Yep, this was the place for John to build a cabin, and blacksmith shop. There was a stream, a wooded area, and of course the mountains to look at. Not to mention that the trail went right through here.

June, and John had talked about living like this, and John wanted to make sure that she was ok with living in a cabin, as opposed to a tipi. She had told him that the tipi was great for traveling from camp to camp, but if they were going to stay in one place, then the cabin was best. John had everything he needed to build a cabin, and if he did not have it, then he would make it himself. The trees were right here, and all they had to do was cut them down, and drag them with Jake's mule, back to the home site.

Jake was a hardened old Mountain Man, but he still was amazed by the fast recovery of his friend John. They had found the perfect place, as John had put it. Now they were cutting down trees, and trimming them to fit together. This was not Jake's kind of life, but he was bound to help his friend, and besides, this would be Jake's place to come visit, after being in the mountains.

As far as John was concerned, he was doing great! It felt good to be working with his hands again, and his muscles were now back to normal. He would put in a full day's work. Mostly, Jake did the hunting, but once in a while June would go out and bring in a goose, or a turkey. She was as good a hunter as the men, but she would not say so.

They had been there a couple of weeks now, and everything was a daily routine. Up early, June would fix breakfast, then the men would go cut trees, and drag them up. The cabin was small, but John figured that they could always build onto it. The side walls were all done, and they were working on the roof. John had just placed a rafter, and was sitting on top waiting for Jake to hand up another one, when he heard a shot!

John had Jake throw up his rifle, because he could see better from up there. The tree line was a few yards away, and John was watching intently, because that is where the shot came from. All of a sudden, someone was hollering, and riding Hell bent for the cabin. It was uncle Jack, and aunt Antelope! John could not help, but laugh at the sound of "aunt Antelope!" *He would not call her that, Hell she was probably Johns own age.* All this was going through his head, but down he jumped, and went over to them, and hugged them both. The fire was always simmering, so it did not take long to build it up, and heat up some coffee. John decided that they needed a break anyway. He knew for a fact that Jake was getting bored, but he also knew that Jake would never let on about it.

Uncle Jack said that they were on their way to Independence to sell, and trade some furs. Besides he wanted to show off his new bride. Antelope had never been to a big city, or any city for that matter. Jack wanted to show her some of the sites, and get her some fufraw. John knew that was a mountain man term for beads, mirrors, cloth, or anything that Indian women didn't get a chance to have while living in the uncivilized world.

They had to tell Jack, and Antelope about their experiences with the

Blackfoot Indians. After listening to John explain about the man who kept hitting him in the wounded chest, Jack thought he might know this man, in fact Jack said that he, himself had, had trouble with him. Jack then told John that they had came across sign of a band of Indians, but had no idea that it was the band that this hated man belonged to.

Jack complemented them on the place they picked for their home, and so did Antelope, for her people had been through here many times. After they had talked a while Jack wanted to know what he could do to help with the house, and shop.

Jake piped up immediately, and said, "Wal ya old varmint, ya kin hep me hand up those there logs to John, I am a gittin to old fer this here stuff!"

Jack gave Jake a shove knocking down, and said, "Ya old fart ya are in better shape than men half yer age!"

Everyone laughed, and got up, and went back to work. The women seemed to get along, and this was kind of unusual, since the Blackfoot, and the Shoshone have never gotten along with each other. They worked for two more weeks, and everything was going great, by John's way of thinking. Everybody took turns hunting. Even the women would take their turn, and they said that it was good just to get out by themselves once in a while. Antelope was very familiar with this part of the country, because her people, the Shoshone just lived a day's ride from here. At first Antelope, and June were quiet with each other. After all, the Blackfoot, and Shoshone had been bitter enemies for as long as anyone could remember. They could not speak to one another in their native tongue, because neither knew the other's language. They both spoke perfect English, so they were able to talk that way, and talk they did! After the two women got to know each other, their tribe's prejudices were forgotten, and they became quite close.

On this day the women were hunting together. There were grouse in the area, and June would walk toward them, and scare them just enough so they did not fly. She would scare them to where Antelope was hiding, and when they were close enough, Antelope would throw a rock, and get one, and then another before they flew. Two grouse were not enough to feed three hungry men, and themselves too!

June aimed her bow at a nice rabbit, and let the arrow fly! It was a good shot! She watched the rabbit run into the bushes with the arrow still in it. She hollered at Antelope, who was hunting just over the ridge, and Antelope answered that she would be right there. As June was parting the bushes to find her rabbit, an Arm went around her neck, and a hand over her mouth! Of course she kicked and tried to scream, but it did no good. The man was just about ready to brain her with a club, when Antelope hollered in his own tongue! The man looked up into the eyes of his sister! Antelope told her brother to let the woman go, and he did. She then told him who June was, and that she was a good Blackfoot.

June asked who this man was, and in English she told her. Antelope's brother could speak a little English, and he apologized to June. She told him that she understood, since she was a Blackfoot, and him a Shoshone. Antelope told her brother that Her husband was just over the hill, and his face lit up, because him and Jack were close friends as well as brothers-in-law. This band of Shoshone had been hunting, and they had a big buck deer draped over a horse. Antelope said the camp will eat good tonight. They now had two grouse, a rabbit, and now a deer.

The two women came into their camp first, just to make sure that nobody got shot accidentally. Jack and his brother-in-law were very glad to see each other, since it had been two trapping seasons now, since they had been together. While the men were back slapping each other, and introducing everybody, the women began preparing the feast they were about to have.

Most Indians did not claim ownership to land, but this was Shoshone hunting territory, and Jack told his brother-in-law that he was on his way to their village to talk to their tribe about John living here. All the man said was John was one of them now, because of Jack being his uncle, and he could not speak for the whole village, but he himself thought that this was a good thing, because maybe now he would see more of Jack, and his own sister. Jack told him that this was true, and they would come visit here more often now. Now June came over to the men, and she told them that even though she was proud to be a Blackfoot, that she would wear the clothes of a white woman, so there would be no trouble. Then she said, "at least until everyone in this area gets to know who I am!" All thought this a good idea, as long as June did not mind doing this thing. After eating, the Shoshone men had to leave, because they had to take the rest of the deer back to their people, and there was time to get another one as well.

The next day the cabin was finished, and then they started on the blacksmith shop. This would be a very small one, because John would still go trapping during the season, after all he now was a "By God Mountain Man!," and that is what they do. The shop would be big enough to accommodate most things that need fixing, here at the base those beautiful Grand Tetons. John decided that when he went trapping, he would be no farther than a half day's ride from home, and June. Jake's story about his own young bride kept haunting John, and he decided a long time ago that this would not happen to June.

Everything was fitting into place now, the house, and shop were done, there was a choral out back for the horses, and they had even built a small outhouse. June laughed for a long time when John told her what this was used for, but after trying it, she decided that this was a good thing.

The trapping season was upon them, and Jake said that it was time for him to leave.

Jack said that he and Antelope were leaving also. He told them that he was going to trap south of here, and take his plews into Taos, since they didn't get to go to Independence. He told John that he would take Antelope to Independence next year.

John told them that he was not going to trap this season, but would go back to it the next season, and both men understood, because they knew what young love was. Before his uncle Jack left, he told John that he would spread the word about this shop at the base of the Grand Tetons.

Two weeks of wedded bliss went by before the first man showed up. John had never been so happy, and he knew that June was just as happy as he was. The man came up leading a limping horse, and John knew immediately that uncle Jack was as good as his word, and this was confirmed when the man told him that Jack had sent him here.

John had enough iron to make the horse shoes that the man needed, and he told the man this. The man said that he was on his way to Taos when his horse threw the shoe, and when he got there he would be glad to pick up some iron for him. John told the man that, that would be payment enough for him shoeing his horse. After the man left, John found ten dollars on the shop table. This happened on several occasions. John would strike up a deal for payment, and when the men left, there would be money on the table. All John ever needed was iron, and coal, and that was brought to him several times through the next few months.

It felt good for John to be back on the forge working the iron, but he did miss the mountains, even though he could see them from his front door. Naturally June could sense this, because she herself missed the thrill of camping in the mountains. That is not to say that she was unhappy, for she was very happy with the life they were living. Most of the people who stopped there were honest working people, such as trappers, hunters, and travelers. All but two men that is. They came riding up while John was in the shop pounding out some iron, and he did not hear them ride up. June had been down to the stream washing clothes, and was returning, when they spotted her. She saw at a glance that these men were not the type she wanted to be around. They looked her up and down, and one said, "hey squaw, is that yer man thet I hear bangin away in thet building?" This man got down off his horse, and walked over to June. They did not see Chick as he was running through the woods in back of the blacksmith shop. John had put port holes all around the shop, just in case there was trouble. Chick jumped up to the port holes in back of the shop and barked. John heard this between hammer blows, so he stopped and looked out just in time to see this man grab June by the wrist.

John burst through the door and was on them immediately! He had left his rifle back in the shop, but this was not a problem, since he had his ever present knife. He need not have worried, because June had already kicked the man in the crotch and he was going down! The other man went for his gun, but was a blink of the eye slower than John with his knife. The man's hand never made it to his holster, and he was looking at the big knife sticking out of his chest!

The other man lay rolling on the ground in extreme pain! The man on the horse toppled to the ground and John walked over and pulled out his knife. The man took his last breath, then his eyes started to cloud up. All John could think of was, Why? Now he had been made to kill another man! He surely was getting sick of this!

Chick had done it again! John thought that he surely didn't know what he would do without Chick. As this thought was going through his head, he looked over at the man laying on the ground, and there was Chick with his mouth over the man's throat, just like he did the bear. John walked up and first asked June if she was ok. She said that she was. Now John looked down at the man and said that all he had to do was say the word and Chick would finish the job. John then pulled the man's gun from it's holster and told him that he would not need it anymore.

June went to the cabin and came out with some rope and handed it to John to tie this man up. After tying him up, they now had to decide what to do with him. John told him that he should turn him over to his wife, because she was a Blackfoot and they knew how to punish an enemy.

This man did not deserve to live, but John was very tired of killing, so he would have to punish in some way that he would never forget. John remembered the man at the trading post who was made to dig a hole for the outhouse, but somehow that did not seem enough. The man wore his gun on his right side like most men, so John presumed him to be right handed.

John grabbed the man by the shirt collar and pulled him over to the chopping block. He then had June untie his hands, but looked at the man and told him that he would not be going anywhere. John called Chick over and had him stand with his head even with the man's crotch! Then he told the man… "remember, all I have to do is ay the word!" At that time John grabbed the man's hand and put it on the chopping block. As quick as you could blink, John brung an axe down, just grazing the man's hand! The man screamed and almost passed out.

"Oops! I missed!," said John.

Then John told him that if he did not do exactly what they told him to do, well then he would not miss the next time. After burying his friend and digging a hole for the outhouse, they let the man go, telling him that if they ever saw him again they would kill him. The dead man's horse was left with John and June as were all the weapons. After the man whined about not having any weapons, John told him that he was lucky they let him keep his horse.

Although June spoke English and acted mostly like a white woman, her Indian side came out with a passion as to the way that John punished the man. She would have at least killed him, though she was brought up with a more explicit way of dealing with one's enemies.

John just could not get it through to her that he hated killing other human beings. Probably because she herself had seen John kill Bull Baker.

Young married couples do not stay mad at each other very long and they were no exception, for after a day went by, everything was back to normal.

CHAPTER XV
Trapping Again

After the incident with the two men, things pretty much got back to the life of living like a working man for John. He loved working the iron, but he was getting the itch to go trapping and June could sense this. So one morning it was no surprise to her when John came in the cabin and said that he was going to go up to the Tetons and find Jake.

June assured him that she could take care of herself, and that he had better leave Chick with her, since his mate was going to have pups.

It kind of made John feel funny, not to have Chick with him, but maybe he would protect June the way that he had done for John in the past. John started rounding up things that he would need for a two week trek into the mountains.

After hugging June and petting Chick, John headed for the mountains. It felt great for John to be heading back to the mountains, but he couldn't help but worry about June. The story about Jake's young wife kept popping into John's head. John knew that Chick would warn her of any danger, and she could handle most things on her own.

At that thought, he could still picture her kicking that man in the crotch and he could not help but grin.

Just as John thought, it was strange traveling without Chick, but he kept reminding himself that this was the best way for all concerned. He did feel great right here where he was truly at home. The mountains!

GONE BEAVER

Since John had been in this area before, he thought that he might be able to find his friend Jake. In fact, from where John was right now, it was just a "hop, skip, and a jump" to the best beaver pond. Just one more hill to climb and the pond was on the other side. Now John was going down the other side, and in fact did see Jake's camp. As he approached, he hollered the traditional "Haloo the camp," but got no response.

As John came up to the camp, he saw Jake's shirt, and then his pants, but the camp looked otherwise undisturbed. He was wondering what was going on here, when he heard the undeniable click of a rifle being cocked! Slowly John turned to the left and there was Jake, just standing there, naked as a jaybird, and pointing his rifle at John.

"You going to shoot me, or make me laugh myself to death?" Said John.

Slowly Jake put down his rifle, and both started laughing so hard that they were crying. After they finally quit laughing, Jake put his clothes back on and told John to pull up a rock to sit on while they palavered a spell.

Now they were sitting around the campfire and Jake told John what he was doing when John rode up on him. It went like this....

"Gawd-a-mighty Youngun, Ya pertneer give me the vapors when I come up fer air."

John broke in to say that he halooed the camp!

At this, Jake said....

"Wal I went divin fer a damned ole beaver wut pulled the peg outten the ground and headed fer deep water. When I come up thar were a man sittin a hoss right in my camp! Course the first thing I done was grab my shootin Iron!"

They both started laughing again and when they quieted down, Jake asked John if everything was ok. John said that it was and he was just looking for Jake to do a little trapping, if Jake didn't mind?

"Glad at have ya," said Jake.

Jake put the coffee on the fire to boil

and they talked small talk for a while, like how have you been, and how is June. At that, John told him about the trouble with the two strangers. Of course Jake said that he should have killed the man, instead of setting him free, and at that point reminded John of Bull Baker's relative.

All John could tell Jake was that he was sick and tired of killing men, and that Jake himself had grown tired of it, because he did not kill Bull's brother.

John asked Jake how the trapping was and Jake showed him his plews. The stack of plews was very small compared to what the two of them trapped in the past. John told Jake that he would go on up to the end of the pond and put in some of his own traps. The water was freezing cold, but it felt good to be back trapping again, although John had to admit that he surely did miss June. He knew that he would especially miss her at night.

When John met up with Jake, he told him that he would be trapping with him for two weeks. Now after only two days he was missing June so much, that he decided to finish out this week and return home to his family of one wife, and two dogs (possibly more than two dogs now.)

Jake had been seeing the way that John was acting, so it came as no surprise to him when John told him that he was heading back after this week. John had been throwing what furs he had trapped on top of Jake's plews, and Jake asked why. John told him that he had made enough money out in his shop, and anyway the fur was getting scarce around here. Jake would need whatever they could take from this area, so as to have enough for trade come rendezvous time.

They were sitting around the fire warming their feet, after wading in the frigid water all morning re-setting their traps. As all mountain men, or anyone living in the mountains, or near them are always in tune with their surroundings, so were Jake, and John. It was too quiet! That was like an alarm going off in both their heads. They looked at each other and both drew their pistols very slowly, then got up and faded back into the trees like ghosts!

It was not long before they heard someone say…."Yohn?" Well they both knew this was Killdeer's version of the name John, so they hollered for him to show himself. Immediately a small band of Shoshone stepped out of the trees directly across from the trappers. Killdeer was the first.

John and Jake stepped out, and Killdeer looked them up and down, and then started laughing. Each were barefoot and had their pants legs rolled up. They too looked down and started laughing. That over with,

Killdeer and John embraced each other in greeting. John motioned for them to set by the fire, and they did.

After all the small talk was over with, through sign and gesture, John asked what they were doing up here.

Killdeer's eyes took on a sad look when he began his story.

Killdeer said that his wife had been taken by a band of Lakota, and she was with child! He also said that he and his men were on their way to the "Stinking Waters," because that was the direction that they took his wife. Killdeer's intension was to steal her back!

At this point John asked him how far ahead of them were they? Through sign, Killdeer told John that they were only a day ahead of them right now.

Immediately John, and Jake started putting things away. Killdeer asked what they were doing, and was told by both John and Jake that they were going with them.

They found a small cave to stash their stuff, and were ready within fifteen minutes. As John was packing stuff away, the thought of June passed through his mind. He knew without a doubt that she would expect nothing less from him, than to go help his friend get his wife back.

They left immediately, and Killdeer acted as if he knew just where to go. Neither trapper questioned Killdeer, after all, he was an Indian. They knew this area better than the white man. After traveling for several hours, Killdeer held up his hand to stop, and all did. He got down off his horse and was looking at some horse tracks, when John walked up to him. John was told that they were getting very close, so they would have to be very alert, and quiet.

They were closer than Killdeer thought, because when they topped the next hill, everyone smelled camp smoke. They all stopped and got off their horses and walked them to about half way up the next hill.

Killdeer told them all to wait, and he went up to the top and peered over. He was up there for quite a while, when he finally came back down. Killdeer said that they were camped just over the next hill, but we would have to wait for the cover of darkness to make our rescue. A plan was formulated and all they had to do now was wait. While they were waiting,

Killdeer made it known to John that him helping was not a good idea, and of course John told him that he would do no less.

While Killdeer was trying to convince John why he should not be helping, Jake had formulated a plan. He broke in on the two to tell them about it.

"All we got ta do is hev two men (meaning John and himself) sneak around ta the other side where the hosses are an spook em. Whilst they are tryin ta cetch em, yore men would swoop down an rescue yore wife!"

Killdeer was skeptical as to whether or not two white men could sneak up on the horses, and he told them so. Jake politely told him that they were "By God Mountain Men," and that he, himself had snuck up on a Grizzly! This pacified Killdeer, and the plan was set.

They decided to wait until just before daylight, when the guards were half asleep.

Killdeer had already told them that the Lakota would not hurt his wife, because she was with child. They planned to raise him as their own just as the Shoshone would do if the situation were reversed.

The waiting was always the hardest part for John. He guessed it was because of his youth, because all the others had laid down and went to sleep Immediately. John just stood there with all these thoughts going through his head. He must have slept some, because Jake was shaking his shoulder for him to wake up.

They left their horses there, because they did not want them to snort and alert everyone in the Lakota camp. John had learned well from Jake and it showed as they made their way around to the other side of the camp. They decided that each would grab a horse just before they spooked the rest of them. That way, they could hopefully escape with their hair intact.

Jake had tucked a small tin frying pan in his belt, and now they were finally close enough to the horse herd. Each knew that there was a guard watching the herd and decided beforehand that one would distract this man, while the other came from behind and clubbed him in the head. It was John who did the distracting by making a small noise just loud enough to make the man curious. It worked. The man was looking in his direction and was hit in the back of the head with the butt of Jake's pistol!

The man was out like a light, and Jake caught him as he fell, so as not to make any more noise than necessary. This was the only guard they could find and both sure did hope there were no more. The horses were a little skittish when they walked up to them, but they wore buckskins that smelled of smoke, just like the Indians did. There was no problem for each man to catch one and tie it to a tree.

This done and all the horses untied, Jake slipped around behind the herd and took out the frying pan, and banged it with his knife! Pandemonium broke out everywhere, as horses ran through camp destroying everything in their path! Almost all the men were chasing horses (and some were catching them).

Killdeer's reaction was immediate as he and his warriors bore down on the camp. Since he already knew which lodge his wife was in, he rode right to it. As he entered the lodge, a man lunged at him with a knife, just grazing his side as he moved out of the way. His own knife was out and they were facing off! He could see his wife out of the corner of his eye and she was tied by the wrists to a stake that was driven into the ground. Her feet were free and she used them when her captor got close to her. As the man was concentrating on Killdeer, she kicked out catching him on the shins! That distracted him enough for Killdeer to stab him in the chest!

Now they were together again and he quicky untied her and led her to their horses. He lifted her up on the horse that he had brought for this purpose, and got on his own. They sped away, back to where everyone had pre-arranged to meet. It would take some time for the Lakota to catch their horses, so they had enough time to make a head count. Everybody was there, including the two white men. There were a few wounded for sure, but all in all, it went as good as could be expected.

It looked like John was going to make it back home before his two weeks were done. He could not wait!

After embracing Killdeer and his wife, they parted company and John and Jake headed back to their camp to collect their things.

Everything was loaded and they were ready to go. John was going home, and Jake said he would head for Taos to trade his furs, then go on down to see his sister. It was very hard for John to convince Jake to take the furs he trapped while there with him. He was finally able to get through to him again that he had everything he needed right there at home, including money and goods.

They hugged each other and Jake headed southwest, while John went east to the bottom of the Tetons. As John was getting closer to home, the butterflies in his stomach were giving him his famous Hissy Fits. The anticipation of seeing June was almost more than he could bear! Almost there now, just one more hill to go over. As he topped this hill and saw his homestead down at the bottom, he thought.... *'Nothing could be more beautiful!'*

CHAPTER XVI
New Family

Everything looked to be ok as he rode up and tied his horse, but no one came running out to greet him and he was starting to panic! He had his hand on the door handle, when this force hit him in the back, and about knocked him down! His knife was out instantly, and as he turned there was Chick wagging his tail and looking at him with that cockeyed look that dogs do! Just behind Chick was June smiling the most beautiful smile that John had ever seen!

She was in his arms instantly and they were hugging and kissing, and telling each other how much they missed one another! Of course Chick would not be left out as he stuck his head under John's hand so John could scratch it. Finally they released each other and went into the house. Each had so much to tell the other, and John had only been gone twelve days.

June had John tell of his trip into the mountains first and as John's tale unfolded, she was shocked, but told John that she would have expected him to go help his friend get his wife back. After John finally wound down, it was June's turn to say what took place while John was away. She told him that there was something that she had to show him, but he would have to come out to the stable. John followed her and Chick out there.

When they built the place, they had put up a small lean-to for the stock and there was a pile of dead grass in the back. June moved the grass out of the way and John found himself looking at six beautiful little puppies!

The proud father kept grabbing John's arm and pulling it toward the puppies. John reached over and scratched Chick on the head, then picked up one that looked just like a small version of Chick. The momma licked John's hand as a sign that she approved.

After spending a few minutes in the lean-to, John said to June, "now there is something I want to show you!"

They walked back to the cabin arm in arm.

Their cabin had only one room, but there was a curtain separating their sleeping quarters. After they entered, John led June over to their bed and said that he had been thinking about this every since he left. They undressed each other very slowly, savoring each other's young bodies. Finally they laid on the bed and melted into each other!

John had never felt so impassioned in his life as he did at that moment, and from the look on June's face, her passion was equal to his. Of course they had made love many times since they had been married. But neither had experienced this total involvement with each giving to the other. Many times John would bring her, and himself to the brink of release only then to back off just enough to keep the passion alive. Finally, when each could wait no more, John drove them both over the edge and into the convulsing release that neither could no longer hold back!

After their breathing returned to normal, they got up and John threw a blanket around both of them, grabbed his pistol and headed for the stream that ran behind their cabin. They spread the blanket on the bank of the stream, got in the water and started splashing and washing each other. This went on for only a few minutes when John told her that they had to go back to the cabin! June reached down into the water, grabbed John, and as she looked into his eyes, said…. "we had better hurry!"

Now, back in bed once again, June looked at her husband and said, "I have something to tell you!" John looked at her for any sign of bad news and found none, so he said, "What do you have to tell me?"

She was smiling as she said that she thought Chick was not the only one who is a father!

The look on John's face was priceless to June, as she saw his expression go from bewilderment to comprehension! John actually stuttered when he said, "Y-You are going to have a baby?"

June told him that she thought so, but it is a little early to tell. Of course John did what any man would do. He bombarded her with questions and was especially worried about what they had just done! With all the patience of her kind, June smiled that beautiful smile of hers and told him that what they had done would hurt neither her, or the baby. John jumped up out of the bed and ran to the door, throwing it open and hollering at the top of his voice, "Woo-Hoo! I am going to be a father!"

Of course Chick came running up from the stable prepared to do battle alongside his friend. When Chick reached the cabin he just sat down and cocked his head at his friend who was standing in the doorway naked as the day he was born, and screaming at the top of his lungs!

John looked down at his friend and saw that sideways look the he was noted for and started laughing so hard that June came to the door to see what was so funny. When she saw Chick she, also started laughing!

After a while June decided that they had better get some clothes on. What would someone think if they came riding up? Here were two young people standing in a doorway completely naked, and laughing at a comical hound dog.

John's mind was racing, as he told June that they had to add on a room to the cabin. He was thinking out loud and June was tickled at the way he worried about this and that, but she just let him ramble on.

Winter was coming on in the mountains and from all the signs this one looked to be a bad one. John had prepared for it as best as he knew how, by cutting enough firewood and hunting more often and jerking the meat so it would last out the winter.

Even though June was big with child, she was right there beside her man, stacking firewood, and even helping him make the jerky. Preparing for winter was not new for June. Her people had to do this every year. She told John that she noticed that the animals fur was thicker than she had ever remembered. The snow started one morning very early, and it snowed all day long. By nightfall there were several inches on the ground. This was expected and the young couple just relaxed and enjoyed each other while staying in the cabin.

Then the wind picked up! It blew with a vengeance for all of the next week, snowing all the while. John had to keep the snow away from the door, so he could open it. Every morning he did this, and the snow was piling up daily. One morning he tried to go outside and could not budge the door! Luckily, he had put two windows in the cabin and kept them covered with a greased skin.

On this morning he took off the greased skin at the window and he could not believe it! The snow had piled up so high that it covered up the window! John started clawing away at it and soon was able to see daylight. He made a hole big enough for him to fit, and through it he went! He had to crawl around to the front of the cabin, because if he stood up, he would sink through to the ground! At this point, the snow was taller than he was. Finally he was able to scrape enough snow out of the way so he could open the door. After warming his hands inside, he told June that he had to go and check on the stock. Good old Jake had showed him how to make snow shoes, and he had a brand new pair.

They had brought all the dogs in with them, so at least they were safe. Now, with his snow shoes strapped on, he headed out to the lean-to where the stock would be. Now as he was walking, he noticed that the awful wind had subsided somewhat.

The snowshoes were hard to get used to, but they kept him on top of the snow and he finally made it to the lean-to. He could see steam coming from the large pile of dead grass that he had put out for the animals, so he headed that way. The two horses were on the other side of the grass just munching away at it. Where was the mule? He had bought a young mule at the last rendezvous.

John knew first hand that mules were hard headed and very notional critters, but they were actually smarter than horses when it came to survival. No way could he go looking for this mule until some of this snow was gone, so he decided that he would scoop out a path to the stream for the horses. Although the wind and snow were terrible things, at least the temperature had stayed fairly decent. The reason for the path to the stream was because the horses were not smart enough to eat a few bites of snow to keep from dehydrating. When he got done, then they could go to water.

John walked back to the cabin and told June what he was going to do, and would be gone all day. Would she be alright? She kissed him and told him to go take care of the animals.

The stream was only about fifty feet from the lean-to, but it did take most of the day, because the snow was just over John's head. He made the path about three feet wide so the horses could fit through. The horses were not wanting to go through this little canyon, but John was finally able to lead them through. The stream was not frozen and therefore had cut a path through the snow. When they reached the water, everything opened up real good and John could actually walk up and down the banks.

While standing there watering the horses, John heard the mule bray! There was a cave just a few yards upstream and John headed that way. He left the horses by themselves, after all, they were not going anywhere. When John came around this enormous boulder, there was the mule, just standing there out in front of the cave. After coming up to it, he scratched it behind the ears and the mule was glad to see him. It was plain to see that the mule had been staying in the cave, but it was probably very hungry, so it followed John, without any trouble, back to the path. The horses were gone when he got back with the mule, but there was no place to go but back to the lean-to, so John headed back also. The mule must have smelled the grass, because he squeezed around John on the path back, and was chomping on some grass when John got there. John left the corral pole down so the animals could go to water when they needed to.

As John was going back to the cabin, he noticed that the wind and snow had stopped for the time being. As he stepped through the door, he could smell the fresh coffee that he had taught June how to make.

She had a deer roast with wild onions and cattail roots (tastes like potatoes) and some of her special seasonings that John did not even want to know about. As he was sitting there eating this delicious meal, drinking his coffee, and looking across the table at the most beautiful girl in the world, he couldn't see it ever getting any better than this.

The temperature stayed warm for the next two weeks and a lot of snow melted. John took advantage of this and went out and cut more firewood, because he knew that they were in for a cold, cold winter!

June's belly was swelling weekly and John was a doting husband, as most are for their first child. Normally at this time John would have had Cabin Fever, but with his young mate there with him, he did not

The snow was still too deep to go hunting. They had enough meat for now anyway. He did not have to worry about the stock, because they kept the path beat down all the way to the stream. They would spend most of the day down at the stream pawing away at the snow for tid-bits of grass, so the pile that he had for them was going to last longer.

The warm weather they had been having did not last, as both knew that it would not. The cold came with a temperature drop of forty degrees! The stream froze over and John had to go down periodically and chop a hole in the ice for them and the animals. While this was a bother, it was an expected part of winter in the mountains.

On this particular day, John was chopping a hole in the ice, when his foot slipped on the rock that he had been standing on! He fell right in the hole that he had just chopped! Under he went! When he came up, he was under the main body of ice! He looked to the left and could see the hole, but his arms were already starting to weaken! The thought of June without him made him call upon some inner strength that he did not know he possessed! When got to the hole and tried to climb out, the ice kept breaking! He then started hollering as loud as he could!

Back in the cabin, June noticed Chick raise his head as if listening to something. Then he ran to the door as if to say "LET ME OUT!" She always trusted his instincts, so she grabbed her coat and she went with him. She followed him down to the stream only to find her husband splashing around in that frigid water! She then ran back to the lean-to and got a rope to throw to John. Just as she started to throw it, Chick grabbed it from her hands and jumped into that icy water! John grabbed the rope and June started pulling him in.

When he could stand, they headed back to the cabin. Chick just shook real hard and acted like it was just another day.

The cabin was very warm so June had John strip off all his clothes and she laid a buffalo robe down in front of the fireplace for him to lay on. After a few minutes his color returned and he quit shaking. He sat up and put the robe around himself and June put a hot cup of coffee in his hands.

She then sat down beside him and looked into his eyes and asked what happened.

John told her that he remembered slipping on a rock and falling through the ice. When he tried to come up through the hole, it was not there! He guessed that when he fell trough the hole, the current pulled him away from it. John took on a very serious look and told her that he thought that he was gone beaver, when he was trying to find the hole.

He told June that he had, had many trials since he came to the mountains, but this was by far, the most terrifying! Then he put his arms around June and told her that while he was scratching at the ice from underneath, the cold was so extreme that he started to embrace it and just quit trying. That was when her face came before him and he brought up a reserve strength from somewhere and did not quit until he found the hole!

As June was looking into his eyes, she noticed tears running down his cheeks. She just wiped them away and kissed him deeply. June knew without a doubt that John loved her above all else, because not any man of her culture would cry in front of a mere woman. Both looked down and there was Chick wanting someone to scratch his neck. After both scratched his neck, he just had to shake one more time, drenching the young couple in the process. All they did was laugh. This made Chick cock his head in his famous sideways look and that made them laugh even harder.

John had to promise June that he would devise a way to break the ice without getting too close to the water, since the bank was on an incline and very slick when icy.

When John had his miss-hap, the axe went flying when he fell. It went skidding out to the middle of the stream. Now John was trying to throw a rope out, hoping to snag it. This method was not working, so he tied a small rock to the rope enabling him to get it out there, and after a few tries, he got it.

This extreme cold lasted another week and when John went down to break the ice, he would tie a rope to himself, then to a tree. This enabled him to get to the edge of the frozen stream without falling in.

One morning when John opened the door to go check the animals, he could not believe it! The wind was calm and the temperature must have been in the twenties, which seemed very warm after what Jake called, "Thet thar tree poppin cold." Plus, the snow had been melting daily, and was now only visible in the low lying areas.

As John was standing there in the doorway pondering the cold, he saw a horse, no two horses, and a pack mule coming from the direction of the Tetons. There was something about the way the man rode his horse.... Then it dawned on him! Uncle Jack! He and Antelope were coming to visit. John turned and hollered at June! "Come, look who has come to visit!"

John hollered, "tie up those animals and come on in. June has coffee ready." They pulled up in front of the cabin and tied their animals to a post that John had just for that purpose. After everybody hugged and said how glad they were to see each other, they went into the cabin.

"Damn nice spread ya got here young'un," said Jack.

June poured them all a cup of steaming hot coffee and they sat at the table and talked. Jack asked John to show him around after they finished their coffee.

Since June was an Indian, there was much she did not know about white man's cooking and John had been teaching her what he knew. In fact she was making pancake batter when the two rode up. June insisted that they have breakfast and Uncle Jack said that he would be mad if she hadn't invited them. He told her that the batter smelled awful good. John then told him that they had some sorghum to put on the pancakes. Jack had been teasing June about how fat she looked, even though he knew she was pregnant. June was very witty and would give, as well as she got. Jack was not going to get ahead of her. It was so much fun to be joking around and everyone who knew Jack, had to be prepared to have a prank of some kind pulled on them.

Breakfast over, now the men were walking outside talking. Jack told John that he had run into Jake back up in the mountains and trapped with him for a week or so. He said that Jake told him about the men who gave John some trouble a while back.

Jack then said, "what in tarnation ya goin to do if the old hound dog dies? Seems like he saved yore bacon a time or two!"

"That is already taken care of," said John

John then took his uncle over to the lean-to and showed him Chick's new family. Even though the puppies' mother did not know Jack, she still let him pick up, and play with the little ones.

After looking at the puppies, they went over to John's shop. Jack was impressed when he saw all the things that John had made with that little forge that he had given him. John told his uncle that he always had plenty of coal and iron. People would want work done. A horse shoe here, a broken knife there, and door hinges for when they built their own place. They would offer him money, but what good was that out here? John just tells them to bring him some coal, or iron the next time through.

John told his uncle that it sure seemed like there were a lot of people coming to the mountains these days. His uncle agreed, and then went on about how it was when he first came out here. He told John that you could go for months without ever seeing a white man. Jack rambled on for a few minutes and John mostly agreed with him. John told Jack that even in the three years that he had been here, the change was staggering. Now that they had all the problems of the mountains solved, they went in to see what the women were up to.

CHAPTER XVII
A Trip East

After they had a big meal and all were sitting around talking, John asked his uncle what they were going to do next. Uncle Jack said that they were on their way to sell furs and decided to come pay a call. John asked if they were going to Taos, or Independence. His uncle said that he wanted to go to Independence to show off his new young wife.

This set John to thinking. June had never seen a white man's city, and besides, there was an old couple he needed to visit with along the way. John looked over at June and said, "how would you like to go to Independence?" June's face lit up! She had heard so many tales of the way the white man lived and now she was going to see for herself.

At that time, John went over and placed his hand on her belly and said, "what about our Youngun here?" June looked at Antelope and both women grinned like they knew some deep, dark secret. Then she told John that her people travel all the time and it was perfectly normal to have a baby while on a journey.

John looked over at his uncle and Jack was grinning from ear, to ear. The plan was set then. John told them that he had a few things to do before he went gallivanting all around the country.

The one main thing John was concerned about was Chick. What was he going to do? John asked his uncle about this and Jack said that Chick would probably follow them for a while and then go back to his family. As for him taking care of himself, well John knew first hand that Chick was a better hunter than he, himself was. One thing for certain, Chick was surely going to be missed.

Everyone decided to leave the next morning. John figured to take the mule too. That way, he didn't have to worry about him, plus they could pack more. June had made a cradle board for the little one, when he decided to come into this world. John was very skeptical about how this would work and when he asked June about it, of course she had the right answer. She told him to remember the white man's own history. Did not Sacajawea carry her baby all over the west with the Lewis & Clark expedition? After this answer, all John could do was wonder why most Indian men treated their women the way they did. They were more intelligent than most men. That is not to say that they did not love them the same as whites. Their culture was just so much different than the white man's.

Dawn found them running around doing this and that and everything involved in preparation for a long trip. Uncle Jack told them that he would go down to the stream and fill the canteens and headed off that way. June was packing things into a bundle, John was in the lean-to, leaving a deer haunch for the dogs. He knew that it would not last, but as was mentioned, Chick would provide for his family. Antelope was getting all the animals together to go to water them.

Jack had just filled the last canteen, when he got this tingling feeling that someone was near! As he started to turn, he was knocked into the water! As he was falling, he saw Jake standing there grinning like a possum. Jake reached out to take his friend's hand and when he did, Jack pulled him into the water as well. They started laughing and patting each other on the back. Everyone back at the cabin heard all the commotion and came running! John even had his pistol drawn, expecting the worst! John made it to the stream first and when he saw who it was, he put away his pistol. The two soaked men were just coming out of the water and Jake gave John a bear hug.

"You got me all wet, you old fart," said John.

Jake looked at Jack and nodded his head and they both grabbed John and threw him out into the water!

John got up spitting and sputtering and said, "what did you do that for?"

"Ya ought not talk at yer elders thet a way," said Jake.

They all started laughing then, even John who was just now coming out of the water dripping wet, just like his uncle and his friend. 'Well, they would not be traveling today', thought John. They had buckskins to dry out and Jake was here, so they would probably drag out the jug later. This was alright with John, even though he did not drink the awful stuff. These two were long time friends and needed this.

Now, back at the cabin, Jake was ribbing Jack about sneaking up on him. Of course Jack was saying that he knew all along that Jake was there. He could feel it on the back of his neck. No one would ever win at this game that they played, but that was ok, because it was usually only about twice a year.

The talk in the cabin came around to why they were packing and Jake asked where in God's name they were going that took so much packing. After telling him, of course they asked if he wanted to go along. Jake politely told them that he had been to a town and he did not want to go back. After discussing it a while, they knew there would be no way to talk Jake into coming with them.

Knowing this, John asked Jake if he would stay on here and keep Chick company. Jake told him that he could think of no better company than Chick. John then asked Jake if he would follow him out to the lean-to. When they got there, Chick jumped up on Jake and was licking him all over. Of course Jake had to pick up one of the puppies (The one that looked like Chick).

After they were done in the lean-to, they headed back to the cabin. When they went in, there was a jug sitting on the table, just as John thought there would be. While the two mountain men were drinking and discussing this and that, John went outside to make sure everything was in good enough shape to travel. This was a good time for the two women to make the pemmican that they would be taking. This was very good for traveling and both women knew how to make it, even though they were from different tribes.

John was not surprised that the two men were already up the next morning, when he got up. Maybe they did not even go to bed. Although upon closer inspection, if either one bent over he would bleed to death! Their eyes were so bloodshot!

It was time to go. They had said their farewells to Jake and Chick, then mounted up and headed East. When John turned around in the saddle, he could see Chick squirming around in Jake's arms. Jake had to hang on tight to keep Chick from following. After all, Chick probably thought they were going hunting. And why wasn't HE going?

John figured that it would take a couple of weeks to reach Independence, if nothing happened. Well…. Happen it did! Three nights out. William Jonathan Tucker was born!

They were all sitting around the campfire, when June said that she would be right back. She was gone only a few minutes, but John decided to go check on her. He heard something in the distance, but could not figure out what it was. Was it a mountain lion screaming? He did not think so. June was out there somewhere, so off he went in the direction of the noise. Now he was in an evergreen thicket and when he parted some bows, there was June, holding their brand new son!

John could not move, but finally was able to ask if she was alright.

"Yes," said June, "come say hello to your son!"

As John started forward, his foot caught on a vine and he fell flat on his face! This made June start laughing and then he, also started laughing. Nobody had seen June take a wet cloth with her, but apparently she did, because she already had the baby cleaned up when John got there. She then promptly put the baby in John's arms. As John held him, June started laughing again and told John that the baby would not break and to loosen up a bit.

When they came walking into camp, June was holding a squirming bundle in her arms and Jack and Antelope rushed over to greet the newborn child. After all had touched and fussed over the little one, Young William started to fuss. June took him over to the edge of the firelight and exposed one of her breasts to him. He quieted immediately! He had more important things to do than cry! Now with young William satisfied, June decided to try out her new cradleboard. In the bottom of this, she had put a bunch of broke open milkweed pods. This created a very soft and absorbent bottom of which she could change as frequently as needed.

The next day they went about their everyday business of traveling. Young William did just fine in the cradleboard strapped to his mother's back. John could not help but wonder at the inventiveness of the American Indian! Simple solutions to otherwise complicated problems.

That was the way of these people, and that, in part was the reason that he was so endeared to them.

They had been on the trail a week now and some signs of civilization were beginning to show on this trail that was once only used for travelers. Now there were homesteads on some of the places where there was water and good ground for growing crops. Gone were all the deer and antelope, gone were the buffalo, and all the beaver ponds were inactive. You did not hear the slap!, slap! of the beaver tails as they rang out their warning to their companions! All the travelers noticed this as they continued eastward.

Just as they rounded a bend in the trail, a shot rang out and just missed Jack's head! Of course all of them were off their horses immediately looking in the direction of the shot! Jack told John that he knew where the man was, cause he saw the sun shining off his rifle barrel. He then said that he would get around behind him, but he needed John to distract the man. When they bailed off their horses, they all hid behind some big rocks. Slowly John peeked over the rock that he was hiding behind. Bang! Rock chips flew just to the left of his head!

John thought.... "at least he is a poor shot!"

He peeked over the rock again, expecting a shot. It did not happen. Uncle Jack came down out of the rocks where the shooter was and he had him by the shirt collar! He was but a boy! About twelve or thirteen years old.

Uncle Jack came up to them with the boy in tow.

"Here is the critter what tried to kill us!," Said uncle Jack.

The wide eyed boy looked at all the travelers and said, "you aint all injuns!"

Jack smacked the boy upside the head and asked if he just shot at Indians for sport, or was he trying to protect his family.

The boy told him that his Pa told him that "the only good Indian, was a dead Indian!"

At that point June turned around to expose William and said to the boy, "would you shoot THIS Indian?"

The boy looked at the baby and tears started to run down his face as he said that he was sorry. John told him that he wanted him to take them to see his Pa. There was a small trail leading off the main one and the boy took them down it. It was not long before they came to a beautiful meadow with a cabin in it.

As they came up on the cabin, they noticed the door was shut as well as all the shutters. Suddenly the door burst open and this man said, thank God you are white men, "I thought my boy was took by Injuns!"

"Some of us are Indians," said uncle Jack. "If you choose to live on their land, the least you could do is not shoot at every one you see!"

Uncle Jack pointed to the two women and little William and said, "do you think THEY are a threat to you?" He then shoved the boy into the cabin and told the man that he needed to teach the boy to shoot better. They all turned as one and left that prejudiced and supposedly civilized homestead. At that point each one of them were wondering why in God's name they were going towards civilization.

A while later, John had the rest of his companions pull up for a few minutes, because they were getting close to where the old couple lived that helped him. Sure enough, the homestead was right over the next rise. Somehow it seemed different to John, but it had been over two years since he had been here. Were those children in the yard?

The children had already ran into the cabin, and as the travelers rode up to the house, John hollered, "hello the house!" As John was sitting there on his horse, he noticed that the place was in good shape for an old couple to be living there. Finally the door cracked open far enough for a rifle barrel to stick out. John told the person that they were friendly and he did not need to point the gun at him.

Slowly the door swung open to reveal a man not much older than John himself.

"You a white man?" Said the man.

"Yes we are white, but as you can see our wives are Indian," said John.

Then the man told his wife to come to the door. She looked to be about eighteen or so, but had the look of despair on her face as most white women do who try to carve out a life on the frontier. The young man told them to get down and come on in. He said that his wife had some leftovers and a fresh pot of coffee.

As they were sitting there drinking coffee, John asked the young man where the old couple was that used to live here. He told them that they had bought the place from them and the last they seen of them, they were headed east. John told the man that he took good care of the place. He then told him how he came to know this place.

The man apologized to them for pointing his rifle at them, then told them that they had been having some trouble with some Blackfoot.

The man was very perceptive as he looked at June and the way she was dressed. John started to tell the man about his wife, but June beat him to it. She told him in perfect English that she was indeed a Blackfoot, but this band was probably the very one that had captured her husband. Then she surprised even John when she told the man that if she had the chance, she would kill the leader herself for what he had done to John. John noticed several rifles placed all around the cabin and asked the man about it. The man said that he had taught everyone here how to shoot and that is why they are still alive. John was looking at the two children that had been out in the yard. They were at least ten and eleven years old. The man saw John looking at them and told John that they were his brother and sister, and that their parents had died of cholera. Of course John sympathized with him on that bit of news.

After everyone was done eating they told the young couple that they appreciated the hospitality and were going down to the stream to camp, if they didn't mind. When they got to the stream, as was June's ritual, she went down to the water and took William out of his cradleboard and laid him on the bank. She then dumped the soiled milkweed fibers out and reached into her pouch and got several more pods. She split these open and the fibers exploded out all soft and silky. These she put into the bottom of the cradleboard.

Now they were all sitting around the campfire talking and deciding how long to stay there. Antelope slowly got up and went over to the bushes. She reached in and pulled out the little boy who lived in the cabin. He was struggling as she brought him up to the fire.

"What were you doing?" she asked.

The boy said that he had never seen any Indians up close before, and the ones he did see, he had to shoot at. Antelope put her arm around the little guy and said that all Indians were not bad. She understood why he had to shoot at them. He was protecting his family. This made the boy sit up strait, and all could tell that Antelope had said the right thing. The boy left their camp and headed back to his cabin. Hopefully with a different attitude toward Indians.

The travelers were all quiet while they were sitting around the fire.

Finally, John broke the silence by saying that he knew why everyone was so quiet. For the same reason that he, himself was......They were all wondering again why in God's name they were heading east!

So far, all they had was trouble with all of these so called civilized people that they had met. Uncle Jack told them that he would turn back, but he had to sell his furs and it was now too far to Taos. They all decided to keep up their journey east, but no farther than Independence.

The next morning the weather was perfect for traveling and they made over twenty miles. John estimated they would be in Independence it two more days. They passed many travelers heading west and most just looked strait ahead, as if they did not see the four and a half travelers. Uncle Jack said that it had been several years since he had been this far east. He finished by saying that it would be a damn site longer before he came this way again.

They smelled it before they saw it! Independence! John could not believe the changes since he had last been here! At least when they rode into town, nobody gave them a second look. John guessed that this was still a mixed conglomeration of humanity, what with the fur trade and all. He had the rest of them follow him over to the Blacksmith shop. He was surprised to see the shop. It looked as if someone was taking good care of things. They tied their horses out in front and John went in.

There was a young man about his own age working the forge. The man looked up from his work and looked John up and down. He then put down his hammer and said, "you're him, aint you?" John had no idea as to what this man was talking about, so he asked, "what do you mean?" The man said that when he saw the knives in his belt, he knew without a doubt that he was John Tucker. The young man could plainly see that John was puzzled, so he told him that his reputation with the knives had preceded him. And also, Jeb had told him all about John Tucker. That is when John asked him about Jeb. The man took on a sad look, then told John that Jeb had sold his shop to him just before he lost his life to pneumonia. He said that he had been working for Jeb just like John himself had.

"What about his wife?" Asked John.

The man told John that she took the money from the shop and went back east to find her sister.

That was that, thought John. Both of the people he knew were now gone.

The young man pushed the door open farther and asked John if that was his uncle Jack.

"Yep," and that is his wife, Antelope, with him, said John. "And the one with the young'un is my wife, June."

"Please come in," said the man. "I want to hear all about the mountains and your experiences! Just come on through the shop to the house out behind. You know where it is."

John went out and asked the others to come on in and go on through the shop. After they all got to the house, the man opened the door and said, "honey, we have company."

The young man introduced himself as Ethan and then said that this is my wife of three months. He said that her name was Greta. She can speak some English, but she is recently from Germany.

Immediately the smells took over John's senses! This young woman was cooking and the smells reminded John of Jeb's wife's cooking.

Greta put out plates for everyone and one could tell by the way that she was just beaming, that she was in her element.

Ethan bombarded the travelers with questions and they seemed not to mind since he was so sincere. He told them that he liked to hear all about the tales that come from the mountains, but unlike John, he had no desire to go there. He was content to just stay there and work the forge. John told him that he was doing a good job with the smithing and that it was a good way to make a living. They talked for a while and after eating an enormous meal, Greta drug out an apple pie and all had a piece.

After they were done, they all thanked her and the two women jumped up and began helping her clean up. They talked for an hour or so and the travelers decided that Ethan and Greta were probably the nicest people they were apt to meet in this smelly, crowded city.

Jack said that he had to go sell his furs and John could take the women over to the General Store and let them pick out what they wanted. John said that was a good idea and they left, after saying goodbye to Ethan and Greta.

When they got to the main street, the women were amazed at the Indians laying around drunk, or passed out. The ones that were not, were just now trying to panhandle money from everyone they came in contact with.

Well, thought John. *This has not changed for the better since he had been here.*

As they opened the door to the General Store, a whole new mix of smells assaulted their senses. There was coffee, candle wax, leather, canvas, and any number of smells that were unidentifiable to the women. June and Antelope went right to the big rolls of cloth and were feeling it and talking about it. Then they went over to the cookware and once again were feeling and talking about it.

John just stood there smiling, until the shopkeeper came up to the women and grabbed their arms and told them that Indians were not allowed in here.

The man was marching them out, until John grabbed him by the shirt collar! The man let the women go and found himself looking into eyes that spelled certain death! After looking John up and down, the man said, "Oh my God! You are John Tucker!"

John pulled the man up to face him and said, "NO ONE TOUCHES THESE WOMEN!"

"Certainly," said the man. "I am sorry, it's just that we don't allow Indians in here."

John then told the man that the women were going to pick out what they wanted, and it was going to be paid for by himself.

The women picked out some pots and pans, and a few bolts of cloth, then told John that they were done in this awful place. John paid the man and they all walked out into the street.

As they were standing in front of the General Store, people were starting to gather around them. This was making John very nervous and he told the women to go to the horses and he would be along directly.

After the women left, John asked the people just what in Hell was going on? One in the crowd hollered, "let's see you throw your knife!" John told them that he would do no such thing, since the people of this town did not respect his wife and aunt. The crowd could plainly see that John was getting agitated, so they broke up and went about their business.

Now, back with the women, they decided as one, that when Jack got back, they would go back west immediately, where they did not have to deal with all this prejudice.

They did not have long to wait. Uncle Jack came up to them just cussing a blue streak! John asked what was wrong and Jack told him that fur prices were so low that trapping was not a good idea! At least not until the prices went back up.

John decided right then not to tell his uncle about the incident in the store. At least not until they were far enough away that uncle Jack could not come back and skin that storekeeper alive.

John asked everybody if they had seen enough civilization and they all agreed to head back west Immediately. They would try to make as much distance from this awful city today as was possible!

As it turned out, they did not make as much distance as they would have liked, since it was late evening when they left. They found a nice camp spot about five miles out. Now, as they were all sitting around the fire, Uncle Jack asked John what all those people were doing standing around him. He said he had seen them when he left the fur dealer.

John told him that they wanted to see him throw his knife. He guessed that they remembered him from when he was here before.

Uncle Jack piped up by saying, "No they didn't, it is because of your reputation!" He then told John how fast the word spreads out here. And since he had killed a man with his knife, he was surprised that no one challenged him to a fight! John just shook his head and said that he never did want to kill anyone, it was just something that he had to do.

"We all know that!," said Uncle Jack.

Both women nodded their heads and said they agreed. Then the women got up as one and said that they were tired and were going to bed. All agreed that this was a good idea and they all turned in.

It must have been two hours later when someone was poking John on the shoulder! Uncle Jack whispered that there was someone out there and he was going to find him. With that said, Uncle Jack left the camp without a whisper of noise. John found himself wondering just how he did that. John went ahead and got up, putting on his belt with both knives and a pistol in it. Now all he did was wait, because he knew that his uncle would bring this person into camp, either walking or over his shoulder!

Crash! Bang! After a small scuffle, here they came out of the trees. Uncle Jack had his pistol pointed at the man's head as they walked out of the trees.

"Here he is!," said Uncle Jack. "Found him hiding and watching our camp! What do you think we ought to do with him?"

John and both women were up and by the fire that he and blown back to life. John told the man to speak and tell them why he was sneaking around their camp. The man responded by saying that he was a nephew of Bull Baker, the first man that John killed. He had come to make things right! The man then said that there were four more men out in the trees, but they only came to witness the fight and would not mix in at all. John hollered at the men to come on out!

Come out they did! All four of them. One among them said that they just came to see their friend beat John Tucker in a fair fight.

John had his uncle let go of this man who made this challenge and asked him if he was ready to fight! The man was very nervous, so John said that it would be just the two of them fighting. They squared off in the traditional fighting pose, then John walked right up to the man close enough to touch him, then said, "make your move!"

As the man went for his gun, John's knife was touching him under the chin! John then flipped the knife catching it by the blade, then knocked the man over the head! He dropped like a POLE AXED STEER! John then looked at the other men and told them, "you all saw this! I could have killed him!" That don't mean that I won't, the next time I see him!" Now drag his sorry ass out of our camp! Don't bother us again!"

John turned to the others and said, "I sure wish I had not learned to handle this knife like I do. I did not ask for this reputation and I am getting mighty tired of defending it!"

June went to him and put her arms around him and told him that she understood and was glad that he did not enjoy killing. He bent down and kissed her and did not care that his uncle and Antelope were still awake.

The next morning dawned bright and sunny. The traveling was very good and they made more miles than any time before. The anxiety was obvious in all the travelers and they all wished they were back in their beloved mountains. If all the days were like this one then they were going to be home a lot quicker than when they were, going east. They were now in the rolling hills of what is now known as Kansas. To John, as it was to all the travelers, even these hills were a site for sore eyes, compared to what they had just came through.

John could remember the first time he had came this way. He had to admit that the anxiety that he now felt was much more than then. Of course that was because he knew now what the mountains had in store for him. He did notice that the homesteads were a lot farther west than when he first came here. As far as traveling goes, it never ceased to amaze John just how good a traveler young William was. What was even more amazing was the seemingly endless supply of milkweed pods that June came up with. The baby was cleaned and the cradle board was changed of it's silky milkweed fibers every time they stopped for something.

June did this so fast that it did not interfere with the traveling one bit.

On this day, as they topped this hill, there in the middle of the trail was a wagon with one of it's wheels off. The man who had been trying to lift the wagon dropped his pry bar and grabbed his rifle! For his own sake, it was a good thing that he did not point the rifle at the travelers, but just held it in the ready position. As they rode up, a little girl of about five years old jumped out of the wagon and came running up to June, shouting, "can I see your baby?"

June got down off the horse and took young William out of the cradleboard and knelt down so the little girl could touch and talk to him. The man with the gun smiled and told his little girl not to be a bother to the lady. John looked at Uncle Jack and both smiled. They all got down and introduced themselves. The men asked the stranger if he wanted them to help put his wheel back on. He told them that he would appreciate any help he could get. Then his wife came out of the wagon. The man looked at Jack and John and said that you never know who is friendly and who aint! So I had the girls get into the wagon when you rode up.

They both lifted the wagon and the man put the wheel back on. The man's wife had some coffee on, over at their fire and she invited them to come over and have some. After the man tightened up his wheel, he came over to the fire and told the little girl not to be a pest bothering the baby and what not. June told him that the baby loved all the attention, because she did not have the time that she would have liked to devote to him while traveling.

The conversation got around to where everyone was going and John told the young couple that they had a home about a weeks hard ride from here, and it was right at the base of the mountains.

The young man said that their thought was to go to Oregon, but this traveling was just too hard on his family. He said that they had come from Tennessee and he knew somewhat about the mountains. He also said that he knew, from talking to others that the Smoky Mountains were nothing like the Great Rocky Mountains! The man said that he was a trapper back in the Smokies, but the kind of fur he took out just wasn't selling any more. He said that he was also a carpenter and was doing that when they decided to head west.

John loved the solitude of the Grand Tetons, but this man called his wife a lady, and in John's book that was a reason to invite them to come and live close by. That is just what he did and the man said that it sure sounded good to him. Of course he would have to see the area before they decided to stay. John asked his uncle if he would show the man the basics of beaver trapping in the mountains. Uncle Jack said that he would do that when they got back. H e then said, "why don't Antelope and me stay with this here family and show them how to get to yore place? The wagon travels so slow and we don't have anything to rush back to, like you do."

"You would do that?" asked John.

"Shore," said uncle Jack. "I kind of like Thomas and Kathleen (that was their names), besides, look over yonder!"

As John looked, there was Antelope swinging the little girl around in circles. It was very plain to see that Antelope was smitten by the little girl. John called everyone over to the fire and explained his uncle's proposal. Everyone agreed, since it would mean more protection for the wagon. Plus uncle Jack would guide them to John and June's place. John, June, and the baby spent that night there and were up before dawn the next morning and ready to go. They bid their farewells and proceeded westward.

To them, it seemed like they had been gone forever and they could not get home fast enough. On the fourth day out, John could just barely see the mountains! Nothing ever looked so beautiful to him! The anticipation also showed on June's face, even though her tribe left and returned often. This was now her home and that made the difference.

Now it was the fifth day out and they were camped at the base of the mountains. These were not their mountains. Where they lived was still about three days north. All they had to do was keep the mountain range on their left as they headed north.

It was late evening and they were sitting around eating pemmican. They did not build a fire this night because there was something disturbing about their surroundings! It was much too quiet! This could mean many things out here, but caution was always best. When it was time to go to bed, John brought the horses up to where they were and staked them down. They then bedded down between the horses. By doing this they would detect any little movement from the horses. Horses were as good for warning you, as were dogs.

All went well that night, but John could not shake the feeling of being watched all the next day. June also shared the same feeling. John had the awful feeling that he was leading someone right to his doorstep! By the next night, that feeling was still there, so the next morning, John made a circle of the camp, looking for sign. He found nothing! They continued their journey and slowly that feeling disappeared. John relaxed a bit and just took in the beauty that the mountains had to offer.

A million things went through John's head as they were within a day's ride from home. He hoped everything was alright there. With Jake watching over the place, he was sure everything would be fine. Now it was their last night on the trail and that darn feeling of being watched returned. He could not get rid of it this time. This night, John decided to pretend to sleep, then in total darkness, sneak around and circle the camp to find out who was dogging them.

This was a very slow process, because whoever was watching them was stationary, while John was moving around. He was just about halfway around the camp, when he could just make out a figure hiding in the rocks. He circled around behind him and as he got close, he could tell that this person was asleep by the way he was breathing.

John lunged forward landing on top of him and pinning his arms! It was a girl! Or more correctly a young woman! She did not try to fight, so John just let go of her. John asked her what in Hell she was doing sneaking around their camp!

"B-Betty, I Betty," she said. "Y-You John Tuck-Tucker?"

"Yes," said John. "I am John Tucker."

"J-Jake's friend?" she said.

"My God," said John. "You are Jake's sister, Betty!"

"Come!," Said John, as he held out his hand to her.

When they entered the camp, June had been hiding behind a rock. As she stepped out, John told her who their stalker was. June introduced herself and turned and introduced William.

Immediately Betty started to cry.

When asked what was wrong, she asked if she could sit by the fire that John had built back up, and then tell her story. When the fire was going good and the light from it shined on Betty, June and John saw her for the first time. She had been beaten badly! Also she was very thin from traveling fast and not stopping to hunt for food.

Her sobbing ceased and she began her story by saying that she was sorry for her slow talk, but it had been years since she had communicated in English. She told them that she knew that her brother had told them about her, so she would not get into why she was now a Comanche. She also told them that the reason that she was crying was that she had a little boy about William's age and a girl much older.

She said that both were taken from her weeks back by Mexicans and other men who raided their village. She said these men were Comanchero and that the children would be sold into slavery. She also said that her husband made her hide, and while she was trying to hide the children they were captured. She fought so hard that a man beat her and knocked her out. While she was laying there on the edge of consciousness, she had to watch as these animals tortured her husband until he died! She knew that if she tried to help, that she too would be captured. Then there would be no one to rescue her children.

CHAPTER XVIII
The Rescue

As June was getting the pemican out for betty to eat, John told Betty that she was in luck, because her brother was just a day's ride north. After Betty had some food, June took her down to the stream to bathe and clean her wounds. She would not want Jake to see her like this, because he would take off immediately for rescue and revenge. Now, back at the fire, John told June that he would be riding with Jake when he went south. Also, since they were going south, they would hook up with uncle Jack and he would go as well.

John knew without a doubt that his uncle would get his nose out of joint if he wasn't invited. Thomas would take care of the women and children on the rest of the journey to the Tetons.

John then asked Betty how in the world did she know who he was? She shook her shoulders and said, who else is your size and wears two big knives on his belt? John told Betty that he felt a little guilty, because he knew that it was about this time of the year when Jake went down to see her. Instead he was watching John's place for him.

Betty said that knowing her brother like she did, John probably saved his life. Had he been there, he would have gave his life defending them! There were just too many of them to fight with, and win. This way, Jake could pick his own time and his own battle ground. John just looked at her, and decided that only Jakes sister would think that way.

Betty asked if they had a spare blanket and they gave her one. She put it around her and said that if they didn't mind, she was going to get some sleep. Of course they told her to go right ahead.

John could only wonder at the stamina of these frontier, or Indian women. He surely knew that he would not have wanted to travel all these miles without something to eat or keep him warm. This was a mother trying to save her children! Only the creator could give them the endurance that it took. John sure hoped God had mercy on the Comancheros, for Quiet Jake surely would not!

As was custom, the travelers were up and ready to go before dawn. There was an even bigger urgency to get home. June knew that her husband would be gone within a day after getting home. But as before, there was no choice, and she would have it no other way. John had to go and of course her and William would miss him, but with Jake and uncle Jack along, then John's returning to them was much greater.

At least Betty was more presentable to her brother, since she made the time to bathe, and to clean her dress. Of course she was still as thin as a rail, but that would pass, now that she would have time to eat some real food.

About mid-day down the trail, found them no more than a few hours from John and June's home. Maybe two hours later, John was pointing out to Betty where he had cut trees for their buildings. Just now they were going through this narrow place in the trail where there were boulders on each side. That was when something hit John in the side with a force that knocked him out of the saddle! He was on the ground and Chick was licking him all over! John reciprocated by petting and hugging him. A half hour later they were sitting on top of the hill overlooking their homestead!

As they rode up to the cabin, Jake stepped out with rifle in hand. At that moment, Betty jumped off her horse and into the arms of her brother. Jake was beside himself and the questions poured out of him. Finally John told him to calm down and they would go into the cabin where Betty would tell her story.

John looked around the cabin and everything was as it should be. Of course he knew that it would be, since Jake was watching the place. John asked Jake if everything was ok and Jake said that it was, with the exception of a big cat that had been trying to get at the puppies. Jake grinned and said this cat now had a big piece of its tail chewed off, thanks to Chick. Jake had a pot of coffee on the fireplace and June poured them all a cup as they sat down at the table.

Betty began her story by saying that the Comancheros raided their village just at dawn scattering the horse herd and running them right through the village. She then said that they started shooting any man who came out of his lodge. She went on to say that the reason that she had escaped was because they thought that she was dead. She was shot while trying to hide the children! Betty then raised up her hair and showed the welt from a bullet grazing her head. She said that she remembered laying in the bushes watching them torture her husband and load up her children before passing out! When she came too, it was hours later and she had to wait for her head to clear up before even thinking about catching one of the horses.

At this point Jake asked if anyone was left alive in their village. Betty said that for all she knew, they were all dead, except for the women and children, which was the purpose for the raid. She told them that she had went through the whole village and they were all dead. Her husband was among them. After thinking about it now, she thought that there were a few men out hunting when the raid took place, maybe they were still alive.

She then told them that it took most of the day for her to find and catch a horse. When she finally did get a horse it started to rain. It rained very hard, washing out all tracks made by the raider's horses. She said that was when she came to find her brother. She then said that it was an accident that she had seen John. She remembered her brother talking about those knives of his.

Jake looked his sister in the eye as he told her about the Comancheros. "Ya Knows thet if'n them thar Comancheros went south inta Mexico, then likely as not ya won't be a seeing yer Younguns agin?"

Betty shook her head yes. After all those years living close to the border, everyone knew the stories about captured women and children. They were sold into slavery to rich Mexicans, or even white people who were not particular where their slaves came from.

The men were up at dawn as was custom and June and Betty bid them farewell as they rode south. Since June and Betty were staying behind, it was decided to let Chick go with the men. Chick's mate and the two women could take care of the pups.

While they were riding south, John told Jake that his uncle Jack could not be more than two days ride south from here. Jake knew that his friend Jack would be ready to go to help find Jake's niece and nephew. He also knew just how hard this quest was going to be. Jake was very fond of those kids, but he was a realist and knew what the chances were of finding them. Especially if they were already bought by someone. That was one thing Jake never understood. How Comanches could sometimes make deals with Mexicans, and sometime join them on raids on unsuspecting villages. This mixture of Mexicans, Indians, and even white men is where the name Comanchero came to be.

As the miles added up, John was watching Chick walking along in front of the horses. He did not seem to be tiring, but John knew that the dog had some age on him. Every once in a while John would get down and pick up his friend and have him curl up on the pommel of the saddle. This worked out very well, because if Chick detected an odor, or heard or saw something out of the ordinary, then he would jump down and go investigate. Just as John predicted, two days out, they spotted the wagon. They continued forward at the same pace so as not to spook uncle Jack. Of course Jack knew who they were long before they were in gunshot range. As they rode up to the wagon the first thing out of uncle Jack's mouth was, "What in tarnation is wrong?"

"What, no kiss my rump, go to Hell, or nothing?" Said Jake.

"I got eyes ya old fart! I can see that John and Chick, plus you means trouble!" Said uncle Jack.

It was late afternoon, so they pulled up and began to make camp. John took this opportunity to introduce Jake to Thomas and Kathleen. And of course Chick, as well. The young ones fell in love with Chick as was expected. And of course Chick was eating up all the attention.

Now, with the fire going and all sitting around it, John explained to his uncle about Jake's niece and nephew. Uncle Jack said that he would go with them and Thomas piped up saying that he would like to go. Uncle Jack explained to him why this was not acceptable. He had a family to take care of, plus he had to make sure they all got to John's place safely. It was plain that Thomas did not like this, but he too was a realist and knew this was the only solution. Since there was not enough daylight to travel far, they decided to stay right here for this night and be gone in the morning.

Jake was stumbling around for words to thank them and uncle Jack politely said, "Oh, shut up ya old he wolf! We would do this for Digger Indians too!"

Yes sir, thought John. This was going to be an interesting trip indeed!

Dawn found them riding south with Jake riding out in front, because he knew where the village was that got raided. He told them that it was about four days ride southwest, traveling like they were right now. The women gave them enough pemican for about a week, if they hunted once in a while. Uncle Jack carried a bow and a quiver of arrows, and it was well known that he knew how to use them. What hunting that was done, was done by him, because the bow was much quieter than a gun. They did not want to announce their arrival to everyone.

They were sitting around the fire eating two rabbits that uncle Jack had gotten earlier. Of course the men did not want the back, so Chick also had a good supper. Jake told them that they were getting close to where the village was and they would probably be there tomorrow. Of course, after all this time there would not be much to go on, as far as tracking was concerned. They all agreed that if the Comancheros went down into Mexico, then they would have to decide whether or not to follow them. Mexico was a very big and hostile country and they had no liking for Americans. John was thinking, that to have come all this way, only to have to turn around, was definitely not to his liking. The three men and Chick were now looking out over the 'Rio Grande'. Each one had doubts about crossing over into Mexico, but the loss of those kids weighed heavy on their minds.

"I see smoke!" Said uncle Jack.

Jake said, "Yup, likely a homestead. Let's head on over thet a way."

They all headed east and came to a cabin setting on the river. It was a ferry. And the people who ran it were nowhere to be seen. John went up and knocked on the door. He banged and banged, but nobody answered. At that time they heard Chick barking. All went running with guns drawn to investigate! Chick was behind the cabin and standing on a little knoll overlooking a ditch. There, in the bottom were three badly decomposing bodies, partially eaten by the critters of the area.

The men went down to the bottom. It looked to be a family. Man, woman, and grown son.

John went back up to the cabin and found a shovel. With all the men taking turns digging, it did not take long to bury the unfortunate family. Afterward, they all went down to the river and washed their faces and hands. It just seemed that smell would not go away.

They went back to the cabin and went inside. Everything seemed intact, so it likely was not a robbery that went on here. As they were standing there contemplating what went on, Chick barked again, but only once as if to say…come here. They all ran outside and could see Chick down at the river's edge with his nose to the ground. When they got to him, John reached down and picked up what had Chick's attention.

It looked like a necklace with a carving of a beaver on it. Jake asked John if he could see it and John handed it to him. Jake sobbed, then turned around very quick, so no one would see him. When he turned to face the men, there were tears in eyes as he told them that this necklace was made by him! He had given it to his nephew two years ago!

That was that then, thought John. Now they had proof that at least Jake's nephew passed this way. Now they would be crossing the river. It was a known fact that the common people of Mexico did not take kindly to the Comancheros. At least the ones who had any morals at all. This being said, maybe they could find someone who would steer them in the right direction. John surely hoped so, because the heat in this country was unbearable to him. He was used to the cooler climate that the mountains had to offer.

They had been on the Mexico side of the river for two days now and Jake was the only one who had ever been there. He told them that they had better put out a guard for the horses at night, because they were now in Yaqui country. He then explained that they were native to these parts and that they liked to steal horses. For food! Not to ride. They took turns watching the horses.

On this night it was John's turn to watch the horses and it was about an hour after the other two men turned in that Chick started that low growl of his. Of course John knew that this meant trouble, but it was so very dark this night that you could not see your hand in front of your face! Something was out there, but John could not make out what it was. As he was petting Chick to quiet him down, he heard a muffled click from under the blanket of both his companions.

So now at least, John knew that his partners were alert to whatever happened.

From out in the darkness, a man said in broken English, "Please don't shoot? I am friendly. Can I come in?"

Uncle Jack threw a log on the fire and told the man to come in slow. As he stepped into the firelight, all could see that he was an Indian, and this one was leading his own horse. John asked who he was and the man said his name was Juan.

Juan could speak some broken English, so as he talked, the men found out that he was half Mexican and half Yaqui. They told Juan why they were down here and asked him if he had any information to share with them. As it turned out, Juan hated the Comancheros because they had stolen his own mother and sold her into slavery. He was very willing to tell the men what he knew, and did so. He told them that the Comancheros passed through here about three weeks ago, and that he had seen some children with them. Juan said that if there were not so many Comancheros, he would have tried to rescue those children.

John offered him some leftover rabbit and some coffee. After eating the rabbit and drinking a cup of coffee, Juan began telling his own story. He said that he was about twelve years old when they took his mother. They raided their small town about ten miles south of this very spot. It was almost daybreak when they rode through the village shooting guns and bows and arrows. All the young men were either dead or wounded, so it was easy for them to collect all the women and children.

At this time someone asked why he himself wasn't taken. Juan told them that they did take him, but could not hold him. He had escaped that same night, stealing a rifle on his way out. Juan got tears in his eyes as he said what happened after that. He had gotten away clean, but did not go far. As he watched from a hill not too far away, he saw these men drag his mother out in the street where there was a fire burning. (At this time Juan broke down). He continued by saying that they held his mother's hands and feet over the fire, just as if they knew that he was watching. The rifle that Juan was able to steal was a muzzle loader and had only one shot. When his mother screamed from the burning fire, he shot her in the head!

After hearing his story, all three men went over and patted Juan on the shoulder and told him that he did the right thing, even though it was the most terrible thing he was apt to do.

The next morning, Juan was gone. Nobody ever heard him leave. This did not bother John, but he could tell that Jack and Jake were disturbed over it. However, they did not dwell on it for their were other things to think about.

They had been traveling for several hours, when Jack had them stop and listen. They were doing just that when Juan and five others rode down from a hill. From the look of Juan's friends, they too were Indians. Juan rode over to the men and said that he and his men were going to help get back those children. He then said that he had been recruiting these men for years, just waiting for the right time. And now was the right time. Juan introduced his friends to the three white men. He told the white men that they did not have to worry about his friends, because each one of them has had bad things done to them by the Comancheros. Even though none of them spoke the white man's tongue, they would do what Juan told them to do.

Uncle Jack had everybody gather around, then asked Juan where the home of the Comancheros was. Juan got a stick and drew in the sand where their stronghold was located. Then he told them that it was protected by mountains on one side and the river on the other. The other two sides were guarded very heavily. He then told the travelers that he and his men have watched and timed every move in and out of the stronghold. Juan said that they were planning to take all the slaves to the coast where a ship was anchored. He had seen this happen time, and time again.

John wanted to know how far it was to this ship and Juan told him that it was only three sleeps away. The next step was to figure out when to make their move. Now at the stronghold?, or wait until they left for the ship. They decide to wait until they left for the ship, as long as it did not take too long. Juan said that they had five days before the Comancheros left for the ship, so they had three days to get to the stronghold. They could then follow them, or there was a way to get between them and the ship and just wait.

They decided to go the short way and get ahead of the Comancheros. Juan led them on some of the most obscure trails that the three men had ever been on. In fact, all three white men were sure that none of their kind had ever passed this way before. After the third day, they came out on a hill that overlooked the Gulf Of Mexico. Sure enough there was a ship anchored out there!

Juan said that they should now backtrack for a few hours. He just wanted to make sure that the ship was waiting for the Comancheros. Juan told the men that he knew where the Comancheros would be camping this night. That was where they were now going. He said that they could get there first and have everything set up before the Comancheros got there.

Now they were at the very spot where the Comancheros would be camped this night. Juan had them all set in a big circle so he could explain his plan. After everyone was down, Juan began by saying that he had been planning this for years, but never had enough firepower, until now! The white man's guns would make up the difference in what they lacked in manpower.

The plan was a simple one, which was usually the best way to go. Juan had some of his men go out and gather some dry grass and some sticks. With these he made some torches. He then produced a goatskin vessel with some kind of oil in it. He told them that this oil would burn a long time. When the bad men were sleeping, (all but the guards, of course) he would have his men light these torches and throw them into the horse herd.

Uncle Jack broke in and asked, "what about the guards?"

Juan told him that this was where he and his two men came in. You will find where the captive were being held and take out the guards. He then said that he would not give the signal for the torches until they and the captives were heading out of the camp. He told the white men that he was counting on their marksmanship as they were leaving the camp. The three white men discussed the plan and could not come up with anything any better. They knew that the Comancheros had them outnumbered three to one, but by scattering their horses, just maybe they had a chance. While discussing the plan, John looked down at Chick and asked, what about dogs? Did they have dogs in their camp that would warn them when we were getting close?

Jake piped up then, telling them that there were no dogs in their camp. When asked why, he said, "cuzz they eat em!" Food is so scarce down here in in this God fersakin country thet they don't want dogs beggin around fer food! When they find em, they jest eat em!"

John got a cold chill and patted Chick on the head. He sure wished that he was back home where he felt somewhat safe. He did not know why anyone would actually want to live in this place.

It just came to John that nothing was said about the captives having horses, so he asked Juan about this. Juan told him that he had two men that were going to do just that. They were going to get enough horses for the captives to ride before they stampeded the herd.

All was set now and all they had to do was wait. Wait, they did! All the rest of that day and most of the next. It was late afternoon when one of Juan's men came in and said that the Comancheros were about two hours out. This gave all the rescuers time to hide. Since John was new at this kind of fighting, Juan told him where to hide. There was a little depression in the ground and Juan put John in it and covered him with tumbleweeds. This made it possible for him to see out, but next to impossible for anyone to see in. John knew this to be true, because he could not see any of the others. They just disappeared from sight and all looked normal. That is, if you could call this country normal.

John heard them before he saw them. They were several hundred yards away, when he detected a noise. It was horse hooves! A lot of horse hooves! Now the hard part was just waiting. Waiting for darkness.

As for their own horses, they were tied up over a hill a couple hundred yards from where they were now hiding. As long as the wind did not change, they would be ok. John thought...*those Yaqui thought of everything.* Horses could smell or hear other horses from a long distance, providing the wind was in their favor. The Comancheros knew this and would be watching their own horses for signs of alarm. With a lot of luck, everything would go as planned. Chick was laying with John in his little depression. John wasn't going to let him out of his sight, after what Jake had said. Chick started that low growl and John patted him on the head to quiet him.

It would be dark soon, but for now, John could see everything as the riders pulled up and began unloading gear and of course, captives. John thought, *those poor captives sure did look forlorn and dejected*

Of course, by now, the captives thought that no one was going to rescue them. There must have been fifteen captives in all, and John had no idea as to which were Jake's niece and nephew. It did not matter, because the plan was to rescue all the captives.

As John was watching, two of the Indian scouts went out and checked the whole perimeter of the camp. They apparently found everything ok, since they went back to camp and made ready for the night's stay.

This waiting was the hardest thing that John had ever done, but he knew that it was essential to the plan and therefore just relaxed. This made Chick also calm down and relax. John must have dozed off for a second, because when Chick suddenly tensed up, he was wide awake. As he was pondering on just what made Chick so tense, a finger was tapping him on the shoulder! He almost jumped right out of the hole, until he saw that it was Jake! Quiet Jake!

It was pitch black out this night and that was a good thing. Jake put his finger to his mouth, indicating to be quiet. Then he motioned for them to go. John had mixed emotions about being able to slip up on an Indian guard, and he expressed these feelings to Jake. Jake had John follow him to a place that was out of earshot and the other men were already there.

All the men were discussing which guard was going to be murdered by who and John felt the bile rise in his throat. This was just not his way of fighting. Everyone there realized this, so uncle Jack told John that he could go with him to get the two guards that were only a few yards apart. That way, if one guard heard the other one being taken out, then John could throw his knife before the man warned the others.

John was just not sure what to think and Jake sensed this.

"Ya jest think too much pard! Ya will do it ifn ya have ta!," said Jake.

John knew that he would. Especially when he remembered the looks of the faces of those poor women and children down there.

It was time! John followed his uncle down the hill where the two guards were sitting about twenty five yards apart. Damn! The moon was beginning to come out and they could see the guard's shadows. John watched his uncle sneak up on the guard and when John turned to check on the other one…he was gone! Panic started to build up in John! Then he saw him! The guard was drawing his bow on uncle Jack! Without even thinking, John's knife was in the air! It found it's mark! The man went down without even a whimper! The timing could not have been better, because uncle Jack was just grabbing his man around the neck, when John threw the knife. Now, their two guards were out of the way. What about the other ones? The thought no sooner went through John's mind, when he heard the signal that meant everything was according to plan. It was planned that John, Jake, and uncle Jack were to start shooting Comancheros, while the Yaquis rescued the captives. The three men placed themselves around the captives and began blazing away at the Comancheros.

The captives had to be protected at all costs! These were very bad men and they would just as soon shoot the captives as let them be taken away by the rescuers. While the white men kept the Comancheros busy, the Yaquis untied the captives and headed over the hill to the waiting horses. The three white men were to follow, while keeping the Comancheros from chasing the rescuers and captives.

One of the captives was walking back to the Comanchero camp! She was a small girl and John guessed that she was scared and just going back where she thought she was safe. John ran out to get her, but a man was suddenly in front of him! They were both racing to get the girl! Since this man was closer, he caught the little girl and was in the process of turning. When he got turned, he had a knife at the girl's throat!

John did not even hesitate! He threw his knife, catching the man in the throat! Of course this made the man release the girl and grab his throat! As was noted, John's knife was also a working knife. Meaning that it was razor sharp on both sides. This being the case, it severed the man's jugular vein. As the man dropped to his knees, John held out his arms to the little girl and she ran to him! He scooped her up and headed for the horses.

All three men shot their assorted guns until all were empty, then they loaded them on the run! This was the hardest thing that John had to learn! As he was loading on the run, he glanced over at Jake and Jack. Both were loaded twice as fast as John! He made a mental note that he would ask Jake to teach him this process. That is, if they ever got out of here alive!

The Comancheros kept right on the heels of the rescuers and captives, and they made it to the horses without any casualties, then headed north. They knew that it would be some time before the Comencheros were able to round up those stampeded horses. They made use of the time by riding hard and fast. They would ride fast, then get down and walk their horses to keep from tiring them.

It was at these walking times that John experienced some pain in his chest. He knew that his wound was healed on the outside, but apparently the inside was not completely healed. He guessed that when that Blackfoot was hitting him on the wound, something broke open on the inside. This did not slow him down for it was minor to what he had already been through. Now, at least, nobody was pounding him on the chest, so it would heal soon enough, to John's way of thinking.

When they finally stopped it was full daylight and John asked where the Indian was going that just rode back the way they had came. He was told by Juan that the man was going back to try to wipe out their trail. John asked how this was done and was told that they used a tumbleweed bush to sweep out the hoof prints for a few miles.

Now they were all sitting around eating pemmican, and or jerky. John was watching Jake hug his niece and nephew, and thought to himself... *This was the Jake that tracked down all those men who stole his sister those many years ago!*

Love! He could see it in Jake's eyes. John swung his gaze to the right and found himself looking into the bluest eyes that he had ever seen! She was maybe three years old and looked to be the only white captive, with the exception of Jake's mixed niece and nephew. She was the little girl that John himself had rescued. John went over and asked Juan about her, only to find out that she was stolen from a white family just on the American side of the border. Naturally they killed her family, then stole her.

John's heart went out to her! He went over and bent down in front of her and she looked up at him with the saddest eyes that any child should have! As he reached out to touch her, she put her arms around his neck and said, "Da, Da!" *That was that!*, thought John. This poor little girl was going home with him! In fact, she was going to ride with him from now on. John knew without a doubt, that when June saw this little girl, she too would want her to live with them. As John was thinking about all this while riding the next day, uncle Jack rode right up beside him and had a big grin on his face.

John said, "ok, let's hear it!"

"For a man who likes the solitude of the mountains, you are starting a small village there at the base of the Tetons."

John started to reply, but uncle Jack threw up his hands and told him he did not have to explain, and that he knew that John would have it no other way, In fact he too would do the same.

While they traveled by day, one of Juan's men would double back occasionally to see if they were being followed. John asked what the news was, and Juan told him that so far no one has followed. He doubted they would. The firepower of he and his companions was so accurate and strong. He went on to say that the Comancheros were not used to that kind of retaliation. He then said that they would just go and steal more of his people. And, of course he would try to get them back again. Juan then told John that tomorrow they would be at the river that divides their countries and he and his men would turn back and take the Yaqui captives with them.

Just as Juan had said, the next morning found them overlooking the Rio Grande river. John rode over to Juan and held out his hand for a handshake. Instead, Juan grabbed him and gave him a hug. John was surely going to miss this man. They crossed the river and headed due north once again. There was still a long way to go, but at least now they could hunt for food, and build a fire to cook it.

Back at the Tetons, life went on, but Betty would be gone for the whole day, every day, June asked her about this and Betty told her that she was just out watching the trail. She knew that her brother and the other two men would be bringing back her children, she just didn't know when. June was every bit as confident as Betty, but it didn't mean that she liked it. She missed John with all her heart.

As far as Antelope was concerned, she was staying with Thomas and Kathleen. She was devoted to their little girl and the parents loved her being there. It freed them up to work on the cabin. Thomas was an excellent carpenter and Kathleen helped him every step of the way. June's only regret was that John was not here to see his son crawling. He just started and he was going everywhere. In fact, when outside, June had to watch him constantly.

This one day, June and William were down at the river. June was washing clothes and William was napping on a blanket behind her. She did not know that William woke up and was crawling toward the rocks behind them. June heard the undeniable rattle of the Rattlesnake! When she turned, there was William about three feet from a full grown Rattlesnake! She called his name, making him stop! Just before the snake struck, June threw a rock hitting it in the head. It struck, but fell short of it's goal! It was stunned and she grabbed William out of harm's way! June went ahead and killed the snake. After all, there were more children in this area. She decided not to mention it to anyone, since this was pretty much everyday life here in the mountains. She finished her washing and went back to the cabin.

Many miles south of the Tetons, the days melted away as they headed north and John was amazed at how the children looked and acted, now that they were free. All had bathed in the river and had been given clean clothes that Juan had left for them. *Good ole Juan thought of everything*, thought John. The little girl that John was smitten over, had herself became enamored with Chick, which was no surprise.

Nobody knew the little girl's name, but John reckoned that he and June would think of something. June and William were never out of John's mind and as they got closer to the Tetons, he could think of nothing else. John did not like leaving his family, but in this case there was no choice. At least Thomas was there to watch over things.

June! Oh to see her and the baby, thought John.

Three days later and they were about a half day's ride from John's little valley at the base of the Tetons, which were now on their left. Everyone's spirits were soaring and they all talked about what they were going to do when they got home.

A scream was heard in the rocks on their left! Betty came running down out of them with her arms outstretched! Both her children jumped off their horses and ran to meet her. Now everyone was hugging and asking questions all at the same time.

John just sat his horse watching and grinning as he noticed Chick running up the trail to home. He guessed he had someone to see as well. After all had quieted down a bit, John asked Betty what in the world she was doing out here. She told him (in much improved English)that she had been coming out here all week long just to watch and wait. She said that she knew that the three men would bring her family back, she just didn't know when.

Now they were topping the last hill that overlooked John's home. When they got to the top and could see the homestead, they could see everyone down there waiting for them. Chick's return notified all that the men were coming home.

John jumped off his horse and ran to meet June! They collided and embraced while kissing long and with deep emotion! John could smell the wild flowers that June rubbed on herself after bathing. He thought, *nothing ever smelled so good!* Finally he was able to tear himself away from her long enough to see little William crawling in the grass.

"Crawling already!" *My God, time flies* thought John.

John noticed June looking up at the little girl on John's horse and told her that he would tell her about her in a few minutes.

As John was looking down the trail, he could see a cabin being started by Thomas and Kathleen, and now even more people were going to be living there. Then he turned and faced the Tetons and thought, *if I need solitude, I could go trapping up there and not be too far away.*

Right now, solitude was the farthest thing from John's mind. He reached up and got the little girl, scooped up William and arm in arm with June, walked to his cabin.

CHAPTER XIX
Wapiti Meadow

The view was magnificent! Thought John. At this moment he was sitting on top of his cabin. John had went up to repair some shake shingles that had gotten damaged in a storm last night. He was looking at the Tetons.

John was thinking that he had not been trapping since last season. He sure would like to go up there. Not that he was not perfectly happy with the way things were. It was just that a man gets the itch to wander once in a while.

With the roof now repaired, John climbed down. As he dropped to the ground, he turned around for one last look at the mountains. He never tired of looking at them, just as he never tired of looking at his equally beautiful wife. June was beautiful, even by white people's standards. After two years of marriage the love that her and John shared had not diminished.

As John started to open the door to their cabin, it burst open and out popped their two children!

"Whoa!" said John. "What's the hurry?"

Young William was running (or trying to) out the door with his big sister right on his heels. Apparently, William had stolen a biscuit from the pan and June had Sarah chase him down.

Breakfast was not yet ready and June was adamant about all of them eating together. John could not help but laugh, neither could June herself after she turned away from the doorway. It was hilarious just to watch William try to run, since he had only been walking for about a little over a year, since their return from the East. The only good that came of that trip was little William being born. They all found out right quick just what white people thought of Indians, by the way their wives were treated.

Both John and June had to laugh again as they watched Sarah try to get the biscuit from William. Even though Sarah was three years William's senior, she was hard pressed to wrest the biscuit from William. Sarah was not their blood relation, but that did not matter. She was loved equally with William, and the two bonded together perfectly.

Sarah was the name of John's little sister who he lost to the dreaded disease cholera, along with the rest of John's family, with the exception of his uncle Jack of course. This Sarah was too young to remember her given name, so as far as she knew, Sarah was her name.

John turned to June and told her that he had been thinking back on all that they have, and all that they have done. As he gazed into her big beautiful ebony eyes, he told her that he would not change a thing and that he was perfectly happy. June pushed away from him and while smiling said, "What is it that you want husband?"

He could not help but chuckle as he was looking at her with her pouting half grin.

"How could you know me so well, in the short time we have been together?" said John.

She told him that she has seen that look on his face before, and wanted to know where he wanted to go.

It never ceased to amaze John at the insight that women possessed. Especially THIS woman. He told her that they needed meat and the hunting was starting to get a little scarce, what with the three cabins of people right here. Tom and Kathleen had a little girl about Sarah's age, so with their family and John's family, it took a lot more hunting. The game just don't tend to stay around when people are shooting at them.

John told June that he knew for a fact that a big elk herd comes down to graze about a half day's ride north of their home. He told June that he would be gone only about two days. Enough time for him to shoot a couple elk and butcher and quarter them before carrying them back home.

June told him to go, and that she would be fine. He should take Chick with him for his own safety. After all, did not Chick have a family of his own? And the biggest male looked and acted just like Chick did. He would warn her of any trouble in the vicinity.

That was that then, thought John, as he went out to the choral and got his horse and the mule for carrying back the elk. When he came back in, June told him that breakfast was ready and asked would he call the children? John stuck his head out the door and called them. Sarah came running back first and she held up a partially eaten biscuit and said that she couldn't get it away from William fast enough. John and June both laughed again and June said that it was ok. She knew that Sarah had done her best and it would not spoil the little one's appetite.

June had them all go out in back and wash up before eating. When they returned, everything was set. The food was on the table. There was eggs from a Prairie Chicken, slabs of venison, boiled cattail roots, and venison gravy. There was some crushed wild berries to put on the biscuits, and last but not least…coffee to top it off.

As John was eating the thought went through his head (as it had many times). *It just don't get any better than this.*

He also knew that these supplies would not last forever, but the Rendezvous was coming up soon and it was going to be held about three day's ride southwest of them. He had discussed this with June and they decided their whole family would go. They would take the tipi that John and June lived in right after they were married. June was excited, because it was rumored that the Blackfoot were coming again this year. She knew without a doubt that it would be her family's village, since they were the ones who started the trade with the white man.

The meal over with, John told the young ones that he would be gone for a day or two and that they were to mind their momma and do what ever she told them to do. Of course they both wanted to go, but they were just too young. Maybe next year John would take Sarah hunting with him. She needed to learn all the tricks on survival. To live out here, this was a must! *She was very intelligent for such a young one.*, thought John. That being said (rather thought), Sarah jumped up and began cleaning off the table. She always helped her mamma with the dishes.

John went outside and began getting things together that he would need for the hunt. He would build a travois to haul back behind the mule for the elk meat. Now with everything all packed and ready to go, he went back inside the cabin to bid his good byes. After many hugs and kisses, he went back outside and called Chick. Chick came running, but so did his whole clan! All the pups (now grown), came running up to John.

John had to ask June to come out and bring all the pups in the cabin until he was out of range from scent and hearing of the animals. He could not go off on a hunt with a half dozen dogs following him around. This development tickled the children to no end, since the dogs were not allowed in the cabin unless there was an emergency. The largest male (the one who looked like Chick) would not be left behind. His name was Juan. Sarah named him from remembering the name of the man who helped rescue them from the Comancheros.

Juan had grown so much that he surpassed Chick in size. No sooner was John gone than Juan jumped up to the door bar and pushed it out in doing so. The door opened and out he went! John had to stop and get down off his horse, pick up Juan and return him to the cabin. This dog weighed in at sixty five pounds and it must have been a sight to see John carrying him back to the cabin, because when he got there, all were laughing! John started laughing as well. He thought, *yep, Chick all over again.*

Chick and John were both finally able to escape the clutches of their combined families. Even though both loved them, it was good to be back out together again on the trail. John knew that Chick had some age on him, but he still acted like he did when John first met him about five years ago. John never did find out if Chick had an owner, but Chick never once tried to leave, so John reckoned he was content. John would never forget how Chick got his name those many years ago. Chick showed up while John was resting, while on his journey westward.

It suddenly dawned on John that he had been thinking back so much that he had forgotten to keep alert. Even though this area was relatively safe, there were still many things that could happen. Many men lost their lives by not paying attention to their surroundings. Living in the

GONE BEAVER

mountains was a privilege for John, and it agreed with him. If one was to look at him you would see a young man of larger than normal stature. He needed to be big, just to carry around all the weapons he had. Most men would shy away from all that weight. There was the normal possible bag, powder horn, and priming horn. Then he carried two throwing knives the same length as the tomahawk that he also carried. Not to mention the Kentucky flintlock pistol that was the same caliber as his rifle, that never was out of his hands.

John had been on this trail before and knew that it only took a half day's ride from his home, but he had been lollygagging. His intention was to get to the big meadow and find a good spot to camp. Then he would go in search of the elk. As it was, it was almost dark by the time he found a good place to camp. From what he could see this spot overlooked the big meadow that John was certain a few elk visited from time to time. Since it was almost dark, John decided not to hunt for camp meat. He had enough pemmican in his saddlebags to make do.

He built a small fire with very dry wood so it would not smoke so much and soon had some coffee boiling. The river was just beyond some big boulders on the edge of the big meadow, so water was not a problem. John had some meat scraps rolled up in an oilcloth for the purpose of feeding Chick when he didn't hunt. John was sitting there petting Chick and drinking coffee laced with chicory. When coffee got scarce you had to make it stretch until the next rendezvous. He had kind of got used to the chicory taste, but no matter, the rendezvous was coming up soon and he would get more coffee then. John took off all his weapons and placed them within reach then laid down and went to sleep immediately with Chick curled up beside him.

Chick was licking him on the face again. John wished he would quit doing that. Oh well it must be time to get up. John opened up his eyes and had the start of his life! A new born elk calf had been licking him on the face. He sat strait up and the critter ran down out of the rocks to it's mother who was definitely looking for it. As John looked across the now dead fire, there was Chick just sitting there with his famous sideways look. He must have watched the baby calf come right up on John, but he knew there was no danger, so he let the calf lick away. It was just beginning to break daylight and John thought that he should have been up about an hour earlier as was usual. He guessed that he was just so relaxed, he just slept in.

John built up the fire and was going down to fill up his coffee pot. He went in the direction that the newborn calf went. When he peered over the boulder, he just about dropped his coffee pot! Out in the meadow there were more elk than he had ever seen in one place before. Of course John knew there were elk up here, but he had no idea that there would be this many. He guessed that with all his day dreaming, he just stumbled in amongst them and neither had known the other was there. *Hell!* thought John! *They may have even come down while I was still abed.*

Now John had to sneak down to the river and back, so as not to spook the elk. He made it without being spotted, so he then put his coffee on to boil. As John sat there waiting for the coffee to get done, he decided that the elk were so busy watching the perimeter of their herd, that they paid little attention to what was already there. If you are trying to sneak up on an elk, or any other wild critter for that matter, it was an iffy business. John made his coffee and even cooked a slab of venison, there, in his little nook among the boulders. The elk did not even stir.

Since John did not have to stalk the elk, this was just going to be too easy and John was not used to things being easy. John picked up his rifle and put on his weapons, along with powder and ball and lay prone on top of a boulder. He picked out two young cows (who did not have calves). Bang! The first one was down and while they were trying to pinpoint John, he was already re-loaded and shot another one.

Now they were on the run! And did they run! In less than ten seconds, not a one could be seen out in the meadow, except the two that John shot. There was never a shortage of cottonwood trees along a river and this was no exception. John tied his mule behind his horse and rode down to the river. There he cut down some saplings big enough for poles and went over to his first kill, where he promptly made a travois. After gutting both elk, he skinned them, then quartered them. Then he lashed it all down on the travois, which he had tied to the mule. Of course Chick was watching the whole process and was fed some prime cuts while John was quartering the meat.

Now they were back at camp and John left the mule loaded while he put everything away and extinguished his fire by dumping the leftover coffee on it.

While heading back home, John got to thinking that this was just too easy. No sooner had the thought left his head! Bang! A rifle shot just behind him! Then a horse was bearing down on him. John let go of the mule's lead rope and took off as fast as he could!

Just as John began his turn in the saddle to confront this person, he was drug off his horse to the ground! Of course his knife was out immediately. All at once his friend Jake started laughing so hard he about cried.

"You damned old fart! I could have killed you!," said John.

Finally Jake quit laughing long enough to say.... "Jest seein ifn ya were a watchin yer backside, young'un!"

Then he started laughing all over again and so did John. As each were hugging and patting each other on the back, the dust was flying from their buckskins. John told Jake that he had to go get his mule. When he turned to go, there was the mule, travois intact, right up next to his horse. The men looked down at Chick and lo and behold, he was looking at them with his look which made both start laughing all over once again. Chick took this moment to jump up and put his front paws on Jake's chest. Of course he wanted Jake to pet him, since it had been a while since anyone had seen ole "Quiet Jake."

Now that Jake's GRAND ENTRANCE was over he commenced to re-loading his rifle (a cardinal rule out in the mountains). Jake looked at the travois and said, "I see ya finally took advantage of the Wapiti herd!"

"You knew about all these elk coming down here in this meadow?" Said John.

"Course!"Said Jake. "Any mountain man worth his salt knows bout this here Wapiti gatherin"

They got back on their horses and headed south.

While they were riding, Jake told John that he had been trapping over by the Green River and the beaver were about trapped out, but what plews he had, he cached and then headed up in the Tetons to find another trapping area. He was on his way down to John's place when he heard the two shots that John made.

"Course when I seed who it were, 'the hair of the bar' come out in me, so I jest had ta test ya!"said Jake. "Even put the sneak on ole Chick this time!"

As they rode and talked, the conversation always came back to the rendezvous. Jake asked John if he was going to the rendezvous this year. John told him that he was, but he didn't have any plews to trade. He did have some cash money though. He surely did need supplies and it would be good to see some old friends again. Jake asked John where Jack was and John told him that as far as he knew, his uncle Jack would be at the rendezvous. He himself had not seen "hide nor hair" of Jack and his wife Antelope. Jake then asked about his sister and her young'uns. John said that they were doing fine and had a new cabin and were happy.

John asked Jake if he knew what the price of beaver was and Jake said that he rightly did not know, but it was way down this year, what with all the companies coming out here trapping.

"Gettin so's a man caint even turn around thout bumpin elbows with a nother white man!"said Jake. Gonna haf ta mosey up ta Canady, jest ta get shet of em! I been thinkin on gettin outta this here beaver trade, maybe so go on up north ta do some meat huntin fer one of them there forts."

"I reckon a man has to do what he can to live," said John. As fer me, I got that forge to work at when the beaver finally peters out. Can't make much cash money, but who needs it out here? I have pounded out many a horse shoe, just for some coal, or some chunks of iron, or a slab of bacon, or any other thing that I can use. People must have the word on me, because somebody is always stopping by my place wanting to trade my work for what they have brought from a town. I almost got enough iron to build a bigger forge, and just use my little one to take to rendezvous and such."

"Sounds like ya got er all planned out," said Jake. "I never was much on plannin, I jest take things as they come. I reckon that's why my only family is my sis and her young'uns. I have been a thinkin, not plannin, mind ya, about gettin myself a nother woman." I be a gittin tired of a ridin round this here "High Lonesome" all by my own self. Ya knows, there is only so much a man can say ta a horse or mule. Sides, a nice plump woman could warm up my nights considerable. Whew!" Said Jake. "I have palaverd the day away. I reckon I have not talked that much in a whole year."

John looked at Jake and stuck out his hand for a handshake. Jake took it and John congratulated him and told him it was about time he settled down. Then he said that Jake could bring his woman(who ever she may be) over to his place there at the base of the Tetons.

"Whoa up there young'un! I said I wanted a woman. A cabin is alright for those that want one, like yourself, but this chile don't cotton ta bein hogtied to one place. Maybe so when I get old, I will live in a cabin."

John looked at him and said, "Waugh! You old fart. You are already two years older than water!"

Quick as lightning, Jake hit John in the arm so hard that it knocked him off his horse!

CHAPTER XX
Wendigo

Jake was on him immediately and they were wrestling around on the ground and laughing, while Chick was barking and trying to get into the fun. Finally they quit and started patting the dust off themselves. All of a sudden Chick stopped barking and was looking to the west at the Tetons. Both men stood looking in the same direction and were wandering what had Chick's attention. Just when they thought it was nothing, they heard it! It was the most "Gawd awful sound" that they had ever heard. It was almost human, but not quite. It sounded sad, and lonesome, but very chilling.

John looked over at Jake and Jake was looking down at the ground and shaking his head.

"You know what in the Hell that was?" asked John.

"Fraid I do young'un," said Jake. "That there was the "Wendigo!"

John said, "I have heard the old mountain men talk of him, but they only heard it when they were alone, so I chalked it up to imagination."

"I have heard it one time my ownself," said Jake. "I were up north trappin on the Yellerstone. It were one of them there tree poppin winters so cold thet critters were a freezin ta death right where they were a standin I were hunkered down inta my wool blanket with a buffler hide on top a that! I first thought that I was a dreamin, cuzz I heard thet thing screamin plain as day! Thought it might be a painter a tryin ta git the horse or mule.

God I hated havin ta git outen those blankets, but I had ta check on the critters The mule was jest standin thar lookin at me, but the stupid horse had tried to lay down to get warm. Thet's whar I found him. Froze to death!"

Jake didn't say anything for a while, so John punched him and said, "What about the screaming?"

"Never did hear it no more," said Jake. "Till now!"

"Well," said John. "We are almost to my place and I don't mind saying that I don't really care for that critter being this close to my family. I reckon I am going to have to go on a little scout, when I get back. Don't really hold with that wendigo stuff, but sure enough something is out there and I am going to cast around for some kind of sign."

"Never said thet I believed in it neither, but thar is sumpin out yonder certain sure," said Jake.

Now they were looking down on John's valley and Jake let out a war hoop.

"Land sake, young'un, you got yourself a little town down thar now. Lookie thar! Ya done built up a cabin fer my sis and her young'uns!"

John told him that he thought that was the least he could do, after all she had been through. After he, Jake, and uncle Jack rescued her children from the Comancheros, they needed some place to stay. Everyone saw them on the hill looking down at the buildings, of course, once again Chick had already went down and announced their arrival.

Down they went into the valley that now had three cabins some various sheds, and a small blacksmith shop. After all hugged each other, June told John that she was glad he did not take the two days that he had planned on taking, and she was glad he had met up with their friend Jake. They could see Jake with his niece and nephew and it was obvious that they were glad to see each other.

After things got back to normal, John asked June if things went well.

"Of course," she said. "But you may have to go up in the mountains to kill a mountain lion or something!"

This got John's attention real quick! "Why?" he said. "Did you hear something?"

"Well," said June. "Juan, Chick's biggest pup, quit playing with the children about three hours ago and started sniffing the air. I had the children quiet down and about then we heard this awful wailing coming from up toward the mountains! To me, it did not sound like one of the big cats. In fact, it did not sound like anything that I have ever heard before."

John then told her that he and Jake had also heard this thing and Jake told him it was a Wendigo. Then he explained about when mountain men were alone for very long periods that some have heard these things. He went on to say that this the first time that he ever knew of where many people have heard it. Then he told June that him and Jake would go on a scout after they had rested and visited for a spell.

John changed the subject and told June that he thought Jake was finally getting lonely for a woman. This pleased June to no end, because even Indian women liked the thought of match making. Of course she was now thinking of someone for Jake. There were many from her tribe who had lost husbands either to war, or natural causes. John could tell all these things were going through her head by the way she had stopped talking and was thinking. He told her not to get carried away with things, because even though his friend had lost his wife a long time ago, he still thought of her. John could tell by the way he acted when around women.

It was a good thing to know that Juan was as good a watch dog as Chick. Especially when John was away. Now he could take Chick with him and not worry quite as bad about things back home.

Most of the day was gone, so John told June that they would just wait until morning to go on their scout. Whatever this thing was, surely there would be some sign. *This was really going to be some hunt*, thought John. Not even knowing what they were hunting for could be a very dangerous proposition here in the mountains. With normal critters, you got to know how they act, and what to look for in the way of sign.

Much later that night, while laying in each other's arms fully spent after making love, the couple heard a scratching at the door and knew this to be Chick. John got up and opened up the door to find Chick and Juan both. Chick made the move for John to follow, but he was going toward the Tetons and no way was John going up there after dark. It would have been a different story had they been camped up there already. He just petted Chick on the head and told him they would go tomorrow.

That was when they heard this awful wailing again! It was coming from somewhere up in the Tetons. John got a chill up his spine! He had definitely never heard anything like that before. June came to the door and said that she heard it also. John knew that Chick and his pup did not understand why John wouldn't follow them. Of course they didn't know a mere man could not see in the darkness like they can, or track by scent, or rely on hearing to follow a trail. John thought seriously about locking the two dogs up for the night to keep them from going up there. He settled on just bringing them inside with him and June for the remainder of the night. No more wailing was heard that night, but neither John or June had that great a night's sleep.

John was up before sunrise as was his custom. After doing all the chores, he came back inside to the smell of fresh brewed coffee. That brightened up the day. June had him sit down to a mess of pancakes with a slab of venison on the side.

Now, with breakfast over, he told June that he was going to Betty's place to fetch Jake and they would go on a little scout up in the Tetons. He said that they would stop back here before they went up there. The next cabin up the trail was Thomas and Kathleen's place. The one after that was Betty's place. John decided to stop at Thomas's place to find out if he also heard that thing last night, or earlier that day.

Thomas was a good man to "Ride the river with," but he was not a mountain man. After talking with Thomas, of course he wanted to go with John and Jake, because he heard that thing also. John politely told him that he would rather he stayed here to protect the families. Thomas said that he surely could do that.

As John pulled into the yard of Betty's cabin, Jake was already saddled and ready to go. John just shook his head and said, "how in God's name did you know I would be here this morning?"

Jake just looked at him and grinned. Then he said, "cuzz thet's whut I woulda done."

"I take it you heard that thing too?" Said John.

Jake said, "Thet critter was some! It surely were! Liked ta skeered the bejesus outen Betty and the young'uns! I aint so sure it is a wendigo, seein as so many people heard it."

"Wendigo or not, are you ready to go up yonder and see?" said John.

"I reckon. Aint nobody gonna rest round here till we find out whut this here critter is."

After stopping at John's place to say goodbye and to pick up Chick, they headed up toward the Tetons. John had never been one to believe in spooks, but there definitely was something up there! Of that, he was certain! They had no way of knowing where to look, so they just headed in the direction where the wailing had been coming from.

About mid day John asked if they could pull up for a breather. Their horses had been climbing for the last two hours. There was a little pool in the rocks with a tiny spring running into it, so they and the horses had a drink. They were sitting there discussing why they had not seen any sign, because they were in the area where all the hollering was coming from. John said that he had been up here many times and knew for a fact that this was the only water around here for quite a way and there ought to be some kind of sign here. Chick had been exploring all around the little pool and suddenly stopped! He began sniffing the air and went immediately up into the rocks.

The men heard Chick let out a bark! Since it only one bark, John knew that he was ok, and that he had found something. They went around this huge boulder and there was Chick standing in front of this enormous cave. Normally it just looked like a big crack in the rocks, but when you went around to the back of the boulder, you could tell that it was a very large cave. Even the two men could smell the odor coming from this cave. This odor was unlike any that either man had ever smelled before. Kind of like rotten meat, but not quite.

Chick started to whine and John had never heard him do that before. It was obvious that Chick did not want to go in there! *What could be so terrible that a dog wouldn't want to explore a cave?* thought John.

This cave appeared to go back a long way and the men had no light, so They each got a cedar branch and wrapped some of the small twigs with needles around it and tied it off with a piece of rawhide string. They knew it would not burn long, but neither planned on staying in this place for long! That much was certain! They decided to go far enough in so they could still see the entrance and no farther.

As they started to go in, John called Chick, but no amount of coaxing could get him to go in there. He let out a bark once and then just sat there doing his cockeyed look, which most always was funny. This time, however, it didn't seem funny at all. John got to thinking that maybe Chick was the smart one here. No matter, they had to find out what was in here and when they entered the first thing they saw were drawings on the walls. Very old drawings! The drawings were crude but explanatory, because you could see where a stick person was being attacked by another very large stick person. The large attacker had what looked to be hair growing out all over it's body. It may or may not have been hair as the drawings were so old and weathered it was hard to tell.

John didn't know about Jake, but this smell was about to gag him. There was a ribbon of water running through the middle of the floor of this cave. John guessed this was the source of the pool just outside. Jake held his hand up in the classic stop position and pointed to the ground at some mud next to the little stream.

Cold chills ran up John's back as he gazed at a footprint about two feet long! A human footprint! Barefooted!

Good God, thought John. *How big was the man who made this?*

Their torches started to flicker, so they headed back to the entrance. Neither man said a thing as they stepped out into the daylight.

Chick was sure glad to see them come out of that dark cave and presented himself to be petted and made over. After petting Chick, John asked Jake if he wanted to fix up the torches and go back inside.

All Jake said while shrugging his shoulders was, "I reckon I seed all I need ta see!"

John shook his head in agreement and said, "Yep, I surely don't want no truck with whoever lives in there! He didn't harm me or mine, so I say we just leave him be."

Of course both men had their own thoughts on the matter, but neither spoke of them, so they just started back down to the cabins. They could tell by the way Chick was acting that this was definitely what HE wanted. As they started around the giant boulder they noticed both horses were gone! Their first thought was that someone stole them, but then they saw them heading back down the trail. As they stepped out on the trail the first thing they noticed was the footprint! Of course this was what scared the horses, but what was worse, this print was behind the big boulder facing where they had just exited the cave! This man (or, God forbid, thing) had been watching them!

The chills returned to John and he could not deny that he was scared. He knew that no man scared him, or for that matter, no animal either if he saw them first. This was something that was beyond both men's reckoning and Jake's version of this was that it was a Wendigo, plain and simple!

Their horses were stopped a few yards down the trail just chomping some grass, so the men had no trouble walking up to them. At least they wouldn't have to walk back down the mountain. As they grabbed the reigns they noticed that the leather had been pulled apart, because the rest was still tied to the cedar trees where they tied them. John looked at Jake and he was looking at him! Both knew that the horses were certainly capable of breaking the reigns, but it was highly unlikely! Something literally pulled them until they snapped, letting the horses go running down the trail. Those Damn chills crept up John's back once again!

The men didn't say much as they headed back, but both were deep in thought. Most men were practical and this was way beyond the borders of practicality.

They traveled the rest of the day with no setbacks or surprises and it was just about sundown when they reached John's cabin. Of course, as usual, Chick had went first to tell everyone they were back, so June and the children were waiting for them. John got down and gave June and the younguns a big hug and Jake rode on, saying he was going on to Betty's cabin.

After taking care of the horses John went inside and June had some coffee on. She had him sit down and wanted to know everything while the coffee was boiling. John knew he could not lie to her, so he told her all that they had found. She just sat there and took in everything he said until he was done talking. She looked at him and told him that her people had talked of these things since she was a little girl. Many times while telling John of the legends of her people, she referred to them as "The old ones" who went before.

She said that she, herself had played in a cave where there were drawings on the walls. She was forbidden to go in there after her parents found out about it. She said that the drawings were not the same as the ones John just described, but they were made by the "old ones" also. John looked at his wife and wondered just how much she knew about these things, and he asked her just that.

June said that her people always spoke of these men who lived in the high mountains where nobody much went unless to hunt for the mountain sheep on occasion. She sad that she remembered one man coming back from one of these sheep hunts. When he left, his hair was as black as night, but when he returned all his hair was as white as snow! He spoke of a man type thing that he saw! He only spoke of it one time then he never talked of it again. She said that her tribe believed that if one saw something that no other had seen, then it was so! No one should question him about it anymore.

John was definitely a practical man, but there are some things that just cannot be explained and this was one of them. So far as he knew nothing ever came of this thing's wailing and nothing was hurt by it, so in John's book it should just be left alone. He told June this and she agreed whole heartily.

June then told John that someone else had some excitement while he was gone!

With a concerned look, John asked, "who?"

"Juan," said June. "Do you know of that big hornet's nest down by the river?"

"Yes, I have seen it."

"I had noticed that Juan was not here and hadn't been for several hours, so I went down to the river and found the hornet's nest laying on the ground. The cottonwood tree that it was in has very low branches and Juan must have jumped up and got in the tree to be able to knock it down. I looked all over for that dog and was about ready to go back when I heard him whine. I finally found him! If he were not in so much pain, it would have been funny, because he was submerged in some backwater from the river. All that I could see was his nose sticking out of the water. And what a nose it was! All swollen almost beyond recognition. I was finally able to coax him back home, but he had so many stings on him that it was hard for him to walk. He is laid up out in the stable and is still swollen, but it has gone down some."

I will go check on him as soon as I get done eating and have some coffee, said John around a piece of elk steak that he was chewing on. Elk was John's favorite meat and June could cook it like no one else. It was delicious! Potatoes, carrots, and onions! *It didn't get any better than this*, thought John. He sure was glad he came across the man selling seeds at the last rendezvous. And he was equally glad that The priest who lived in June's village taught some of them how to plant a garden. Now June would have her own seeds to plant next year, and to give some to the neighbors. There were still some things that they needed, but could get them at the rendezvous.

Ah! The rendezvous, thought John. This would be his third one, and he could not wait! He had many experiences at the other two, including Killing a man (in self defense of course), and last but definitely not least, his proposal to June. This was also a good time to see people who you have not seen for a year or more. it has been several months since John had seen his uncle Jack and his lovely young wife, Antelope. Uncle Jack would not miss the rendezvous for nothing. He and Antelope left this valley right after they returned from the rescue of the captives from the Comancheros. Also there would competition in shooting and hawk and knife throwing. John had no equal when it came to throwing the knife and tomahawk. He was a legend at his young age, but he never bragged about it.

Competing would be fine, thought John. As long as he didn't have to kill anyone. He just did not like to use his skill in that way.

June suddenly broke into his thoughts and asked him if he thought the trappers at the rendezvous would like some fresh vegetables from their garden.

John's reply was with a question of his own. He said, "how did you know that I was thinking about the rendezvous?"

"I know that this has been on both our minds for the last few weeks. It is a time to see old friends, and in mine and your case, relatives, I hope. Your Uncle Jack will probably be there along with Antelope who I miss very much." Even though the Blackfoot and Shoshone did not get along, June and Antelope became quite close while traveling together back east.

They had been discussing the coming rendezvous for weeks and now the time had come for them to pack what they would be taking and head south. The trip would take three days at the very least, but the weather could not have been any better. John had been teaching Sarah to ride and in fact she had her own small pony. John had broke the pony himself and knew it to be gentile, so she would hang on to young William and they would ride double. John was kind of worried about Chick. He did not know how old he was, but he was getting some age on him for sure. Six traveling days may be a bit much for the old hound, even though he wouldn't show it. Juan, on the other hand, would be a good choice, providing they could make Chick stay home. As it turned out, that problem solved itself. Chick's mate tangled with a coon down at the river and it drug her into the water! Anyone who knows anything knows that if a coon gets a dog in the water.... well the dog will have a bad day for certain. She would be fine in a few days, but Chick would not leave her side, so getting away from him was not a problem anymore.

They were almost done packing and John was getting nervous waiting. Jake had said that he would be going with them, but he was not here yet. John was just getting ready to tell June that he was going over to Betty's place, when he noticed movement on the trail. It was Jake, and he had Betty and both her younguns with him. When he got close to John all he did was roll his eyes and John knew that Jake had been waiting on Betty.

Jake said to John, "I tried ta tell her thet a rendezvous were no place fer her, but she had ta come anyways."

Betty broke in at that time, saying that she needed things that she just knew Jake would forget and she wanted to see other people now that she was no longer a captive.

John reckoned that he could not argue with that, anyway, his family was going too, so he couldn't say a word. John asked Jake if he spoke to Thomas and Jake said that Thomas had no intentions of going and that he had everything he needed right here at home.

At that time John said to the group, "let's head south folks!"

It took about a day for everyone to get into a routine of some kind, but by day's end everyone was in good spirits and there were no miss-haps to speak of. They just had one communal fire as opposed to separate family fires. Mostly the only thing cooking was coffee, as everyone had brought pemmican or jerky. Jake told everyone that he would go hunt up a small deer, or antelope tomorrow. That way, they could have at least one meal while traveling. That suited everyone since they were only going to be on the trail two more days.

Later that night while everyone was asleep and all was quiet, John began stirring around and finally woke up. He could not figure just what it was that woke him up. As he was lying there on his side pondering this, Juan came up behind him and put his cold nose against the back of John's neck. John was sitting up immediately with his pistol pointed at Juan! All Juan did was cock his head just like his father, Chick! John stifled a chuckle as he put his pistol back under the blanket. Of course June who was laying beside him was wide awake now and she also had to laugh at the way Juan was looking at them. That was when both John and June noticed the odor! John got up and put another log on the fire, so he could see better.

The smell was getting fainter and in a few minutes it was gone altogether. John looked over towards Jake's family and noticed that Jake was gone! John squatted down and told June that he was going to go looking for Jake and she told him to be very careful. Just as John was getting all his weapons together, Jake came into the camp. He motioned for John to come away from the camp so they could talk and not wake everybody up. "What did you find?" whispered John.

"Couldn't find a thing in this here dark, so I follered my nose. Whatever it were, it be a headin back up ta the mountains."

Those cold chills returned to John as he knew this to be the same smell that was at the cave the other day. He had made up his mind to leave this thing alone, but if it was going to dog their trail, then it would have to pay the consequences. John asked Jake what he thought they should do. All Jake said was that there was nothing that they could do right now, but if they smelled it any more then they would have to go on a hunt. John agreed whole heartily. They decided to stand watch the rest of the night. John said that he would take the first watch and Jake could relieve him in a couple hours.

The morning dawned bright and clear with the smell of the mountain air and nothing else. All the travelers were up and had breakfast over with by the time the sun was all the way up. They were about ready to go when Juan was heard barking just outside the camp. John rode over there and just sat his horse looking down at the giant footprint that Juan had found. it was pointed to the camp. This thing had been watching them last night! Well, the cold chills returned to John, but he turned his horse and told everyone that Juan had found a gopher hole. John thought there was no need to alarm everyone. Little did he know that Jake and June knew something was wrong, but each figured that if John did not want to tell them, then they would not say anything to anyone either.

The traveling went very well and they made very good time. Jake said at this rate they would be at the rendezvous by tomorrow at mid-day. This pleased everyone, because the closer they got the more excited they all became. Each had their own reasons for going to the rendezvous. John and June would camp in the lodge that they had their honeymoon in. they had been dragging it behind the mule on a travois. Jake had said that he would put up a lean-to type of lodge for Betty and her younguns. He knew that "Trader Bob," who was Jake's brother would be there and he had an extra canvas cover to make a lean-to with.

That night the men stood watch again, but nothing out of the ordinary happened and it was quiet all night.

Once again the sun found the travelers about a mile down the trail. Jake had shot a small buck deer the day before and all had dined on steaks, but this morning not a soul wanted breakfast. All were in a hurry to get to the rendezvous and did not want to take time to cook. In fact they were eating pemmican as they rode.

They made very good time that day and while sitting around the fire that evening, Jake said that if they kept at this pace, they would be at rendezvous by mid-morning the next day. They decided to roast the last of Jake's deer meat that evening and put it on a spit over the fire. The smell of the meat cooking was tantalizing to all the travelers and apparently to a cougar who made himself quite vocal off to the west. This time it really was a cougar screaming and not whatever made those tracks a while back.

It must have been about an hour before dawn when John awoke as usual, but this time he had this feeling that he could not explain. it was kind of like when you know that you are being watched. Apparently Juan sensed something also, because he came over and sat by John and was just looking at the trees just outside of the camp's perimeter.

Suddenly Juan emitted this low growl and John reached down and stroked his neck with one hand while bringing his rifle up with the other. A shape began to materialize in the pre-dawn darkness! John could tell it was a man and he had his hand in the air in the sign of peace.

"Who's there?" said John.

As the man came up to the dying embers of the fire, John could see that it was his friend Killdeer.

With all the commotion everyone was up and curious to who was here. After they got through hugging each other, John and Killdeer began talking in sign language since neither could speak the other's tongue. Now Killdeer made a motion and about ten of his fellow tribesmen came into the camp. Killdeer explained that they too were on their way to the rendezvous for their yearly trade. Of course the fire was built up and coffee was put on to boil. They were out of fresh meat to offer the men and told them so. Killdeer made another motion and a man came up carrying a small antelope. The antelope was butchered immediately and cooked over the fire.

John and his friend had a lot of catching up to do, since they hadn't seen each other since last rendezvous and that is just what they did the rest of the way to the rendezvous site. Through sign and with Jake's interpreting they were able to find out what each had done the previous year. Since Killdeer's arrival had slowed them down a little, it wasn't until mid-afternoon when they arrived at the rendezvous. As they topped this last hill, the view was breathtaking as usual. There, nestled in this huge valley was the rendezvous! About a thousand, or more horses and many, many tipis, and of course there were the white man's marquis tents and various types of shelters. The camp smoke hung like a cloud over the large encampment. And as usual there was the smell! Horses, manure, camp smoke, green beaver hides, roasting meat, and many other odors as well.

CHAPTER XXI
Third Rendezvous

As was the custom, all the men changed into their best buckskins, and adorned themselves with necklaces, slicked down their hair, and primped and preened themselves until they deemed themselves fit to ride down into the me-lee that was rendezvous. This was done by white men and Indian alike. After all had themselves ready, they raised their rifles and shot in the air! Then went racing down to the rendezvous, hollering at the top of their lungs! The women knew this was the way things were done and they did not mind, so they just watched and went down at their own pace. They knew their men would be there waiting for them when they got there.

There were several Indian tribes attending this rendezvous, but the closest to the travelers were the Shoshone, and that is where the men waited for their families. Of course Killdeer knew most of these people, but they were not his tribe. He said his family and most of his people were just a little ways behind them and would be here within the next day if not sooner. There was one tipi, however that John recognized. His uncle Jack was camped with his young Shoshone wife, Antelope, just a little way from the main encampment.

John waited for his family to catch up and they all headed for Uncle Jack's lodge. John walked over and rattled some elk hooves that were hanging there for that purpose. After several tries, he decided there was nobody home. John was just getting ready to get back on his horse, when he heard his uncle holler. Jack and Antelope were walking toward them and when they got closer, Antelope ran to meet and hug John! Of course by then June was off her horse and Antelope hugged her as well. After everyone was done hugging and backslapping, Jack said they had just come from trading his plews. John could tell that his uncle was not happy and asked how it went. Uncle Jack frowned and said, "beaver just don't shine no more, I pertneer had ta give em away!" He looked at John and told him it was a good thing he knew a trade such as blacksmithing, because he sure could not make a living trapping beaver this day and age.

Jake had taken his sister and her children to the trading area, since that was where Trader Bob, his brother had a table set up. Jake could not wait to show Bob their sister and her children. Bob had not seen their sister for many years. He was staying at a friend's house when some bad men raided the home of their parents, knocking out Jake and kidnapping Betty. Of course thanks to John. Jack, and her brother, Jake, Betty had her beloved young ones back.

As for John's uncle Jack, he told John that he was so disgusted that he was going to look up Jake and his brother to "crack open a jug," as he put it. Although John did not like to drink, he quite understood why his uncle would want to. A man spends all season wading around in ice cold water trapping, skinning, and stretching those plews, just to have them sell for next to nothing! *Besides*, thought John. *This was rendezvous! a time to "let er loose!"*

It was time to go shopping! Antelope grabbed June and the little ones, then led her to the trading area. And since her and Jack had been there a while, she knew where all the stuff that would interest June, (or any woman for that matter) was. John already had in mind where he wanted to go, so he told the women that they would meet back here at Antelope's and Jack's lodge. This done, John headed for the blacksmith area. He wanted to see who was here this year and was shocked to the core to find the man who ran the shop back in Independence, just pounding away at some horse shoes. They had their greetings and John asked if he brought his wife, Gretta. The man pointed behind him to a marquis tent and there was a line of men stretched as far as John could see! John asked him what was going on and the man said Gretta's cooking is a big thing to these men who have ate their own cooking for so long. John looked inside the tent and saw her hustling and bustling around and he could see that she was in the height of her glory. John bought a small keg of nails for repairs around the cabin. Drilling and pinning was very time consuming and nails were so much faster.

There was so much to see, as this rendezvous was much bigger than the ones John had already been to. There were big and small Marquis Tents, and tables, and many, many blankets laid out with trade goods on them. John walked around looking at all the blanket traders that he could. It seemed that they were more apt to cut a deal than the larger Marquis traders. As John walked up to this one blanket, he noticed a man squatted down looking at the trade goods on it. More appropriately, he noticed the large knife that was in the man's belt.

"Jim Bowie!," said John.

Jim turned and looked John up and down, then smiled real big saying, "well I'll be damned! John Tucker! Aint seen you since Independence. I shore have been hearing about this man who throws a knife real good. Might that be you?"

"I reckon," was all John said." Then he stuck out his hand for a handshake.

Jim noticed the knife that John had strapped to him and asked if he could see it. John handed it to him and Jim checked it out extensively, noting the balance and weight, plus the sharp edge that most throwing knives lacked. Jim knew good steel when he saw it and this was the best. With the exception of his own, of course.

They walked on together checking out the various trade blankets and making small talk. John found out that Jim was just up here for the rendezvous. Being a southern man, as Jim was, this climate was not to his liking and he told John that he was going down to Texas and Louisiana, his home state, just as soon as the rendezvous was over.

There were always competitions of some kind going on at a rendezvous and this one had many. The two men saw a bunch of men out on the edge of the main encampment shooting at targets. John noticed that his friend Jake was there. As he got closer, he saw his uncle Jack taking aim at a playing card out about twenty five yards out. The real kicker was...the card was turned so all you could see was the edge. Of course Jim had seen this many times before and he was not surprised when Jack cut the card in half with his first shot. Everyone patted Jack on the back. Jake stepped up to the line and primed his rifle, took aim and fired, doing the same thing. Several men were able to cut cards and it was now down to who could cut one exactly in half. When it was all said and done, Jake came out the winner. John knew that his uncle was going to be in for a hard time now.

The two men walked on to the next competition. This was shooting an arrow at some bunched grass with a paper target attached to it. They watched this for a while, noticing the Indians were more proficient at this. No surprise there.

It was the last competition that got their attention. Knife and hawk throwing!

Of course when all the men saw who was watching, they could not believe that the now famous Jim Bowie, and the almost as famous John Tucker were at their very own competition. After much handshaking and pats on the back. Jim and John were asked if they would compete with each other. At first they declined, but eventually gave in, since everyone was so enthused about it.

The rules were simple. A line was scraped on the ground about twelve feet from a cottonwood block. The rules stated that you could not step over the line, but could throw from anywhere behind it, as long as the hawk or knife only turned over one time before sticking in the block. The block was on a stand about three feet from the ground. a Playing card was placed somewhere close to the center of the block. For the tomahawk, the card was placed horizontally. This allowed the blade of the hawk to cut the card in half, if you were good enough. You were allowed two practice throws if you wanted them. Then the next five throws counted as points. If you just stuck the hawk anywhere on the block, you got one point. If you cut or nicked, or damaged the card in any way, you got three points. If the card was cut anywhere in half, you got five points. Twenty five points was a perfect score.

The knife was scored much the same way, but the card was placed vertical and you had to get the knife point all inside the card for five points. A cut or damaged card was three points. A stick on the block was one point. When throwing a hawk, one could tell without even looking when the card was cut in half. It sounded like an egg shell cracking.

There was a five cent charge for entering, or the trading of something that the judge deemed fit. The judge of the event was a man who watched from the side, and would go up and inspect the card for damage, or in case of a tie, there was a tie breaker throw. In this, the competitors would each get one throw apiece. The closest one to the card was the winner. If both cut the card in half, the judge would determine who was closest to the middle of the card. This worked for both hawk and knife.

Both men paid their admission fee, and Jim stepped up to the line first. Jim had just gotten to the rendezvous and had not practiced this day, so he opted to take his two practice throws. He chose the hawk first and let go with the first throw sticking it on the side of the block's face. He did this, again sticking it on the side. Now he was ready, and told the judge so. Since the card was not damaged, they left it up there. "Crack!" His first throw cut the card in half about a half inch from the left side. A new card was placed up there and "Crack!" his next throw cut the card in half a little closer to the middle this time. another new card was placed up and he cut it, but not quite all the way. There was about an eighth inch holding it together at the bottom. His hawk was a little high. This was a three point shot. A new card was put up and CRACK! another five pointer. The last throw was also a five pointer. This got Jim twenty three points for the hawk throw. Now for the knife.

Jim was loosened up now, so he declined the practice throws for the knife. A card was placed up on the block in the vertical position, and Jim let go with his first throw, sticking his famous knife right in the middle of the card. The crowd could hold it no longer as they hooted and hollered. Jim done this four more times and everyone was just dumbfounded. No one had ever had a score like he had just done. Forty eight points total for knife and hawk! There was a blanket laying off to the side with numerous trade goods on it that the trappers had donated for the prizes, but Jim could not go pick out his prize just yet, because John had not threw.

John stepped up to the line and when asked if he wanted the two practice throws, said he would take one throw, just to loosen up. John had already had a round of throwing earlier that morning as was his daily routine. John also chose the hawk first and stuck it off to the side on his practice throw. Now he threw and cut the card in half making the famous eggshell breaking sound. Four more times, he done this, not quite in the middle, but close. Twenty five points! This was just unheard of with a tomahawk, and the men gathered around John patting him on the back and telling him he had beat the famous Jim Bowie in the hawk part of the competition.

This heady feeling of accomplishment was new to John, but he was smart enough to realize that he still had the knife to throw, and he was throwing against JIM BOWIE! When you throw your knife in a fight for life or any other emergency, it was totally different from competition throwing. In competition, you have time to think! In an emergency you don't!

John took a deep breath and let it out, slowly calming down. Now he let go with the knife sticking it inside the perimeter of the card. John did this four more times, but the last throw was questionable and the judge along with everybody standing around crowded around the block looking at the knife that just barely was breaking out the side of the card.

A tie! Jim missed one on his hawk and John missed one on his knife! Now they had to throw off a tie! How were they going to do it, someone said. Were they going to use the hawk or the knife, since each had missed with one or the other. This had never come up before, so the judge said he would flip a coin to see what weapon was to be used. He did this and it so happened to be the knife was to be used. A card was placed vertical on the block and Jim took his throw. The judge decide to use only aces for this throw, since both men were so good. Jim's throw was dead center into the ace of hearts. John took his throw and nailed the ace of spades dead center.

The crowd was cheering both men so much that the judge determined that the competition was a draw. These two men would just keep throwing dead center, so they might just as well go pick out their prizes off the blanket. Both men did so and everyone was satisfied.

This competition would be talked about for years around the

campfires! John could not believe that he had just tied with his mentor, Mister James Bowie! They shook hands and John told him that he had to go find his wife, and that Jim and himself would be running into each other for a couple of weeks here at the rendezvous.

The prize that John picked was a large cast iron kettle. He knew that his wife would just love this piece of cookware, since it was bigger than the one they now have.

As John walked over to the side of the encampment where he told June and Antelope to meet him, there was a large group of people standing around someone who was in the middle. When John was able to see who it was, he was surprised to see his wife and Antelope being harassed by some other Indian women. John knew that June and Antelope could take care of themselves, but there were men egging on the other women. Just as John started to go help, one of the men grabbed June and was holding her for the other women to hurt her! Without even thinking, John swung the big cast iron kettle, and hit the man in the back, knocking him down!

John grabbed his wife and yelled at the crowd, "anyone touches this woman or this one(pointing at Antelope), they answer to me!"

"She is a Blackfoot!," hollered a man.

"Aye! She is that!, And damned proud of it, yelled John!"

Now that John had all their attention, he told them that he was ashamed to be a white man right now, and did they think that this woman was going to scalp them right here at the rendezvous? He went on to say that all Blackfoot were not bad, just like all whites were not good, while pointing his finger at the whole group. John went on to say that he thought a rendezvous was a place to come and feel safe.

By now, most were hanging their heads and breaking up. That is with the exception of the man that John knocked down! This man came up off the ground at John's feet! He lunged at John with a knife in his hand! John sidestepped just out of reach, or he would have been gutted like a deer. No one saw John draw his own knife! One minute, he was holding a kettle, and the next, a knife! John had his knife out before the kettle he had been holding hit the ground. The man lunged at John again! This man was very fast and did manage to slice John's arm a little bit. John told the man that they did not have to do this! Of course the man thought that his honor was at stake now, and no amount of talking would do any good.

All John had to do was to think of this man when he was holding the women a few minutes ago, then he had no problem dealing with him. Every time the man lunged, John was able to sidestep out of the way. Most knife fighters just moved in on their opponent, and this man was no exception. John pretended to stumble and the man thought he had him. As he made his move with his knife aiming for John's chest, he found himself impaled on John's knife. John's stumble was calculated to have John move his body, but not his feet, therefore enabling him to be stationary and use the other man's momentum. John looked into the man's eyes and he saw total surprise. As he pulled his knife out of the man's chest he told him that he should have listened to him. Then the man collapsed and was dead.

All the ones who had not left the scene came over and started to pat John on the back. He moved out of the way and told them in no uncertain terms how he felt. By this time June and Antelope were pulling on his sleeves and heading back toward there camp. When they reached their camp, June had John take off his shirt so she could see to his wound. As it turned out the wound was not deep and would be no problem as long as it was treated right away. While June was treating John's arm, Antelope went back to her and Jack's camp. Jack was standing in front of the lodge when she got there. He looked at his wife very serious and said, "What's this I been a hearin bout this fight?"

Antelope had to tell the whole story and when she was done, Jack suddenly left the lodge and headed for trader Bob's place. Antelope thought he was going to go drink some more, but as she watched he jumped up on Bob's table and pulled both his pistols and fired into the air. Of course there were shots all the time, but it did get most everybody's attention.

"Gather round!," hollered Jack. "I got somethin ta say!"

John and June, plus Antelope were standing at the table. John's uncle pointed down at June and told everyone there that she was his niece, and then pointed to Antelope and said that she was his wife. He went on to say that anyone who threatened these women in any way was going to have he, himself to deal with. Jack told them that he was ashamed of his so called friends acting this way, and how could any of them think that they could trade with the Blackfoot if they treated one of their people this way. Jack then pointed to John and said, "look what happened to my nephew! Come to the rendezvous for a good time, only to have to defend his wife's honor! Thet don't shine with this here chile!"

There was total silence as Jack jumped down off the table, and got his family, and headed back to their camp. As they were walking Jack said, "Y'all kin do what ye want but I got me a sour stomach over this here rendezvous, and we'll be a headin out, come mornin."

John looked at June and asked her what she wanted to do. "Leave," she said. "Just as soon as possible." June told them that she was used to seeing people getting killed, but her children had to witness how they were treated, and later the fight to the death between their father and another man. Antelope also agreed, and about that time Jake and his family were walking up to them. After talking with them, they found out that they were on the outside of the ring of people during the fight, but missed the ill treatment of June and Antelope. Jake and his sister decided they also would leave in the morning.

After John and his family were back at their camp for a while sitting around the fire outside the lodge, a man came up to them. It was Jim Bowie, and John welcomed him into his camp. Jim told them that he got in on the fight but missed the reason for it. John explained all of it to him and when he was done, Jim said that he too was ashamed that those people acted that way. Jim said that he came by to say good bye, and he was heading for Texas. The men shook hands and Jim got up on his horse and rode off. Little did John know that Jim Bowie would be killed three years later at the "Fight of the Alamo."

June wanted to leave, but she did want to see her family and the Blackfoot had not come in yet, so John told her that they would leave in the direction that her family would be coming from. That way they would probably meet up with them.

The morning dawned bright and warm. All the travelers were packed and ready to go within an hour after a small breakfast of biscuits and some ham that the women bought at the rendezvous. June was certain that her family would be coming from the north, so John told the others that was the way they were going to go, and if they wanted to go on home, he would understand.

"We will go with you.," said uncle Jack.

"I reckon we will tag along as well.," said Jake. "Someone has ta watch out fer yer uncle, peers he jest caint hear like he used ta."

At that remark Jack went through many names for Jake, and none of them good.

John just grinned and thought to himself...*At least this was going to be an interesting trip!*

As it turned out, they had only to travel for about three hours. The small village that was June's was camped right on the trail, and had been there for at least a day. When you live around horses, you can tell how long they have been in one spot by how much, and how old their droppings are. With June out in front, they rode up to her parent's tipi. Her father came out first, followed by her mother. Of course June was off her horse immediately and hugging them both. By that time, Sarah and William were also there with her. June's father picked up young William and said something in his tongue. June told the rest that he said, "who is this strong young warrior?" Naturally Sarah was not to be outdone, so she presented herself, and was picked up as well. June would explain later how she came to have a child as old as Sarah.

June conversed with her parents extensively and finally turned to the rest of her group and said that someone had met her parents and told them how she was treated and now they were not going to trade here. When they absolutely needed something, then they would go down to the trading post, where they had been before.

They visited all that day and the travelers decided that the Blackfoot were a friendly people, once you got to know them. Jack, Jake, and even John himself had, had many fights with the Blackfoot through the years, but come to find out, those were some of the more warlike part of the tribe. June's village was peaceful, unless provoked of course.

They decided to stay the night, so they pitched camp just outside of the Blackfoot's camp. As most people travel, they like to camp close to a stream when possible and this stream was just a five minute walk from the travelers camp. As was custom, June was up before anyone else and took an elk skin down to the stream and laid it out on the sandbar. Then she took all her clothes off and waded out into the stream. She bathed and washed her hair and then just went back and laid out on the elk skin to dry off.

June was not the only one who was up early. John had watched her leave and followed her. Now he was behind some bushes just marveling at how she looked in the pre-dawn light and getting very excited in the process! John had no way of knowing that June knew that he was watching her, and she rolled over, facing him. She grinned when she heard him grunt. June knew what she was doing to him and she was doing it on purpose.

John could stand it no longer, so he stepped out of the bushes and June acted like she jumped and was startled. John walked over to where she was laying and June pointed to his manhood that was very prominent in his buckskins. She said, "why don't you take off your pants?" She then asked if the children were still sleeping and John told her that they were. Since it was not all the way light yet, they made love there on the sandbar, a very quick, need to kind of love. Then they went down and bathed and both came back to the elk skin to dry. Of course this lasted only a few minutes, because John got excited again and this time they took their time, making each other feel the passion that had been pent up for too long.

The sun was peeking up over the surrounding mountains and the two lovers decided that they had better get back to camp. When they got to the fire, the smell of fresh coffee was overpowering. Antelope was up and she had the coffee done. As the two approached the fire, Antelope grinned and said that every couple needs some alone time.

Everyone was beginning to stir in the camp and Betty came up to the fire. John asked her where that no-good brother of hers' was hiding. Betty told him that Jake left to go hunting quite some time ago. John looked at Antelope and asked where his uncle was.

She told John that Jack went out hunting also. As amazing as this was, what was more amazing was the fact that both hunters just emerged from opposite sides of their camp. Jake had a young deer over his shoulder and Jack had a very large turkey. This started all over the question of who was the quietest. Jack said that he was up before Jake, and Jake said that he was up first. Before the two came to blows, John stepped in and said it don't matter who was first, what does matter is you got critters to butcher. John knew without a doubt that he would be hearing all about both men's morning hunt. John respected both these men more than anyone in the world and he would not mind hearing all the details of both hunts.

The turkey was ate that morning and the deer was quartered and rolled up in it's hide to eat along the way. What was left would be made into pemmican by either June or Antelope. Since it was only about three days travel to their valley, most of the deer would be left to be made into pemmican.

The good weather held for the remainder of the trip and they made about as good a time as they did on the way there. When they topped the hill that overlooks their valley, everything looked to be ok. Naturally Chick was the first to make an appearance. He had heard them coming and went up to greet them. John jumped down off his horse and hugged and made over Chick. While he was trying to pet Chick, Juan kept getting right between them, wanting his share of the attention. Chick had to greet everyone and the children were next, then June and Jake and all the rest.

CHAPTER XXII

All had went to their own homes, (with the exception of Uncle Jack and Antelope)who's home was some miles south. Everyone had already said their good byes to Jack and Antelope and they were on their way home by now. Thomas and Kathleen were sitting at John and June's table talking about how things went while John and June were at the rendezvous. Thomas told John that Chick had been leaving most days and would be gone for a long time. John asked about Chick's mate and Thomas told him that she was doing fine and the coon didn't do too much damage. At least she was up and around now. John said that if Chick left tomorrow, that he would follow him to see what had so much of his attention.

John was up before anyone the next morning and had already been down to the stream and bathed. Of course Chick was with him and on the way back to the cabin, Chick acted like he wanted John to follow him. John had everything he needed for a short trip. Always in his possible bag were pemmican and fire starting equipment. And his Knives tomahawk, and guns were always with him. He did go to the cabin long enough to tell June that he was going to follow Chick.

Chick was heading for the Tetons and it was very apparent that he wanted John to follow him. John followed him for about three hours when Chick stopped and put his nose in the air and was sniffing. Satisfied that he had the right direction, he headed off to the right. They must have went about a quarter mile when Chick stopped at this thicket and was whining. John parted the bushes and was shocked to see a small hand sticking out of the ground. Most of the meat was gone but it looked human to John. The smell was not good surrounding this little grave or whatever it was.

Apparently Chick was waiting for John, or he would have dug this up himself. John took out his tomahawk and proceeded to dig very carefully, so as not to disturb anything. He had almost gotten it dug up when he heard this awful screaming again. Immediately he grabbed his rifle and looked in the direction of the scream. The hair on Chick's back was standing up, and John thought, *surely mine is too!* The screaming stopped and John looked back down at the grave. He was shocked to the core and was surprise that he did not see it before. There right next to the grave was a hand print! Not just any hand print. This print was enormous! It looked like this man, or thing was on it's knees and put one hand on the ground and dug this grave with the other.

The only thing that came to John's mind was the Wendigo that Jake had talked about, and he himself had heard.

Very carefully, John dug all around this little thing and was able to see the whole body now. It did not look human, but in a way it did. John carefully tucked away the little arm that was sticking up, and went ahead and buried the whole thing. He then smoothed the dirt and put leaves and sticks all over it, so as to make it look like there was nothing there.

This little creature was a baby to the thing that had been screaming! Of this, John was certain. John did not know what these creatures were for sure, but he wished they lived somewhere else. They were just too close to home to suit John. John watched Chick all the way back to the cabin for any signs that the thing was following them. He made it home without incident and hollered before he went in the cabin. He didn't want to get shot by his lovely wife. Everyone was up and June was just finishing up cooking breakfast. June laid out a place for John and put a tin plate full of pancakes on it. John just picked at his food, so June knew that something was wrong and John told her that they would talk when the children went out to play. Immediately after breakfast, June had the children go out to feed the dogs and then she said that they could play, but not to go far from the cabin.

Now that they were alone, John told her what Chick had found. June looked sad as John explained what he had seen. John asked her why and she told him that she did not know what this thing was, but animals don't bury their dead. She said that she knew that bears would partially bury their prey with leaves an a little dirt, so they could come back to finish eating it.

This was getting a way too complicated to John's way of thinking. He knew that the screaming that he had heard sure could have been a mother morning the loss of her child, but that thing was no normal child! He told June that since this thing had not harmed any body that he knew of, then he would go back to his original way of thinking. Just leave them alone! June agreed, but she made an unusual request. She asked John to take her up to the grave!

"Now why on earth would I want to do that?" asked John.

"Because I want to take some food up there as an offering, then go back later to see if they took the food. If this is truly a mother, then she will be back often to this grave."

Only a woman would think like this, thought John. "Alright," said John. "We will take the children over to Betty's place and let them play with her younguns. The bundle of food we will be carrying, will be used for our little outing. At least that's what we will say."

This being decided, June started gathering up food and put it in a small bag. When they went out to tell the children, they were elated. They loved to go anywhere, even though they had just gotten back from the rendezvous. June and John knew that Betty would just love for the children to be there, even though it was only for a couple hours.

John was not so sure of June's idea, but this was better than having to hunt these creatures down and destroy them. If by some small chance they could get on the good side of them, then maybe they could live in harmony in these beautiful mountains. As for hunting them down, that would be a monumental task, for as far as John knew, nobody has ever seen one.

All plans set into motion, they went up to where the baby was buried. When they got there, June found a bunch of small rocks and placed them in piles, one at the head, and one at the foot of the grave. This done, she then placed the food at the center. This was an offering, plain and simple. Then she raised her hands to the heavens and spoke in her native tongue. John did not know the words that she spoke, but it was her way of making an offering to the spirits. Of this, John was certain.

After a few minutes, June turned to John and said that they should go. They headed back down the mountain toward their home. Neither spoke for a long time, and finally John broke the silence by asking her if she thought that this creature would understand what she had done. June told him that she did not know, but it surely could not hurt. John knew that her culture was as one with the spirits and he sure did wish that most white men were that way. Maybe then he would not have had to kill another human.

When they reached the cabin, John's uncle was sitting in front of the door waiting. After greeting each other. Jack told them that Antelope was over at Thomas and Kathleen's place. Jack then said that they had some serious business to talk about. Of course this got John and June's attention. Jack went on to tell them what they had seen about a day's ride south of here. He said that there were a large group of men riding this way, and they did not look like the kind that would be up to any good.

Jack said that when they all split up after the rendezvous, that he and Antelope went south looking for a place to trap, come the fall. They had just came to this little pond, when they heard the horses. They moved into the trees on the edge of the clearing and waited. Soon enough these very hard looking men came riding up to the pond. As they were stopped letting their horses drink, Jack was able check them out more thoroughly. What he saw was not good. He saw some scalps hanging from some of their saddles and some of the scalps were blonde and red. He told John that since they were headed north, he thought it wise to come and warn all of the people here at the base of the Tetons.

John did not hesitate! Immediately he went from cabin to cabin telling them what his uncle had said and also telling them to pack some water and pemmican and meet him at his cabin. He also said to bring any weapon they could lay their hand upon. Betty and her family were the first to arrive at John's cabin, then Thomas and Kathleen with their young ones. John had them all assemble out in front and commenced to telling them of his plan. He thought to place the men in crucial places around the edge of the timber. The women and Betty's girl would load the guns for them and stay hidden behind the rocks. Betty asked why they did not go to John's blacksmith shop, since it had gun portals in it. John told her that it would be too easy to burn out, and this way they would be able to partially surround these men.

No sooner had everyone gotten into position than they heard the horses! When they rode up to the cabin (John and June's were the first from the south), anyone could see that they had been punishing their mounts, because the horses were blowing and sweating profusely. Since they were all in a bunch John decided to go talk to them, knowing full well that he was covered by Jake and his uncle, plus Thomas.

They were still mounted when John stepped out of the trees and none saw him until he was among them. John had his hand up in the traditional sign for peace. The leader who was a small ferret looking man was looking at John with his beady eyes and said, "this here your spread?"

"It is!, said John. "What can I do for you?"

While John was talking to the leader, someone in the group pulled a pistol and was aiming it at John's chest.

"Bang!" A hole appeared in the man's forehead right between the eyes and he was knocked off his horse. Jake's fifty caliber Hawkin was dead center again. The men hollered and the leader looked at his fallen comrade. When he turned to face John, there was nobody there! John had faded back into the trees without being noticed. From his concealment, John hollered to the men saying to ride on and nobody else had to die. Immediately they all started firing into the trees and rocks and then dismounted and proceeded to hide behind the cabin. That was a mistake, because Thomas was on that side and he was almost as good a shot as the mountain men. As luck would have it the woodpile was back there and John was wishing now that he had not cut and stacked so much. Now they had cover.

Two of their number was able to slip away while Thomas was reloading. They melted into the trees on the north side of the clearing.

Somehow one of them was able to circle around and come up behind where Jake and Betty were stationed. Jake was firing and Betty was reloading for him. Betty's daughter was back a little ways looking at the cabin siege, when this man grabbed her and put his hand on her mouth to keep her quiet. He drug her back to where his horse was tied and the other man was waiting. John was re-loading while standing behind this tree, when a hand touched him on the shoulder! His knife was out immediately and he found himself looking into Betty's eyes.

How did she do that?, thought John. After a quick thought, John dismissed it, because, after all she had lived with the Indians all of her adult life.

She whispered into John's ear, "Willow is gone!"

CHAPTER XXIII
Jake's Revenge

That is the name of her daughter and she was a pretty teen age girl/woman. John asked her to show him where she was last seen and Betty did so. Jake came up to see what was going on at that time. When Betty told Jake that his niece was missing, John could see him visibly shake a little bit.

The bad men were apparently gone and all the families were coming out of hiding. They all gathered in front of John and June's cabin. John told them about Willow and they all decided that they had no time to waste and got together their plunder and some pemmican for the trail. Once again Thomas said that he wanted to go help find the girl. This time John said that he could go. The women and children would be safe until they returned, since the bad men were heading south and away from their valley. John had the women hold all the dogs, because he wanted them to stay with the women.

John was sure glad his uncle Jack was with them, But his friend Jake was as good a tracker as anyone and this was his niece. To John's way of thinking, this was getting old. Chasing after bad men who have stolen away decent folks. That is exactly how Betty and her children came to be living in this valley.

They found where Willow had been hiding behind this boulder. Her little knife that she uses in cooking and helping Betty was lying on the ground. There was blood on it! Jake had everyone stop so they did not disturb the scene. He then was looking to the right and left. It was not long before Jake raised up and said that they went that way. He was pointing to the south. It was plain for everyone to see that a horse had been there and this man drug Willow to it, mounted and rode off to the south.

John was thinking that he sure hoped this man did not go too far south, because John had seen enough of the far south to last a lifetime, when he was helping search for Betty and her family.

As far as Jake was concerned, he did not care how far this man went. He would follow him into Hell to get Willow back. Since the man was on the run, he was not trying to hide his trail. They would dog him until his horse dropped! *From the way these men treated their animals, this would not be too long,* thought Jake. So far this man had not hooked up with his partners yet, and was still traveling alone.

Sure hope Willow is ok, thought Jake. He knew that this man must have knocked her out, or she would be fighting for her life. At least there was some satisfaction in knowing that Willow wounded the man somewhat with her knife. Jake had been out in front checking all the sign and had everyone stop. Here was where the rest of the men met. At least all that was left of them. They had not had time for a body count back at the cabin, but all knew that many of those men would not be stealing people anymore.

John could not help but wonder how this poor little girl felt. After getting stolen by the Comancheros, then rescued and living happily, only to have it happen again.

Several miles to the south, Willow was just coming too from having been hit on the head. She knew immediately what had happened and how she got there. These men had no idea what they had gotten themselves in to. For sure, they knew they were being followed, but they had themselves a girl and they were going to have some fun come nightfall. At least they thought they were. Willow was not an ordinary teen age girl. She had been through so much already that fear did not even enter the picture. Anger is what she felt right now, but she was tied over a horse and could not do anything. She relaxed and tried to match the horses movements in order not to be too uncomfortable. Since she had been rescued earlier her uncle Jake had been teaching her how to defend herself and she was devising a plan as they rode along. The fringe that went all around the top part of her dress normally just hung over her chest, but was now hanging down and tickling her nose. She was able to reach it with her hands and pull off a couple strings. These, she would drop every once in a while for her uncle Jake to find.

Meanwhile, a few miles north of Willow and her captors, Jake was having trouble finding sign. It was apparent that these men finally decided to try to cover their trail, because they were traveling on rocky ground, plus riding down the middle of streams when possible. Jake and his friends were having a hard time finding sign and they were running out of time. They knew that when darkness came, those very bad men would be doing very bad things, because even Jake could not trail them at night. Jake found the first piece of fringe and now knew the direction that they were traveling.

The light was beginning to fade as darkness was almost upon them. They had found the other piece of fringe and were heading in the right direction, but would not be able to overtake them before full darkness. Jake was sure hoping that Willow would be able to remember what he had taught her. If she could get one of their weapons, she may have a chance. If not, then they would use her unmercifully, then kill her. Of this, Jake was certain.

It was now full dark! The outlaws stopped and one of them came over to Willow and grabbed her by the hair and pulled her head up. he looked her in the eye and told her that if she so much as made a whimper, that he would gut her like a deer! Then he showed her his big knife. Willow looked at the knife and acted like she was terrified! In fact, she was trying to think of a way to get that big knife. Her uncle had showed her how to use a big knife. For fighting in close, and also for throwing. She had learned fast and was very good with the knife of her uncle's. This one appeared to be about the same size and weight.

The man put the knife back into his sheath and began untying her. When he untied the rope that went under the horse's belly, Willow acted like she fainted and just fell to the ground. She heard the leader tell the man who untied her to take her over there and stake out her arms to the ground. To do this, they had to untie her hands. She had but one chance!

While the man spread one arm out to stake it, Willow made her move! The man thought that she was still out, so while he was busy with one arm, she grabbed his knife with the other!

Without hesitation, she plunged the knife into his heart! He grunted and died, then fell right on top of her. One of the other men came over and said get off her you damn fool! Wait until you get her staked out, then we can all have a turn! He then kicked the dead man off! At that moment, Willow pulled out the knife and jumped up! The other man was stunned and that was his mistake! Willow threw the knife and scored a hit right where his heart should have been! She did not wait around to see if she killed him! Into the woods she ran! As she was running, she heard the definite click of a pistol being cocked, but another man said, "no, you idiot, there are men following us!"

Now it was full dark and she was in the heavy timber. This was her element. She was one with the forest and no man in this group would be able to find her. Slowly, she walked, making no sound that could be heard by a man. She knew from which way they had come and was heading in that direction. She could hear the men bumbling around in the woods like a heard of buffalo. Finally the men following her stopped. They knew that there had been men following them and did not want to walk right in on their camp.

A couple hours later, Jake was sitting at their camp without a fire naturally, when he detected something amiss! Slowly he turned in the direction of the ever so slight noise that he heard. He cocked his pistol and was prepared, when from out of the darkness the unmistakable voice of Willow said. "are you going to shoot me uncle Jake?" Of course John and Thomas were both up from a sound sleep at the cock of Jake's pistol, and they watched as Willow threw herself into Jake's arms.

They talked well into the night and Jake found out there was only three left to deal with. Willow was not sure about the man she threw the knife at, because she did not stay around to see if he was dead. She did tell her uncle that she hit where she aimed to. Jake said that it did not matter anyway.

The next morning Jake asked John and Thomas to take Willow back home. He had a job to do and he was going to enjoy doing it. John shuddered, because he knew just what Jake was capable of doing. Willow wanted to go with Jake, because she said she had a score to settle with those men.

John thought to himself, *yep, this is Jake's niece alright.*

Thomas started to protest to Jake, and John looked at him and shook his head ever so slightly. Thomas said no more about it and they all turned in. John had seen the look on Jake's face and he knew there would be no way to convince him to take someone with him. John remembered the story of when Jake tracked down his sister's captors when he was but a boy. Those murderers met with horrible deaths at the hands of Jake. A Bible passage came into John's head from out of nowhere "Vengeance is mine, sayeth the Lord!" Of course the vengeance in this case was going to be Jake's! John thought that he surely would not want to be in those three men's shoes.

The next morning when John woke up, Jake was gone. This was no surprise, and he just let Willow and Thomas sleep a little longer. Now they could have a fire and it was not long until John had the coffee boiling. Thomas got up to the smell of the coffee. Willow got up and went down to the little stream to clean up. There was no danger from those outlaws, because they were long gone with Jake dogging their trail. Willow returned to the fire and looked "no worse for the wear," after all she had been through. She definitely knew hardship at her young age. To live in a village of Comanche Indians was bad enough in itself, but then to have been drug around all over by the Comancheros was worse. This little excursion with the outlaws was not comparable. She had escaped before anything bad had happened to her. She knew without a doubt that her uncle Jake would catch those men and deal out his own kind of justice. That was fine with her.

Thomas had thrown some biscuits in his saddlebag and he offered them. John was packing along a slab of salt pork that he had gotten from the rendezvous, so they feasted on these for their breakfast. As soon as they were done and everything cleaned up, they headed for home.

A few miles south of John and his fellow travelers, Quiet Jake was doing what he was noted for. He had found the men's sign and been tracking them since sun-up. These men were *"Damn Idjits,"* thought Jake.

They were killing their horses trying to get away! Jake actually found horse sweat on some weeds, so he knew that those poor beasts would not last very much longer. This riled Jake even more! Certainly it was bad enough to take human hostages, but to treat animals this way was inexcusable. His thoughts were confirmed just a little while later, when he found the horse laying in the trail. it was still alive and it's sides were heaving. Jake took out his pistol and shot the poor animal in the head. He did not care if they heard, in fact he hoped they did. Now one horse was riding double. Jake could plainly see that the imprints were deeper. About another two miles and Jake saw another horse in the trail.

This one was different! It had a man pinned under it! Jake got off his own horse and let the reigns dangle. It was trained to stay where he left it. He then went around to the backside of the man, because he could see that this man was waving a pistol around. This man was waiting, for he knew that he was being followed. From what Jake could see, this man's left leg was pinned under the horse. This horse was not going anywhere, because the man had rode it to death! There was blood around the horse's nose where it's lungs just blew up!

Jake was twenty feet from the man and threw a looped rope around his wrist, and jerked so hard that the gun went off!

"What ya goin ta do now, feller?" said Jake.

The man could not turn around enough to even see Jake. He told Jake to go to Hell! Jake said that he probably would, but he would have plenty of company.

"Yore good friends done run off and left ya.," said Jake. "Ifn yer mad at em, don't fret, cuzz I will be catchin em shortly."

"What are you going to do to me?" asked the man.

"I don't reckon ya really want ta know, ya piece of human garbage! First, I reckon I will free ya from this here horse."

"How are you going to do that?" the man said.

"Wal I caint lift this here critter, so they is only one other way," said Jake. He went over to the man and jerked the pistol out of his hand. Then he took his finger and outlined his trousers.

"I think Ifn I cut right here, that ought ta do it."

The man passed out!

Jake wasn't going to cut the guy's leg off while he watched, but the man did not know that. Normally, Jake would have spent more time with this man and found out what he was all about, but he had two of the man's buddies to catch up with, so he just shot him between the eyes! That was more than the man did for this poor horse. Now for the business of tracking. Jake just left the man and horse laying right where he found them.

By this time, John, Willow and Thomas were just topping the hill that overlooked their valley. Of course the first thing they saw was Chick and his whole family. They all came running up to greet them. Everything looked ok down in the valley, and this was confirmed when June came running up the hill to greet them as well. Before June could get up the hill, Betty let out a scream right behind the rescuers! She had been waiting in the rocks just like she had done when they returned from the last rescue. Now everybody was hugging and kissing, and dogs were licking the men and Willow. *It was good to be back home again*, thought John.

While John was re-united with his family, his friend and mentor was many miles to the south. Jake was closing in on his query! He found some weeds with blood speckles on them. This was from the one horse left that was riding double. It was blowing hard and the blood was from it's lungs. When Jake found this bright red lung blood, he knew it would not be long before he found another dead horse. He could not believe that people could be so stupid! Not to mention the cruelty to these poor animals!

About a half hour later, he found the horse. Naturally it was dead. He found where the riders were walking. If they were trying to hide their trail, it did not matter. Jake could follow them anyway. A bent weed here, an overturned stone there, a partial footprint. It did not matter what they did. Now Jake could actually hear them talking! *What Idjits!*, thought Jake.

They were sitting on a big rock arguing about which way to go. Jake slipped right up behind them and said, "Theys only one way yer a goin!"

One man started to draw his pistol and Jake hit his hand with his tomahawk that he already had out. Jake's knife and hawk were both very sharp! The man screamed when he saw his hand dropping to the ground with the pistol still in it! The other man tried to draw his own pistol, but after seeing the hand on the ground, he got so shook up that he dropped his pistol! Jake told the screaming man that he had better put something around his wrist or the blood was going to pump away! He threw a leather strip at the man and he grabbed it and began wrapping it around his stub of an arm!

Jake tied both men up and went about building a fire. The man with two good arms asked him what he was going to do. Jake just kept gathering twigs and limbs. Finally the fire was going nicely and Jake put on some coffee to boil. Then grabbed a burning branch from the fire and went over to the one handed man. Both men screamed! Jake said this is for my niece, who you were going to violate. He raised the man's arm up and put the burning branch on the stub! The man fainted dead away! Jake looked at the other man and told him that he had to cauterize the wound and this was the only way. This was all true, but the other man could plainly see that Jake enjoyed this procedure very much. When the wound was sufficiently sealed, Jake turned to the other man. The torch was still in Jake's hand and this man fainted as well!

Damn cowards!, was what Jake thought. Jake then went about cooking something to eat. He had brought a slab of venison with him and now was as good a time as any to cook it. As he was eating, the men started to come around. The one with two good arms started acting funny and talking to himself. Jake got up and went over to him. He looked the man in the eyes and there was nothing there. That is to say that this man had lost his mind. The other man was looking at Jake with a hatred that knew no bounds!

Jake finished eating, then cleaned up and put out the fire. Before he left, he went over to the men and untied them. He told the one handed man that he was going to let him live, and that he could look at his hand and think of the young girl he was going to violate. Or, Jake said. "Ifn ya caint make it, I will leave yore pistol with one charge in it."

Jake then looked over at the other man. What he saw was nothing. The man had a blank look on his face. Jake had seen this before, so he knew this was real. He figured the man was touched in the head even before he met him. After pondering the situation, Jake figured that there had to be something wrong with these men, to do the things they do. No matter, he would just go off and leave them to the mountains. Jake knew the mountains had their own way of dealing with people. He was certain that these two would not be bothering the women again, so he headed for home.

Back in the valley below the Tetons, life was beginning to get back to normal. John finished the repairs to his roof, then went over to Thomas's place to help build a barn for the stock that they had accumulated. This was where John was when Jake finally made it back. Everyone had seen him riding down into the valley and all were waiting for him when he pulled up in front of John's cabin. He got down off his horse and June handed him a cup of steaming hot coffee. As soon as he set the cup down, Willow was in his arms! They hugged, then Willow wanted to know what happened. Jake was tired, so he just told everyone in as few words as possible just what took place.

Much later, when John and June were in their bed, June told John that Jake should have killed the last two men. This was Indian logic and John did not know how to explain that men get tired of killing. At least the decent ones do. While they were laying there talking, John tried to explain this to her. The Indian believed that when something was threatening you, or your family, you got rid of it! He tried to tell her that he, himself was tired of killing other men, but would do so in a heartbeat, if they were threatening his family. He went on to say that the two men that Jake left in the mountains were no threat anymore and they would very likely die right there in the mountains. John was not entirely sure this pacified his wife, but he was tired and turned over and went to sleep. Apparently she was satisfied for now, because in a short time John heard the slow, even breathing of her sleeping.

It was much later when John heard the unmistakable sound of Chick scratching on the door. June heard it too, and both got up immediately. John got his gun and possible bag, put on a coat and opened up the door. Chick and Juan both greeted him and wanted him to follow them out to the lean-to where the other dogs (they were no longer pups) stayed. John made a head count and noticed one was missing. Chick and Juan wanted John to follow them, but it was too dark to go stumbling around in the woods. John reached down and petted both dogs and told them that they would go in the morning. Of course he knew they would not understand but they did settle down a bit, so he went back in and told June what was going on, and they both went back to bed.

CHAPTER XXIV
WOLVERINE

John was up and out before dawn as usual and got his morning chores done. The morning dawned bright and clear and John thought this to be a good morning for tracking. He had a dog to find and now that it was light, he got to it. When he left, he took both Chick and Juan with him. Who better, to find their own? John was half expecting to find a very large human type footprint, but so far he had seen nothing to make him believe that the big creatures had anything to do with this. He had only been gone a few minutes when he smelled it! Not the same as the Wendigos, or whatever they were, but similar. He knew he had smelled this before and after thinking about it, he remembered. The "Glutton!" That was Jake's term for the wolverine. He had a first hand experience with one of these back when he and Jake were traveling together for the first time! These critters were not much bigger than Chick, but could "gut" a man in the blink of the eye.

His suspicion was confirmed when he found the track! It was a wolverine! A very big male, to be exact. Jake had told him that the males have a stronger smell than the females. What was worse, this one was dragging something! The tracks were easy enough to follow, but the smell made it a lot quicker. John just followed his nose. This smell was getting stronger, so John had to be on his toes and not miss anything. One definitely did not want a wolverine to get the jump on you. They were the most vicious animal in the world for their size. At least here in John's world. John stopped dead in his tracks! Right there in front of him was a small clearing. it was what was in the clearing that made John stop. There was a large pool of blood with a dog's foot laying in it. John had played and wrestled with all the dogs enough to know that this was Chick's pup. Chick and Juan were up ahead somewhere barking! They were on to something. of course they had already been in this little clearing and this drove them to plunge ahead! John sure hoped they kept their senses about them, because even though there were two dogs, that was still not enough to fight a full grown wolverine.

The dogs barking was getting closer, so John figured that thing had led them in a big circle. He just started to step foreword, when he heard a grunt from above! Very slowly, John looked up into the only tree that was out in this clearing. There, on a fork was what was left of the dog! John's eyes moved up a little higher and he found himself looking into the most fearful, meanest eyes that he had ever seen!

John jumped to the side just as the wolverine jumped out of the tree! There was no time to draw and cock the pistol, so his knife was in his hand in an instant. When the wolverine hit the ground, it sprung immediately at John. The movements were so quick that all John had time to do was raise the knife in front of himself! This worked as far as stabbing the beast, but in no way did it stop the charge! John's big knife was buried in the thing's chest and yet it was still slicing with it's claws, and biting everything it could! The shear fury of it knocked John to the ground! He was able to hold the knife and keep the thing at bay, but his arm was giving out! This thing was tearing it to pieces!

The hand that was on the knife handle was losing it's grip from being so slick with the wolverine's blood and John thought he was "Gone Beaver," when from out of nowhere came Chick and Juan! Both jumped the wolverine and got it off John! Chick would keep it occupied from the front while Juan would get to it from behind. Finally Juan was able to hamstring it and it could not move it's back legs!

Even though John was laying there with a bleeding arm full of gashes and puncture wounds, he could not help but marvel at the stamina of this creature! Here it was, a knife sticking out of it's chest, and it's whole back end crippled, but still it charged forward, using it's front legs! Finally the thing just collapsed! It was dead! It literally died on it's feet!

Now that it was all over, John started feeling weak. He had lost a lot of blood and he had to get a tourniquet on his arm! He fished a leather lace from his possible bag and wrapped it around his upper arm very tight. he would have to loosen it occasionally to keep the circulation going. He began eating some pemmican, because he knew that he had to build up his strength in order to make it back home. After taking off his buckskin shirt, he saw that his arm was not as bad as he thought. The shirt kept most of the wounds from being too deep. The worst thing he had to fear now was infection! Wolverines ate anything! Even dead animals! Their bites and the wounds from their claws would probably invite infection.

There was a small stream a few yards away, so John made his way over to it and began the painful job of cleaning his wounds. By the time he had them all cleaned, he was feeling stronger. This was a good thing, because from over in the woods came the unmistakable grunt of another wolverine! Chick and Juan were on to it immediately! Running full bore toward the noise. John knew that he could not go through this again, so he called the dogs back. They definitely wanted to go get the other one, but John was able to convince them to come home with him.

They had not gone far when another grunt was heard! This thing was following them!

Well, thought John. *I reckon I can't lead the critter back home!*

John checked the priming in his rifle and pistol and told the dogs to lead the way. That was what they were wanting to hear, for off they went in the direction of the last grunt that was heard. After the dogs left, the first thing John did was check all the trees around him. He was not about to let this one creep up and get in a tree. This was a strange feeling for John. Now he felt like HE was the one being hunted. Once in a while John could smell the awful smell of the wolverine, but it was all over him from wrestling around with the big male. Was this the other one's mate? John did not know, but it did not matter, since it would have to be dealt with as well.

John's arm was starting to stiffen up from all the wounds and this was not a good thing, since he may be using it before long. He was now following the dogs, because it sounded like they had something treed. When John got to where all the commotion was coming from, he was surprised to see that the dogs had a very small wolverine treed. John raised his rifle and was about to blast the critter into oblivion, when he heard yet another grunt from just on the other side of the dogs! The large female that suddenly appeared gave John chills! Instead of shooting the baby out of the tree, he called the dogs off. This was a mother trying to defend her young and there was no telling the amount of damage she would do to the dogs. Immediately, John brought his Hawkin to bear! Bang! one shot, and it was right between the eyes!

Since her head almost exploded, this one died instantly. John quickly re-loaded and aimed up in the tree. Bang! He got this one in the head as well, and it came crashing down through the branches of the tree. The dogs went wild biting and barking at the two dead wolverines. Finally John was able to calm them down enough to pull them off. John knew that he should skin them, but he did not think that he could, with his arm the way it was, so he left them lay and headed toward home.

Traveling was easy, because he did not have to stop and inspect everything like he did when he was tracking those critters. John made it home while it was still daylight. Juan ran ahead to tell everyone they were coming. Chick stayed with John, because he knew John was hurt and would not leave his side. One more hill to climb and they would be there. John could move no more! He was so weak from blood loss that he sat down on a log to rest. He leaned back against another tree and just passed out! Sometime later, John awoke to chick licking his face. As his eyes began to focus, he saw that he was in his own bed. He sat up and immediately wished he hadn't, for he got dizzy again. June was there and she told him to lay back down, which he did.

"How long have I been here?" asked John.

"About two hours," June told him.

June told him that when Juan came home by himself and acted like we should follow him, that was just what they did. She went on to say that Thomas hitched up the wagon and followed Juan back to where you were sitting on that log passed out with Chick standing guard. John started to reach down to pet Chick, but his arm did not move too well. Instead, he used his right arm to scratch Chick behind the ears. John was left handed when it came to throwing his knives and tomahawks. And like most left handed people, he was ambidextrous. Meaning he could use either arm for most things. Such as stabbing a wolverine. He looked at his right arm and noticed that it was all bandaged up. Other than being stiff, it did not feel too bad. He could see that June had worked her magic on it by using her famous cures for prevention of infection, and fast healing. Now all he had to do was wait. That was the worst part for John, who was a man of action, and did not like laying around.

Two weeks went by and John was about out of his mind. This laying around had taken its toll. This morning he announced to June that he was healed enough to go hunting. After which he flexed his arm a few times to show her. At this point in time, June knew it to be hopeless to try to stop him, so she packed him some biscuits and cold slabs of leftover deer meat. John got his guns and grabbed his possible bag, and was off.

First he walked down to Betty's place to see if Jake wanted to go. Chick was by his side as always and John figured the pup Juan had been out hunting when he left, otherwise they would have been hard pressed to leave without him. As John walked into Betty's yard, she was hanging some clothes on a line. John asked if Jake was home and Betty told him that Jake had been gone for three days. She told John that he went hunting, and wanted to go ask him to go, but then he changed his mind and said that June would probably shoot him for asking.

CHAPTER XXV
Eventful Elk Hunt

John laughed and said that he was probably right. He bid Betty farewell and returned to his place for his horse and mule. John was able to get away without having to tie up Juan, because he still was not back yet. He decided to go back up to that big valley where all the elk came to graze. It was only about a half days ride and although his arm was much improved, it was still a little stiff. This would be a good break from the routine of home life which has been taking up all his time. He kept the animals at a slow walk and was in no hurry. As he topped this little hill, Chick suddenly stopped and was sniffing the air. John stopped as well and he himself detected the odor of camp smoke. The river that runs the length of the valley here at the base of the Tetons was on John's right, and that was where the odor was coming from. John veered off the trail to the right and headed for the river. He figured maybe this was Jake camped over by the river, but when got within sight of the camp, the first thing he noticed was a wagon. Not just any wagon, but a huge very well built one. John admired good craftsmanship and this was the best he had seen. As he was sitting on his horse looking the wagon up and down, he heard splashing and laughing down by the river. He dismounted and went down there. As he approached, he could see two young women swimming and bathing, so he turned away and said he would stay that way until they came out and got dressed.

They screamed and hurried out and dressed. While John was standing there, he noticed a man standing there behind the wagon holding a shotgun. The muzzle was pointed in John's general direction. This man was a giant of a man! He had a beard and no mustache, so John immediately pegged him for a Mormon.

In a booming voice, this man said, "I see that you are an honorable man, so you can come into my camp."

John followed him back to his wagon. That was when John noticed the horses in a rope choral. These were Draft horses and they were magnificent animals, by any standards. The man leaned his shotgun against the wagon and turned to face John. He offered John a cup of coffee. John accepted it and they stood by the fire. John told the man that he lived only a little way back up the trail. John was totally surprised at what he said next. He told John that they had passed his place just the other day and took a wide berth around it, so no one would see them. John asked him why he did not want to be seen, and the man said that Gentiles just do not understand us and our beliefs, and it is easier to avoid being around them. John told him that he understood.

John asked about the wagon and the man said that he had built it himself. He told John that he had a shop back in Pennsylvania, but the people got to be too much for him and his two wives, so they came west. He said that he was going to Oregon, but was in no hurry to get there. He and his wives loved this country and the lack of persecuting people in it. John told the man that he was on his way to the valley that they would be passing through in a few hours. He told the man that there were plenty of elk in that valley, but the man said that all he had was the shotgun and they had done fine on ducks and an occasional turkey. John shook hands with the man and when he put his hand in the man's hand, John's hand disappeared.

As John was riding away from the camp, he decided that he would bring an elk back for this family. They needed something besides small animals to eat. For sure they could stay alive, but the body did much better when it had the larger grease saturated meat. John thought that when he did come back here, he at least would ask the man's name. John was not an overly religious man, but he did not hold with the idea of having more than one wife, therefore understanding why people did not accept the Mormon belief. He was thinking that maybe Oregon might just be a good place for this family. Besides, he had enough people in his valley at this point in time.

John was now entering the same place that he had hunted elk the last time he was up here. He was now far enough away from the Mormons so as not to be smelling their camp smoke, but he still smelled it. No, John decided the smell was coming from up ahead somewhere. Someone had beaten him to his favorite hunting camp! And that someone was Jake! John thought he would sneak up on him, but this was not going to happen! Before John got to within 50 yards from him, Jake said, "Bout time ya got off yer duff!"

"Had to come and check you, ya old fart!"

By this time John was within reach of Jake, so they gave each other a bear hug. Of course Chick was right there wanting some attention from Jake as well. Jake asked John if he saw the Mormons. John told him he did, and asked if he talked to the man. Jake told John that he made a wide berth around their camp when he saw they were Mormons. He told John that he did not want any truck with those people. John said that he talked to the man and he seemed ok, but he himself felt uncomfortable what with the two wives hovering around.

John saw the elk all quartered and wrapped in its own skin, and mentioned it. Jake told him that he had gotten it about three hours ago and was just getting ready to break camp and head for home when he heard John coming up to the camp. They talked for a while, then Jake started loading up his possibles, John helped him load up the elk and told him to watch his top knot. As Jake was leaving he turned in the saddle and said. "keep yer powder dry, Pilgrim."

With all the noise that he and Jake were making, John did not think there would be any elk down in the valley, so he went over to the rocks and peeked over. Sure enough, the elk were gone, but John could see some on the other side just coming down, He did not figure it would be too long before this valley filled up with them like it usually did. John did not have long to wait. In a short time there were elk appearing from all sides of the valley, and soon enough the valley was covered with them. He knew that there were other valleys with good graze, so he could not figure out why they always returned to this one. this was just one of the many mysteries of nature, and John did not beat himself up over it. He just accepted it the way it was.

There was movement to John's right and he swung his gaze that way. There coming out of the forest was some painted ponies like most Indians ride. As he looked closer, he noticed men walking on the off side of their horses from the elk herd. Indians on the hunt, and they were getting close to the herd by hiding behind their horses. He did not recognize this tribe, so he just watched the whole hunt from his position in the rocks. He had plenty of time, so he would not hunt this day. The way he figured it, the Indians have to eat too, and they were here first, so he was content to watch. As he watched, he did notice that these horses were not the painted horses like he originally thought, in fact these were the famous spotted horses of the Nez Pierce. These horses were treasured by all men in the mountains. They were perfect in every way. John remembered the same kind of horses that he acquired for trade with his wife's father. At this thought, John could not help but wonder if this was the same tribe. As they got closer, John could tell that they were not, so he just watched. And it was a grand spectacle to see!

The men walked right down among the elk, then mounted their ponies and started shooting arrows into the herd. Soon enough they had all they wanted, and a signal was made. At the signal, women rode into the melee and dismounted to begin the skinning and quartering.

John marveled at the efficiency of this family unit. The men stalked and shot the elk, then the women rode in and helped with the skinning and butchering. In a half hour there were several carcasses laying around and the Indians were riding off. What was left, would serve to feed the vultures and coyotes. This was not much, for the Indians used most everything on an animal.

The elk were stirred up for now, so John went back to Jake's camp where the fire was still burning. He put some coffee on to boil and just waited. He knew the elk would return. This was an age old story played out between the hunter and the hunted. It had been going on long before John was here and hopefully long after he was gone. He did not think those Indians he saw would pose a threat, since they were on the other side of the valley, and anyway, they had to get their meat back to their people. John was sitting there drinking his coffee and pondering on the past wolverine attack. His arm was still a little stiff, but he himself was as strong as usual. Lord he hoped he saw the last of those critters. John always begrudged an animal his due, but he just hoped those critters stayed away from his valley. He would never kill an animal for nothing, but these were a threat to his family and friends, so he felt no remorse.

Of late, John had been pondering a lot. He was now a family man, so he would not take the chances that he used to take when confronted with danger. He was also a practical man and knew that he would do what was necessary when the time came. Good ole' Chick and his son Juan, saved his bacon this last time. Maybe he would not be so lucky the next. The only thing that he should have done differently was to take another man with him on the trail of the wolverines.

Chick was suddenly looking in the rocks behind them! He was growling real low! John picked up his rifle and was looking in that direction. Suddenly the large head of a big cougar appeared on top of the rocks right above them. Up came John's rifle! He could have shot the thing right between the eyes, but he held off. Instead, John grabbed Chick to keep him from getting killed. The cat and John just stared at each other for what seemed like hours to John! Finally the big cat turned and deftly jumped to another rock and was gone! John watched him for a long time, making sure he was leaving the area. Chick looked at John as if to say, "why didn't you shoot him?"

John just scratched Chick behind the ears and he settled down. He decided the cat was just curious as to who was hunting his territory. When the cat saw it was a man, he left. Most animals don't like humans, and this cat was no exception. John could understand this, because a lot of men would just have shot this cat because, he was what he was.

A couple hours later John was riding down to the elk herd that had came back into this valley. He dismounted and walked on the off side of his horse. When he got within range, he laid his Hawkin across the saddle and got a bead on a nice cow. John was not concerned about his horse jumping from the shot, because he trained him not too. Who knows what the elk thought with this strange looking critter with a bunch of legs. It had worked before and it should work now.

"Boom!" His cow was down and kicking. The rest of the herd scattered into the trees and were gone. By the time he reached the elk, it had stopped kicking and was dead. John expertly field dressed it, skinned it, and quartered it. This was a small cow, but it still weighed in at around 600 lbs. so one didn't just pick it up and throw it on the mule's back. John laid the elk skin flesh side up on the mule's back, then proceeded to put the quarters on, then roll the skin around them and tying it off.

Of course the whole time John was busy, Chick was wolfing down his favorite morsels from the gut pile. such as liver, heart, and anything else that smelled good enough.

Everything was ready to go, so John went over to the river and washed himself off. As he turned, there was Chick face to face with three wolves! John had committed a cardinal sin in the mountains! He had left his rifle on his horse! His two pistols were in his belt, but there were three wolves. Slowly, John pulled out both pistols. The distance was only about twenty yards, so he did not worry about missing. They had smelled the blood and were able to pinpoint their location and sneak right up to both him and Chick. The situation was about to explode when the mule decided he had enough of these stalking critters and kicked out catching one right in the head. This wolf yelped and it got the attention of the others for a split second. John chose this moment to fire! He got one and it was dead before it hit the ground! The other one was starting to run, but was hit in the spine, and could not go anywhere. Chick was on it immediately! Killing it with his powerful bite to the neck! The wolf that was kicked by the mule was now running for all that it was worth, with Chick right on it's heels! John called Chick off, but he was reluctant to quit. Finally, Chick came back and acted like he was the "King of the hill!" He even put his foot on the wolf he thought he finished off, then lifted his head and howled real loud.

John could not help but laugh at his friend's antics, but in reality, Chick was a descendant of the wolves and reverted back for an instant. John decided that he better take off right away, because these three wolves may have been a forward hunting party to a pack. Normally, he would have skinned the wolves, but the need to be out of this area immediately was strong, so he left them lay and loaded his pistols and headed south. He figured that if there were more wolves, they would stay at the elk kill site and clean up what was left of the elk.

As John was nearing the camp of the Mormons, he could hear hammering. His intention was to deliver this elk to them, then go back and get one for his family. Between the pounding, John hollered at the camp to let them know he was coming. The man said to come on in. John sat his horse as he told the man that he had brought some good elk meat for him and his wives. The man said he was welcome and to get down and come sit by the fire. John off loaded the mule before he went over to the fire. One of the women was over inspecting the elk and told her husband that they would dine on some delicious steaks tonight.

This giant of a man stuck out his hand to John saying his name was Daniel. John told him his name and put his hand in the biggest hand he had ever seen. Daniel told John that they had seen his family from a distance and noticed that there was a very young boy playing out in the yard. John looked at the man with a puzzled look. Daniel just grinned and went over to a table. when he returned he was carrying a small chair.

"This is for your boy," said Daniel.

John was shocked! This little chair was beautifully hand crafted by this man.

Daniel told John that they thought one of his wives was with child, so he made this chair. He then said that he would make another one, for that is what he does. John thanked him and went over to where there were other items the man made. There was a cradle, a small wooden wagon, and numerous other items. John could see that Daniel was pleased that his work was being praised. That was important for an artist, or craftsman. Daniel had his wives come over and introduced them to John.

Daniel told John that although he was a Mormon, he did not hold with the way his people were acting now-a-days. He said that he was born a Mormon, and would die a Mormon. He also said that he knew what people thought about polygamy, but he would not give up either of his wives, and they were happy the way things were.

Live and let live, thought John. It was not his place to judge this family.

The conversation got around to wood working, and Daniel was in his element as he told John about how he built his wagon. he would point to a board here and then to a joint there, and John found it all very interesting.

The women declared the steaks done and Daniel and John went back to the fire. A plate was offered to John and there were real potatoes, not cattail bulbs, and also carrots. John dug in and never tasted anything any better. He told them so. He knew that these people were either Dutch, or German, and nobody cooked any better. After the meal was over they tried to talk John into staying the night, but he declined, saying that he wanted to go back and get another elk before dark.

John did go back for another elk, and was pleased to find them back in this valley once again. He and Chick were walking on the off side of the horse just like before and it was working perfectly. They were able to get within 50 yards from the herd. All john had to do was pick out the one he wanted. They were a little south of where they were a while back, and therefore could not see the wolves that he had shot. Perhaps they had already been drug off by other critters. John had his cow picked out and shot her in the heart area. She was down and not moving. The other elk did not run, but just stood there looking around for what put the cow down. John turned and was walking toward them and as one they turned and were gone into the trees in no time.

This time, after skinning, gutting, and quartering the elk, John wiped his hands in the grass, grabbed his Hawkin and went down to the river to wash up. Chick had smelled all the leavings, but decided he had, had enough to eat for now, and just followed John down to the river. John had rolled up his sleeves before skinning, and now after washing his hands, and arms was rolling them back down. As he was doing this, he was looking upstream and noticed movement about two to three hundred yards away. He looked down at Chick. but apparently Chick did not see, hear, or smell anything out of the ordinary. The wind was wrong, or he surely would have.

Curiosity could get you killed out here and John knew that, but he had to find out what he had seen. He had his rifle, both pistols, and knives and hawk, so he just started walking that way. *Never a dull moment out here,* thought John, as he approached with caution. He could see that it was an Indian woman sitting on a rock by the river. As he got closer, it was apparent that this was a very old woman. She had been watching John approach, and as he got close, he could see her looking him up and down. John used the sign for friend and was rewarded with the woman speaking some broken English.

"I...know...who...are," she said in a very shaky voice.

After looking closer, John decided that she was Blackfoot. He asked her if she knew his wife.

She told him with some English and a lot of sign that she was not from his wife's tribe, but was acquainted with them.

John asked her if she would come with him back to where he shot the elk. She told John that her hip was broken and she was just sitting here waiting to die. She said that her tribe had been camped behind her, but had left to go back to the main village. She went on to tell John that they had been hunting the elk and the men got a few down and the women were riding in to help butcher. That was when her horse stepped in a prairie dog hole and she went flying off to fall and break her hip.

John had to break in at this point. "They just rode off and left you?"

"You are married to one of our own. Do you not know that it is custom to leave a very old and useless woman?"

He had heard of that custom and told her so.

She then told John that it was her decision to stay behind. That is the way of their people, and had been since anyone could remember. John then asked her if she was hungry, and would she mind if he went back and got his horse and mule? She told him that she would like that very much.

John returned to the kill site, loaded everything up and went back to the old woman. She was slouched over and John thought she was dead! When he got to her she sat up strait and smiled. John told her that he was going to camp right here if she did not care. He had to camp anyway for it was getting dark. After he built a fire, he got out a skillet and commenced to frying the elk liver. He still had a small piece of bacon from the rendezvous, so he sliced a couple slices for grease in the skillet. He had brought along some biscuits that June had baked. They were hard now, but it did not matter, since they would be sopping up the grease in the skillet with them.

When it was done, John gave her his plate and he ate out of the skillet. As he watched her eat, he guessed she would die another time, because she was consuming this meal like it was her last, and John supposed that it was. He would leave in the morning and not look back. *But Damn it was going to be hard to leave her like this*, thought John. This was their custom and John would not interfere. Besides, to try to move her would probably kill her. He would have to quit thinking about her when he left, and that was going to be a hard job to do.

This custom sounds cruel, and it is, but the women do it knowingly to keep the tribe strong, just like a buffalo herd, or elk herd will leave an old or cripple one behind. John decided that he would enjoy the old woman's company tonight, and could learn many things from her before she passed. The pain from her hip was etched in her face, but it did not stop her from talking and signing to John. They talked way into the night, until they got sleepy. Then they covered up and went to sleep.

John was up at daybreak, which was very unusual for him to sleep this late. He went over to check on the old lady and found her sleeping peacefully. As he looked closer, John could see that she was not breathing. She had passed in the night. John was told by her, not to interfere, and just leave her as he found her. That was their way. At least, John remembered her name, so he could tell June who she was. He knew that after he told her, June would never speak of her again. That was the way they dealt with death. It was impolite to speak of the dead. John did as he was asked. He did not disturb the old lady in any way. He packed his things and rode off. This was a very hard thing to do for a man like John, who would have buried her, or built a scaffold, or done anything but just ride off and leave her.

Nothing out of the ordinary happened on the way home, and they made good time. As was now custom, when they got to within about a half mile from home, Chick took off running and would be the first to get there, plus alert everyone that John was coming. As John topped the last hill and looked down at his place, everything looked to be in order. Children were playing out in front of the cabins, Jake was down at his sister's cabin sawing wood for the fireplace, Thomas was out in back building something.

June stepped out the door and saw John riding into the yard. He jumped off his horse and June was in his arms immediately. He had only been gone a short time, but his homecoming was great. Both children ran up to him and he had to hug them as well. Of course Juan and the other pups were right there demanding some attention also. Jake and Thomas came over and asked if everything went well. John told them all at the same time about his encounter with the old woman. Jake had already told them about the Mormons.

John asked Thomas what he was building out back and Thomas told him it was a smokehouse, and he had just finished with it when John rode up. John asked if it was ready to try out and Thomas said that it was. John said that was good because he had an elk haunch to hang in it. As luck would have it, when they cleared this land for the cabins there were some hickory trees that had to be cut down. Of course they all had been using it for their fireplaces but there was plenty left for smoking meat.

CHAPTER XXVI
Jake's Woman

All three men were out back hanging the elk haunch and starting a smoky fire when a shot was heard and a horse was thundering down into their valley! The men immediately drew their pistols and went around front to see what was going on.

Jack Tucker was riding like the devil was after him! As John and the other men looked behind him, all they could see was Antelope and another woman sitting on their horses and shaking their heads. Uncle Jack came skidding to a stop right in front of the men! He was smiling that mischievous smile of his and said, "did ya all think ya was being attacked?"

He jumped off his horse and gave all the men a hug. By this time, Antelope and the other woman were there, and got down off their horses. All the children ran to Antelope and were hugging her before anyone else could greet her. After the shot everyone in the valley was alerted, and all came to see what was going on. Uncle Jack said he had a story to tell. John said to forgive him his manners and come inside and have some coffee. As they started to go inside, John could not help to notice the woman with Antelope. Someone else noticed her as well. John saw Jake looking at her with a look he never seen on his friend. Jake was following the men inside, but not paying attention to where he was, and ran into the side of the doorway. John had to stifle a laugh, but none of the others saw it, except the strange woman, who was looking at Jake with the same look he had. John saw her smile when Jake hit the doorway.

Antelope was able to break away from the children enough to come into the cabin and the strange woman followed her. June poured everyone a cup of steaming hot coffee and they sat at the table. Uncle Jack stood up and said the lady with Antelope was her sister, and her name is "Looks through." John could easily tell why this was her name, because when she looked at you, it was like she was looking right through you. Also, anyone in the room could tell there was something between Jake and Looks through.

John saw that Jack was just busting to tell his story, so he told him to go ahead. The room quieted as Jack began his story. Apparently, Antelope's sister was taken by some bad white men. Jack and Antelope were just on their way to the Shoshone village, when a group of men rode up on them. These were Antelope's tribesmen on their way to rescue her sister. Since Jack knew most of the men, he was allowed to go along. At this juncture, Jack said, "my young bride sittin over there would have none of it!"

He continued by saying that Antelope talked the men into letting her go along, since it was her sister and Antelope was as good a shot with a bow as any of the men. John had heard of some WARRIOR WOMEN among the different tribes. It was not common, but there were a few. John turned his attention back to his uncle. Jack was telling everyone that he sure did not want to make his wife mad at him. Antelope hit him on the shoulder and he said, "see what I mean!" Everyone laughed at that. Now the story got serious again as Jack continued by saying that they tracked these bad men for three days through some very rough country. Finally, on the third evening the camp of these bad men was found. There was still enough light to see, so they climbed up this hill and peaked over the side at the camp below. At this time Jack said that this was a stupid thing for the men to do. They had to figure they were being followed, and still they camped in a little depression with hills all around them.

Jack said that was when his wife told the men that she had a plan. Her plan involved her going down to the camp and demanding her sister be released to her. All the men laughed, even me, said Jack. Antelope then told the men that these bad white men would not harm her, but would try to take her as well. That was what she wanted them to do.

Antelope broke in at this point. She said, "first I have to tell a little story of my own. My husband may want to pay attention, since he does not know this story. There was a reason that the men let me go with them to find my sister. It is because of the way that I fight. They all know me and my sister." She said that she would have to go back in time to when she and her sister were very young girls. Her Father did have one boy, and the two sisters were always trying to better him in ways of war, or any kind of fighting.

She went on to say that their tribe came upon a small man of Chinese descent, just sitting there waiting to die. He could not speak their tongue, or English, but they found out that he had worked in a hole in the ground for white men. He had fought with them so much that they had stabbed him and left him to die. She said that her father respected his strength so much that they took him to their village, where she and her sister nourished him back to health. After he got all healed up he showed us how to fight in his way. This was to stay completely focused and concentrate on what you were doing and of course the moves we made were so surprising, that most times we won the fight. This man still lives in our village, but is now an old man. Antelope said that the things her and her sister learned from this man were used by them when they wanted to get the best of their brother, or any man in the village. "No one bothered us mere girls after that." She then said that her husband would continue with his story.

Everyone looked over at Jack and he was sitting there with his mouth hanging open, until he realized he was being called upon. He finally tore his gaze away from his wife and cleared his throat and began again.

Jack said that he did not want his wife going down there with those bad men, but no amount of talking was going to persuade her not too. All the men had the little depression surrounded and Antelope assured her husband that she would be fine and just wait for one hour, then if she did not come back, they were to come get her. Jack said that he did not like it one damn bit, but his wife was very stubborn, when she decides something. Before Jack could say anymore on the subject, Antelope went

GONE BEAVER

running down the hill yelling her sister's name. It was almost dark by now, but Jack said he could see a man grab Antelope and lead her over to the fire where her sister was tied up and lying on the ground. Now Jack said he waited the hour that was agreed upon, and was just getting ready to go down the hill with guns blazing and killing anyone who got in his way, when he heard Antelope say, "you can come down now."

All Jack did at this point was shrug his shoulders and say, "we went down there expecting trouble, but the four men who took Antelope's sister were all dead! John started to say something then, but his uncle put up his hand and said, "I will let Antelope tell the rest, since I was not there."

Antelope said that it went as she expected it would. When she got down there one man came out and grabbed her and held a knife to her throat in case anyone was watching. He then led her over to the fire and him and the others began questioning her about how she found them and who was with her. "Of course I told them that I was alone and would take my sister's place if they would release her! I was acting very submissive, so they had not tied me up yet. I then asked them to untie my sister, which they did.'" "As soon as my sister was loose, I winked at her and then the fun began!"

"The one untieing my sister was bent over her when she kicked him in his man parts! I was busy myself, twisting the knife out of the hand of the one who grabbed me! The other two men had been out on the edge of camp watching, when they heard the commotion, they came running! I stabbed the man with his own knife, and my sister done the same with the man she put down!" These two men were not expecting women to fight like this and we used the force of them running and grabbed their rifles while falling backward, therefore catapulting them over us! Then we just went over and stabbed them in the hearts! It was nothing and was over in less than a minute!"

Now John realized that he had his own mouth hanging open, so he cleared his throat, just like his uncle had done. He could not believe what these two women were capable of. He had always thought of Antelope as a quiet, but intelligent person. This brought out a whole new respect for her, and it made John wonder just what capabilities his own wife had. He looked over at June and saw no emotion at all. She was not surprised at all about how these women escaped.

Finally the conversation got around to what has been happening around John's neck of the woods. John told his uncle about running into the Mormons. Jack started cussing a blue streak, and John asked him what was wrong. Jack told them all how he did not like the Mormon people. He said that they would help a person in need, but were so clannish that you always left thinking you owed them something. Then there was the thing with more than one wife. Jack said that he was not a religious man, but that just did not set well with him. Everyone agreed with him, but John showed them the chair and told them that Daniel gave it to him for the elk meat John gave them. John also said that he did not think Daniel was a normal Mormon, because he left the fold, so to speak. John finished by saying that it did not matter, they were on there way west anyway.

John told his uncle Jack to come on outside and check out the smokehouse that Thomas made. All the men got up and started for the door. Except Jake. Jake was over talking to Looks through. John sneaked a peek at his wife, and June was smiling her knowing smile. After everyone was outside, Jake and his new friend came out. Jake told them that he and Looks were going for a walk. He was going to show her his sister's place and introduce her to everyone.

Antelope came over to the smokehouse where all the men were gathered and reminded Uncle Jack(as he was called by everyone, except Jake), that they still had to get to her parents village. Uncle Jack then told everyone that after they got the girls back they were closer to this place and had not been to the village yet. He said everyone at the village would wonder where we were, so they had to take off right quick. Jake and Looks Through were just walking up, and heard what was said, so Jake piped up saying that he would like to go along.

No surprise there, thought John.

Jake went over to his sister's place and got his possibles and horse and was ready to go. They all hugged and said their good byes, then they were gone. June said to John, "The next time you see your friend Jake…he will be a married man."

John looked at her and said, "you think so?"

"Did you not see the way they looked at each other?"

"You know I did, but this is too fast."

June told John that Jake would have to go through the process of courting, and then offer the horses to Looks through's father, then wait until her father said it was good. She said that her and Antelope talked a lot about each other's customs, and found out that they were much alike in most ways, this being one. She told John that Jake would be back in about a Moon or so. Then she changed her wording and said, "I mean a month or so."

John looked at her and said that she did not have to completely convert to the white man's language, in fact he kind of liked it when she used the Indian way of talking once in a while. John then said, "since we on the subject of you, how much do you know of the way Antelope and her sister fights?"

June got that devilish grin and told John, "do not challenge me, husband!"

At this time John realized that it was the mystery of this woman that attracted him, as much as her beauty. He let the subject drop and told June that he had to finish building the fire at the smokehouse, since they were interrupted. When he got around in back, Thomas already had the smoky fire going and declared that the meat would be ready in a day or so. This was a new process for the men, so they would have to experiment with spices to rub on the elk, but June could definitely help in that department.

CHAPTER XXVII
Little Storm

John went back around in front where the children were playing and was watching Sarah. it would be time to start teaching her how to defend herself, and to live off the land. He would be thinking of a time to take her into the mountains. William was still too young and would get his nose out of joint over this, but disappointment was something he had to learn. John would think of some way to appease him, without being too obvious. At the time, young William was busy playing fetch with one of the pups, so John called Sarah over to him and asked her if she would like to take a little trip into the mountains. Just her and him. Sarah's eyes lit up, as she said, "you mean, not take William?"

"That's exactly what I mean, said John."

Even though Sarah loved William dearly, she welcomed the chance to get away from him. John knew that this was common for brother and sister, because he still remembered his family the way they were before the dreaded cholera claimed them. Now, with this in mind, John went and found his wife. June warmed to this idea, because out here, if you did not know what to look for while on the trail, or in a camp, and even at home, things could happen at the blink of an eye. Sarah was at the age that she needed to know these things, and who better to teach her than her father?

They decided to go the next day. John began getting things ready for the trip. As far as clothing goes, Sarah did have some leggings that June had made for her. These, she would wear under her dress to protect her from briars and limbs that swing into the path, and also for warmth. William had to be told, so John did not waste any time trying to avoid it. He just got him off to the side and told him that he needed to stay behind so he could protect his mother. Although he did want to go with John and Sarah, this did please him, because he now was important and had a job to do. June had told John that she would play along to a point, but if anything did happen, then she would be the real protector.

Full daylight found them about a half mile from the valley. The day was beautiful and travel was very easy. John remembered his first day on the trail. of course he was eighteen years old and not seven or eight like Sarah. He started explaining things, just like Jake did with him. He was surprised to see how much Sarah adapted to this way of life. She was a natural at traveling in the mountains. Since she had spent all her young life in the mountains, either up here or down in the southwest, things just came easy to her. She remembered everything John told her, such as what plant that was, and what kind of footprint this was, and even how to find directions from the moss growing on certain sides of trees.

Of course Chick was with them. John would have been hard pressed to leave him home. John and Chick had a traveling routine and each knew what the other would do in certain situations. John was not going to leave Sarah's side even to go hunting. She had to learn that as well. Even though Sarah loved the animals, she knew that they needed their meat to survive on. When setting snares, John had taught Chick how to stay away from them. When John set a snare and Chick happened up on it, he would sniff it and know it to be John's, then go on about his business. John taught him the same thing with Sarah's scent, so he would not get caught up in it. Sarah was taught to use what she had, but if something else was needed, then they made do. Like, if you had no string, then you could strip willow bark off small branches and they were flexible enough, until they dried out. Of course this was for small animals. He told her that larger animals were caught in a different manner.

On this morning they were traveling on a narrow trail with trees on both sides, and if it were not for Chick John would not have came on this trail. there were too many places to hide and ambush unsuspecting travelers. John knew that Chick would warn them if there was anything out of the ordinary. This is just what he did! Chick was out in front, then John, next was Sarah. they stopped their horses and John pulled his pistol. His rifle was already in his other hand.

"Thwack!" A knife was sticking into the tree right beside John! One of John's own knives. Killdeer's knife. John's long time friend stepped out on the trail along with several other Indians. Killdeer and John hugged each other and began talking in sign language. Killdeer had learned a few white man's words, but this was much easier. Sarah watched like she knew what they were talking about, and in fact, she did. She learned sign language at a very young age, while being a captive of the dreaded Comancheros. Apparently the Indians had been hunting in the elk valley just north of John's place, and were on their way back to their small village. They had been on their way to the main village which was many miles from here. Killdeer invited John and his daughter, plus Chick to come with him to his hunting camp. Killdeer was petting Chick, because they also were friends. John agreed and turned to Sarah who signed that she would love to go to their camp.

When they rode into the small hunting camp, Killdeer's wife came running out to greet them. It had been a long while since John had seen her, so she gave him a hug, then looked down at little Sarah and said, in sign, "Who is this?" John told her in English, and after e few times she could pronounce it well enough. Since this was a hunting camp, there were no children. Just the men to hunt and the women to skin and butcher the elk. John noticed several elk hides stretched out on the ground and signed to killdeer that it looked like they had a good hunt. Killdeer told John that they were done now and would be going back to the main village before long.

Sarah was in awe of all the people going here and there, scraping hides and preparing meals, and numerous other chores that come with camping outdoors. Of course she remembered the Comanchero encampment, but she was not allowed to wander around and the people there were dirty, while these were clean. These people even smiled at her. Sarah walked around the whole camp talking to this one and that one. If she would have thought about it, she looked just like their children. Even down to the way she was dressed in her buckskin dress and leggings. Chick was following Sarah around the whole time. Some of the men would pet him, because they remembered him from when he saved John's life at the rendezvous.

John was talking to Killdeer out in front of Killdeer's lodge when they all heard a roar and then a scream! Everyone brought their weapons to bear, then ran to the edge of the camp! There, about ten feet from Sarah and a woman who had been scraping a hide, stood an enormous Grizzly Bear! John guessed that it smelled all the blood and came over to investigate. All the men standing there knew that they could kill it with all their arrows, but it would still have time to get to the woman and Sarah. The problem was solved immediately as Sarah grabbed a burning branch from a cooking fire and charged it with full force screaming at the top of her lungs and waving the torch under the thing's nose! John's heart skipped a beat and he was ready to fire, when the Grizzly dropped down on all fours and turned. Then it took of running into the forest!

All the villagers were trying to touch Sarah as she was now regarded as a warrior woman, and not just a girl. John was shaking so bad he did not know if he could even walk over to her. He finally did and when he got there, he scooped her up in his arms and asked just what did she think she was doing? Sarah told him that she just acted and did not even think about it. All the people were talking in their tongue so fast that John or Sarah could not understand what was being said. John asked Killdeer what was going on and Killdeer told him they wanted to have a celebration in Sarah's honor for her bravery. John looked at Sarah and she was blushing. He told her that it would be an insult if she did not go along with this. About a half dozen women came over and got Sarah and took her down to the river. Through sign and what little Antelope taught her of the Shoshone people, she understood what they wanted. They had her undress, then two of them began bathing her. When this was done, one of them gave her a pair of white leggings and a breach clout. She knew that the breach clout was for men only, and she asked about this. They told her that she was now a warrior woman and she could dress any way she wanted. She could be a woman when she wanted, or also a man when the need arose. Then they slipped a war shirt over head. When Sarah looked into the water, she saw a small warrior looking back at her. She was pleased.

When they got back to camp, John had to look twice to recognize his daughter. She did indeed look like a small warrior. *But a very pretty one*, thought John.

Sarah looked at her father, and John saw that she was just beaming. This obviously pleased her very much, so John was happy for her as well. *After all*, thought John, *she had plenty of time to be a woman. For now she might just as well enjoy this warrior status.*

They feasted and celebrated the rest of that day and well into the night. Before John and Sarah were able to go to bed, Killdeer had them come over to his lodge. Everyone gathered in a big circle(the sacred symbol to most Indians) and put Sarah in the middle. Since Killdeer was most familiar with her, it was he who was selected to re-name her. John knew that this was a very important ceremony to the Indians, and so did Sarah. Killdeer had Sarah kneel in front of him, then he put his hand on her head. He then looked to the sky and said some words that neither her or John understood. Finally he looked down at her and signed that the re-naming was done. Her new name was "Little Storm," because, Killdeer said, when she grabbed the burning branch and was waving it under the bear's nose, it reminded him of lightning coming from her hands. This pleased Sarah and John as well. They thanked all who was there and made the sign for bed. John was dead tired and knew Sarah, rather, Little Storm had to be worn out as well. They bedded down that night to the soft beat of drums that were still beating when John and his daughter went to sleep.

CHAPTER XXVIII
Mountain Justice

As always, the sun found them a little way from the hunting camp. They had said their good byes and were headed for home. John figured that his little girl had learned enough for this session. Besides, neither could wait to get home and tell June what all took place. Chick always got to their home before anyone else, so as usual, everyone knew they were coming. While they were setting their horses overlooking the valley, John had an Idea. He gave Sarah his rifle(which she knew how to use), and told her to point it up in the air and he pointed his pistol up also. He then said to touch it off and holler at the top of her lungs while riding hell bent down to the cabin. They did just that and went riding down the hill!

When they got down there, June was shocked to the core to see her daughter wearing men's clothing. John held up his hand and told her he would tell her all about it over a cup of coffee. John and Sarah sat on the front step and June went and got both a cup of coffee. The whole bunch were there. Thomas and his family, Betty and her young ones and of course all of Chick's clan. John told the story and left nothing out. He could see the transformation on June's face as it went from fear to surprise, and finally to pride. Sarah asked her mother if she was mad at her for chasing the bear away. June said that she should be, but all she felt was pride for her, and she earned the new name she now had.

Life got back to the everyday routine and was normal for the next three weeks. This one bright cool morning Chick let out a bark and went running up the hill. John had heard him, but was not overly concerned, because he only barked once. That probably meant someone he knew, was coming. As it turned out, the someone was Jake and his brand new bride, Looks Through. The whole clan turned out to meet them. Everyone was asking questions at the same time. Finally. John asked them to dismount and come over by the fire. John always had a fire going outside the cabin. Naturally there was a pot of coffee ready and after all who wanted some were sitting around the fire, Jake told the story of his wedding. Jake did not leave out any details, and John noticed that the Shoshone wedding ritual was very similar to his and June's wedding. When Jake finished his story, John asked him if they were going to build a cabin here in this valley. Jake told John that he and Looks(as he called her), were not fond of having a roof over their heads. They had discussed this somewhat and came to the conclusion that they would be happy to just put up a tipi when they were here in the valley. Most of the time they would be traveling, trapping beaver along the way. Looks broke in at this time, saying that she was happy to go with her husband and loved the mountains as much as he did. Now it was June's turn to break into the conversation. She asked Looks about children. All Looks said was even though she was still in the child bearing years, she would rather travel with her husband. Then she said maybe some day her and Jake would talk about it, but not any day soon.

 Things got pretty much back to normal. Sarah stowed her breach clout away for a time when she would go with her father again. She went back to wearing her little buckskin dress and acting like a child of her age should. Her and young William would fight like cats and dogs, but this was typical sister/brother rivalry. This one afternoon, June and the children were down at the stream so June could wash some clothes and let the children play around the water. She noticed William trying to get something away from Sarah and went over to investigate. When June got to them, she noticed something shiny in Sarah's hand. It was a little gold nugget, and Sarah said she had found it under a rock in the stream. June told her to keep it, but not to show it to anyone. Sarah did not understand, but she always did her mother's bidding and stowed it away.

That same evening, back at the cabin and the children in bed, She told John about the gold. June had seen the way white men covet the yellow gold, and told John that was why she had Sarah put it away. The less anyone knew about it, the better. John agreed with her whole heartily. They would let Sarah keep it and she could use it when she got older.

As for Sarah, when she went to bed that night, she already had a plan for the nugget.

When Sarah awoke the next morning and had bathed and done all her other daily rituals, she waited for young William to take his nap, then she went over under the big cottonwood tree out in front and began drilling a hole in the nugget. She had seen the Comanches, and even her mother putting holes in things by turning a small metal rod (which she acquired from her father out in the blacksmith shop). John knew what she was doing with it and did not mind. She had told him she was going to hang it around her neck and keep it hidden under her dress. This process took all day, even though gold is a very soft metal, it was still very hard for a six year old girl. The nugget was about the size of an acorn, but flattened and smooth from rolling around in the gravel on the bottom of the stream. When she was satisfied the hole was big enough, she went in the cabin and showed her mother. June got a leather string for her and put it around her neck. Sarah promised to keep it out of sight.

Sarah loved the outdoors and her mom and dad had a very hard time trying to keep her inside. Finally John sat her down and told her that they were going to let her go riding on her own, but she always had to keep the cabin within sight. She was absolutely not to go out of range where she could not be seen from home. She was beside herself with joy! To think her folks trusted her enough for her to ride by herself. Almost daily, Sarah could be found riding the perimeter of the home place. This day she rode a little faster, and made her gold nugget bounce out to the outside of her dress. There was nobody around, so she just left it out. As she was coming around this huge rock,(the only thing blocking the view of the cabin,) a man stepped out in front of her! This startled her horse, who bucked her off! She knew how to land and was fine, but this big ugly man was standing in the trail! She had a knife and knew how to use it, or throw it, but as she started to draw it, an arm went around her from behind! There were two of them!

They disarmed her and now she was at their mercy. The first one came up to her and grabbed the nugget that was very visible now. He pulled it lose and inspected it very carefully. Finally he demanded to know where she got it! "Over in the stream," she said.

The man said, "My god you are a white girl!"

The only thing Sarah could think to do was holler Chick's name! She did this, and the one holding her put his hand over her mouth.

Down at the homestead, Chick had been drinking out of the stream when he heard his name ever so faintly coming from up on the hill above the house. Away he ran! He knew the voice was Sarah's, and as he ran past the house heading for the hill, he let out two barks. This was heard by John and June as well. Immediately John grabbed his loaded rifle, strapped on his belt with knives and hawk, then headed for the door! He was in time to see Chick running over the hill! He knew Sarah was out riding and also knew she was in trouble.

The two bad men heard Chick let out a couple barks and drug the kicking and screaming Sarah toward their horses. Before they could get her up on one, a brown blur came flying through the air! Chick's weight was thrown against the man who was holding Sarah! The man had to let go to protect himself from the fury of Chick's attack. He was not fast enough! Chick had him down and was biting down on his neck when the other man shot. The force of the bullet knocked Chick off the man! This gave Sarah enough time to pull her knife and finish the job Chick had started. She stabbed the downed man in the chest! The other man who was mounted started to raise his gun toward Sarah and was blown from his saddle as John had topped the hill and saw what was taking place. Both men were down now and as John walked up, he made sure they were not capable of doing more damage. As he reloaded his Hawkin, he saw Chick for the first time! Sarah was up and had Chick cradled in her arms.

John asked Sarah if she was ok and she said she was, but she was not sure about Chick. John made sure there were no other bad men around then he went back to Sarah and Chick. Chick was breathing, but he had a bullet hole in his side. John took him from Sarah and carried him back down to the cabin. June was there to meet them, for she had heard the shots. She grabbed Sarah and asked if she was ok, then all three went in the cabin. June took Chick from John and examined him. She said the bullet went on through, but she did not know if it hit any organs, or not. John made a pallet on the floor in front of the fireplace and June laid Chick on it. She went and got her medicinal powders, and roots and whatever else was needed to make Chick well again. Chick had lost a lot of blood, but June did not think any major organs were damaged.

John was sick to death for his old friend, but he had some bodies to get rid of and he went back to the place where it all happened. He knew something was not right as soon as he topped the hill. One of the bodies was gone! He knew he made a kill shot on the man on the horse, and he was still laying there where he fell. John felt for a pulse and found none, so he would have to bury this one. The other *one* could wait until he knew if Chick was going to make it, then he thought, *God have mercy on his soul, for I will follow him into Hell if need be!*

John went ahead and buried the dead man, then retrieved his horse and headed for home. He would go through the man's saddle bags to find out who he was. He unsaddled the horse and turned it loose in his choral, then went in to see about Chick.

Two days went by before June would say if Chick was going to make it, or not. On the third day, Chick opened his eyes and wagged his tail. John and the rest of the family were overjoyed! Of course, he was not out of the woods yet, but this was very promising. It was all John needed. Now he had a job to do. Tracking was something he was very good at, but he would enlist the help of Jake, for there were none better, when it came to tracking men. John's only fear was that if this man got to a settlement and spouted off about finding gold before John could silence him, then his precious mountains would be teeming with people tearing up the Earth, and killing each other all for the sake of the gold.

He found his friend right where he knew he would be. Jake and Looks Far were up in a high basin where he and John had trapped the most beaver ever. Jake had just came back into their camp when John rode down into the basin. He looked at his friend and said, "I reckon ya aint here ta trap beaver. What happened?"

John got down off his horse and told Jake the story of the men who would have hurt Sarah, and almost killed Chick. Before he even finished the story, Looks was breaking camp. He looked at Jake and said, "I reckon she will be good to ride the river with!"

Jake told him that they were going to break camp and head to her village anyway.

John said that was good because that is the way the wounded man went.

In no time at all they were traveling toward Look's village. She would visit until Jake returned from this quest. John asked Jake if they were always going to be tracking someone.

Jake looked at John and said, "These by God mountains er fer most everyone to enjoy, ifn it's up ta us ta clean em up a bit, then so be it. I've always knowed there was gold in these here hills, but I never tolt a soul." Jest like you, I don't want a bunch of idjits out here scrapin up the ground."

All John could think of to say was, "Amen brother, amen."

Also available from PublishAmerica

Thoughts and Second Thoughts

By Barry Clapsaddle

From the claustrophobic dreams and interminable drudgery of a worker in the not too distant future to a young man's fantasies about a sexy convicted killer, the stories in *Thoughts and Second Thoughts* portray people caught up with both themselves and their situations, sometimes of their own making and sometimes not, but caught nonetheless. Influenced by an eclectic literary heritage, Barry Clapsaddle describes, among other stories, the indelible antics of some oddball street cops and the vagaries of modern warfare with equal insight and intensity. Combining experiences and creativity, the vignettes in this collection offer glimpses into and raise questions about life and death and the struggles in between, in settings that gradually fade into their own, often roughhewn backgrounds, but told always with the quick wink and nod of a crafted storyteller.

Paperback, 57 pages
6" x 9"
ISBN 1-4137-8601-4

About the author:

In addition to *Thoughts and Second Thoughts*, Barry Clapsaddle has written two screenplays, *Elysian Fields* and *Picking Up the Pieces*. He has undergraduate and graduate degrees in literature, and is the President and CEO of the IT firm CTGi. He lives near Washington, D.C., with his wife, Laura, and their four children.

Available to all bookstores nationwide.
www.publishamerica.com

Also available from PublishAmerica

DAY OF THE SHADOW
By Ronald W. Knott

Meet Joseph Parrot, a Native American living in the Canadian northwest. An ordinary man with a bit of history, he thought his dreams were dead at age forty-two, with a family and working as a simple surveyor of the land. A highschool sweetheart, now an FBI agent, comes knocking, offering Joe the job of a lifetime…tracking terrorists that have eluded the Feds with their intentions for years. Joe was unknowingly groomed for two years by the FBI. Now with wife Hanna's blessing, a bad relationship with teenage daughter Cameron and mother Twila suffering from Alzheimer's, he is off to track the enemy around the world. Traveling from Hong Kong to London and on to Moscow, he ultimately interrupts the successful takeover of the entire nuclear arsenal! Joe Parrot returns home a wounded and changed man to a surprise ending.

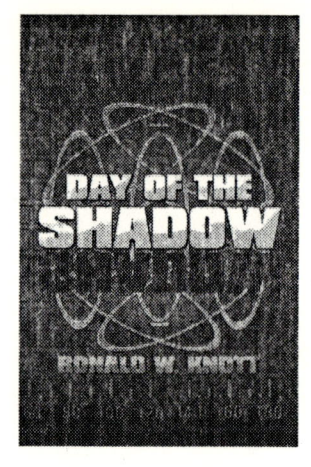

Paperback, 295 pages
6" x 9"
ISBN 978-1-60749-188-0

About the author:
I published my memoir, *Jaundiced*, with PublishAmerica, and wrote three feature screenplays including *Day of the Shadow*. I had a part in the movie *The Alphabet Killer* starring Timothy Hutton and Eliza Dushku. I am Native American and currently work as a behavioral health technician. I live with my wife, Carol-Aynn, in Rochester, New York.

Available to all bookstores nationwide.
www.publishamerica.com